Lightning Source UK Ltd.
Milton Keynes UK
UKOW07f2302030616
275567UK00009B/22
9 781909 640139

SST
YOUNG, HIGH AND DEAD
DON'T CAMP THERE !
A LUKE BRADY FILM
MISSING
SST
AVAILABLE ONLINE IN THE UK FROM FRIDAY 13TH SEPTEMBER 2013 EXCLUSIVE TO
vimeo
IMDb
You Tube

HORROR FICTION & DARK ART

COLUMNS, INTERVIEWS & REVIEWS

BACKGROUND ART BY VINCE NATALE

Editorial

Paul Fry

A warm welcome to the first issue of *Beware the Dark*.

This really is a very special issue for me. I have the honour of publishing fiction and non-fiction by some of the greats, and some of the best newcomers and up-and-coming authors and artists working today.

Firstly, we have truly amazing cover art by the fantastic and multi award-winning Vincent Chong, and we also have a brief interview with Vincent and a gallery of some of his best work to date. We also have some brilliant interior artwork and story illustrations from some really fantastic artists.

Now for the fiction: It's a *real* honour for me to be able to publish an excellent rare reprint by the legendary Ramsey Campbell ("Potential" was originally published in *Demons by Daylight*. Arkham House, 1973.) I'm also *really* honoured to be able to publish fantastic reprints by Bram Stoker Award Winners Jack Ketchum ("Twins" was originally published in *Peaceable Kingdom*. Subterranean Press, 2003) and Kealan Patrick Burke ("Empathy" was originally published in *Corpse Blossoms*, edited by Julia & R.J. Sevin. Creeping Hemlock Press, 2005.) We also have some fantastic new stories by James B. Carter, Timothy McGivney, Jeremy Terry, Aaron J. French, Sheri White, Russell C. Connor and Terry 'Horns' Erwin. All the stories include artwork and illustrations by Alfred Klosterman, Luke Spooner, Glenn Chadbourne, Eleanor Bennett, Stephen Cooney, Allen Koszowski and Daniele Serra. We also have some fantastic artwork on the Contents Page by Vince Natale.

If all that wasn't enough, we have some seriously fantastic regular columnists. It *really* is an honour for me to be able to publish one of my favourite authors of all time, Ray Garton. I'm also honoured to publish non-fiction by Nancy Kilpatrick, Robert Morrish and Ty Schwamberger. Ty also interviews singer-songwriter, actress, editor and author Kasey Lansdale. Plus, Vi Reaper talks with writer/director Luke Brady about his debut film *Young, High and Dead*.

I know I use the word "honour" a lot. But I really mean it, I really am honoured to be able to publish all these amazing people in my mag. So thanks to everyone for being a part of *Beware the Dark* and I hope you, the reader, will really enjoy what's within.

By the way, issue #2 is going to be a *very* Special Issue, so I'll see you all soon!

Beware the Dark Issue #1

Publisher: Short, Scary Tales Publications

Editor: Paul Fry

Fiction Contributors:
Ramsey Campbell
James B. Carter
Timothy McGivney
Jeremy Terry
Jack Ketchum
Aaron J. French
Sheri White
Russell C. Connor
Terry 'Horns' Erwin
Kealan Patrick Burke

Cover Artist: Vincent Chong

Artwork Contributors:
Vince Natale
Alfred Klosterman
Luke Spooner
Glenn Chadbourne
Eleanor Bennett
Stephen Cooney
Allen Koszowski
Daniele Serra
Vincent Chong

Non Fiction Contributors:
Ray Garton
Nancy Kilpatrick
Robert Morrish
Ty Schwamberger
Vincent Chong
Paul Fry
Kasey Lansdale
Luke Brady
Vi Reaper

Magazine Design: Paul Fry

ISSN: 2053-0307
ISBN: 978-1-909640-13-9

Mail enquiries: SST Publications, 15 North Roundhay, Birmingham, B33 9PE, England
Please remember to include a SASE or email address for a response.

Email enquiries: info@sstpublications.co.uk

Marketing Enquiries: sstpubmarketing@gmail.com

Advertising Rates, Subscription Info, Submission Guidelines are available online at: bewarethedark.sstpublications.co.uk

Please Note: The opinions expressed within are not necessarily those of the publisher.

SST

Ramsey Campbell

Potential

Illustration by Alfred Klosterman

On the poster outside the Cooperative Hall, forming from the stars twined in the foliage, Charles had read: 'BRICHESTER'S FIRST BE-IN—FREE FLOWERS AND BELLS!' But in the entrance hall, beyond the desk where a suspicious muscle-man accepted his ten shillings, two girls were squabbling over the last plastic bell. Searching in the second cardboard carton, Charles found a paper flower whose petals were not too dog-eared, whose wire hooked into his button hole without snapping. "Bloody typical," a boy said next to him. "I'm going to write to the *International Times* about this."

He meant it wasn't a true love-in, Charles supposed, fumbling with terminology. He'd once bought the *International Times*, the underground newspaper, but the little he had understood he hadn't liked. Uneasily he watched the crowds entering the ballroom. Cloaks, shawls, boys with hair like dark lather, like tangled wire: Charles adjusted his Make Love Not War badge, conscious of its incongruity against his grey office suit. He glanced up at the names of groups above the ballroom door: the Titus Groans, the Faveolate Colossi. "Okay, guys and gals, we've got a fabulously faveolate evening ahead for you," he muttered in faint parody. "Come on," said the boy at his side, "let's go in."

Through the entrance Charles could see swaying figures merged by chameleon lights and hear drums like subterranean engines; as they entered the guitars screamed, a spotlight plunged through his eyes to expand inside his skull. "Let me adjust," he said to his companion: anything to gain time. Threads of joss-smoke curled into his nostrils, sinuous as the hands of a squatting girl, Indian-dancing for an encircling intent audience. A middle-aged man left the circle, which closed, and wandered ill at ease: a reporter, Charles thought. He searched the vast ballroom; groups of thirteen-year-old girls dancing, multicoloured spotlights painting faces, projectors spitting images of turbulent liquid on the walls, on the stage the Faveolate Colossi lifting guitars high in a faintly obscene gesture. "Ready?" asked the boy at his side.

They danced towards two girls: sixteen, perhaps, or younger. A crimson light found Charles; when it moved away his face stayed red. Each time he moved his foot it was dragged down by a sense of triviality; he thought of the file left on his desk last night, to be dealt with on Monday morning. He sensed the reporter watching him from the shadows. The music throbbed to silence. The two girls glared at Charles and walked away. "Not much cop, anyway," said his companion—but then he seemed to see someone he knew: he vanished in the murk.

On the balcony above the ballroom a girl wearily blew bubbles through the shafts of coloured light. They settled, bursting when they touched floor or flesh: Charles saw his life. "Are you a flower person?" a voice asked: it was the reporter, twirling a paper flower.

"No less so than you, I should think." Charles felt cheated: the boys with flowers behind their ears, the girls dancing together like uneasy extras in a musical, the jagged lances of sound, the lights excruciating as the dazzle of scraped tin, gave him nothing: less than the fragments he'd retained from books on philosophy.

"I'm not one—Good Lord, no. I'm just searching."

Charles sensed sympathy. "You're not a reporter?"

"Never have been. Is that what I look like? No wonder they've all been watching me."

"Then why are you here?"

"For the same reason as you," the other said. "Searching."

Charles supposed that was true. He stared about: at the far end from the stage a bar had been given over to lemonade. "Let me stand you a drink," the other said.

At the bar Charles saw that the man's hands were trembling; he'd torn the paper petals from the wire. Charles couldn't walk away; he searched for distraction. On stage the leader of the Titus Groans was staggering about, hands covering his eyes, crying "Oswald, Kennedy, James Dean, Marilyn Monroe—" The speakers round the ballroom squealed and snorted. "Kill, kill!" screamed the Titus Groan, setting fire to a cardboard amplifier. Charles glanced away, at caped figures in a corner. "Sons of Dracula," he muttered in a weak Karloff parody. The other laughed. "You're a good mimic," he said. Charles thought of the office: moments when he'd felt the conversation move away from him and improvised an imitation to hold attention. He stared at the figures smoking gravely in the corner, until he saw the flash of a packet of Woodbines.

"If someone had given you LSD or hashish, would you have accepted?" the other asked, sipping a Coke and belching.

"I don't know. Perhaps." Something to set him apart from the people at the office, though they'd never know: he hadn't even dared to wear his badge among them.

"You feel empty. You're looking for someone to fill you, to expand your mind as they'd say." The man's hands were shaking again: the glass jangled on the bar.

"Ja, iss right, Herr Doktor," but it didn't work. "I suppose you're right," Charles said.

The Titus Groan was casting flowers into the crowd. Suddenly Charles wanted one—then immediately he didn't: it was trivial. Girls scrambled for the flowers; as they converged they changed from red to green. "Gerroff!" yelled one. "I think—" Charles said. "I know," the other agreed. "Let's leave."

In the entrance hall the pugilist behind the desk peered at them suspiciously. "By the way, my name's Cook," the man mentioned. "Charles," Charles said.

They emerged into the main street; behind the blue lamps the moon was choked by clouds. A passing couple eyed Charles' flower and 'Make Love Not War' and shook their heads, tut tut. "I know you bought that badge for the occasion," Cook remarked. "You might as well take it off."

"I do believe in it, you know," Charles said.

"Of course," Cook said. "We all do."

Tomorrow Charles might say "Last night I met a philosopher"—but once he'd claimed as his own a description of a robbery told him by a friend, only to be taunted by his neighbour at the office: "Yes, I saw that too. Last week on TV, wasn't it?" Two boys passed, tinkling with beads and bells. Charles was about to offer Cook a drink: he'd formed vague friendships at the office thus. But Cook was struggling to speak.

"I wonder—" he mumbled. The moon

fought back the clouds, like an awakening face. "I don't know you very well, but still—you seem sympathetic . . . Look, I'll tell you. I'm meeting some friends of mine who are experimenting with the mind, let's say. Trying to realise potential. It sounds dramatic, but maybe they can help you find yourself." His head shook; he looked away.

He was nervous, Charles could see: it was as if he'd drained Charles' unease into himself, leaving Charles the power to calm him. "I'll try anything once," Charles said. Blinded by the lamps like photofloods, the moon shrank back into the clouds.

They walked towards a side street where Cook's car was parked. In the unreal light the shops rose to Victorian facades, annihilating time. Charles wondered what they'd give him: LSD, lights, hypnosis? In the Be-In the pounding sound and leaping lights had reminded him somehow of brainwashing. He didn't like the idea of hypnosis: he wanted to be aware of his actions, to preserve his identity. Perhaps he'd simply watch the others.

Down a side street, on a stage of light from a pub door, two men fought. Charles couldn't look away. "I thought so," Cook said. "You're one of us."

In the next street Cook's car waited, its headlights dull like great blind eyes. "I hope you're not too perfect," Cook mumbled, unlocking the door. "They can't abandon me, not now. No, I'm just suspicious by nature, I know that." Savagely he twisted the ignition key, and shuddered. "They're in Severnford," he said.

Darkness spread again over the last house like decay, and the road dipped. As they swept over a rise Charles saw the distant Severn: a boat drifted quietly and vanished. Hills were lit like sleeping colossi; over them the moon bounced absurdly before the clouds closed. Suddenly Cook stopped the car. The darkness hid his face, but Charles could make out his hands working on the wheel. Cook rolled the window down. "Look up there," he said, pointing an unsteady finger at a gap in the clouds exposing the universe, a lone far frosty star. "Infinity. There must be something in all that to fill us."

In Severnford they pulled up near the wharf. The streets were lit by gas lamps, reflected flickering in windows set in dark moist stone. "We'll walk from here," Cook said.

They crossed an empty street of shops. On the corner of an alley Cook stopped before a window: socks, shirts, skirts, bags of sweets, tins of Vim, along the front of the pane a line of books like a frieze. "Do you read science fiction?" Cook asked.

"Not much," Charles said. "I don't read much." Not fiction, anyway, and retained little.

"You should read Lovecraft." Next to the tentacled cover a man fought off a razor, hands flailing, eyes pleading with the camera: Cook almost gripped Charles' arm, then flinched away. They entered the alley. Two dogs scrabbling at dustbins snarled and ran ahead. In a lighted window, above the broken glass which grew from the alley wall, someone played a violin.

Beyond the houses at the end of the alley ran the Severn. The boat had gone; tranquil lights floated against the current. Gas lamps left the windows of the houses dark and gaping, shifted shadows behind the broken leaning doors. "Over here," Cook said, clearing his throat.

"Here?" Cook had headed for a disused pub, its dim window autographed in dust. Charles wavered: was Cook perhaps alone? Why had he lured him here? Then Charles looked up; behind the sign—THE RIVERSIDE—nailed across the second storey, he glimpsed the bright edge of a window and heard a hint of voices, mixed with some sound he couldn't place. Cook was swallowed by the lightless doorway; the two dogs ran out whimpering. Charles followed his guide.

Beer-bottles were piled in pyramids on the bar, held together by Sellotape; in the topmost candles flared, their flames flattened and leapt, briefly revealing broken pump-handles on the bar top like ancient truncheons, black mirrors from which Charles' face sprang surprised, two crates behind the bar cloaked in sacking. POLICE ARE PEOPLE TOO was painted on a glass partition; for a moment it appeared like the answer of an oracle. "Oh, the police know about this," Cook said, catching Charles' eye. "They're used to it by now, they don't interfere. Upstairs."

Beyond the bar a dark staircase climbed; as they mounted past a large unseen room, through whose empty window glimmered the Severn, the voices hushed, giving way to the sound which worried Charles. Cook knocked twice on a panelled door. A secret society, thought Charles, wondering. The door opened.

Sound rushed out. Charles' first thought was of the Be-In: a united shriek of violins, terrifying. Inside the long room faces turned to him. "Take off your shoes," Cook said, leaving his own in the row at the door, padding onto the fur which carpeted the flat.

Charles complied uneasily, postponing the moment when he must look up. When he did they were still watching: but not curious, clearly eager to know him. He felt accepted; for the first time he was wanted for himself, not a desperately mimicked image. The young man in black who had opened the door circled him, shoulder-length ringlets swaying, and took his hand. "I'm Smith," he said. "You're in my flat."

Cook hurried forward. "This is Charles," he stuttered.

"Yes, yes, Cook, he'll tell us his name when he's ready."

Cook retreated, almost tripping over someone prone on the fur. Charles surveyed: boys with hair they shook back from their faces, girls already sketched on by experience, in a corner an old couple whose eyes glittered as if galvanised—writers, perhaps. They weren't like the people at the office; he felt they could give him something he sought. Against the walls two speakers shrieked; several of the listeners lay close, crawling closer. "What's that?" Charles asked.

"Penderecki. *Threnody for the Victims of Hiroshima.*"

Charles watched the listeners: in the violins the imaginative might hear the screams of the victims, in the pizzicati the popping of scorched flesh. Near one speaker *Beyond Belief* protected a veneer from a pub ashtray; next to it lay *New Worlds Speculative Fiction*, *We Pass From View*, *Le Sadisme au Cinema*, an *International Times* and a pile of Ultimate Press pornography, above which, mute, stared Mervyn Peake's Auschwitz sketches. "Smoke?" Smith asked, producing a gold cigarette-case.

"No thanks," Charles said; when he knew them better he'd try the marihuana, if that was what it was.

"I will," Cook interrupted, taking a black cigarette.

The violins died. "Time?" someone suggested.

"I'll make sure," Smith turned to Charles apologetically: "We don't use words unless they're meaningful." He padded to a corner and opened a door which Charles hadn't noticed; beyond it light blazed as at the Be-In. Charles thought he heard voices whispering, and a metal sound. He glanced about, avoiding the faces; outside the window loomed the back of the pub sign. A wall hid the river from him, but he could still see the quiet boat in the moonlight. He wished they'd speak instead of watching him; but perhaps they were waiting for him to declare himself. He wished Cook wouldn't stand at the bookcase, his shivering back aware of Charles.

Smith appeared, closing the door. The faces turned from Charles to him. "Charles has come to find himself," he said. "In there, Charles."

They stood up and surrounded the door, leaving a path for Charles. They were eager—too eager; Charles hesitated. He'd wanted to be a part of something, not alone and acted upon. But Smith smiled deprecatingly; the fur lulled Charles' nerves like a childhood blanket. He started forward. "Wait," Smith said. He stared at Cook, still trembling before the bookcase. "Cook," he called, "you want to participate. You be guide."

"I feel sick," said Cook's back.

"You don't want to leave us after so long."

Cook shuddered and whirled to face them. He looked at Charles, then away. "All right," he whispered, "I'll help him." Beckoned by Smith, he preceded Charles into the other room.

Charles almost turned and ran, he couldn't have said why; but he was inhibited against rejecting people he'd just met. He strode past the

eyes into the blazing light.

At first he didn't see the girl. There was so much in the way: cameras on splayed tripods, blind blinding spotlights climbed by cords like Lovecraft tentacles, in the centre of the floor a rack of knives and razors and sharp instruments, carefully arranged. He heard what must be the whimper of a dog on the wharf. Suddenly he peered through the twined cords and thrust Cook aside. A girl was tied to the wall. Her arms were crucified high. She was naked.

The jigsaw fitted—*International Times*, pornography, the cameras, pornographic films—but Charles felt no revulsion, simply anger: he'd come so far for this. Then a glimpse of crimson drew his eye to the gap where the girl's left little finger should have been. Unbelieving, he stared at the floor, at the pattern of crimson tracing the agonised flurry of her hand.

"Make your choice," Cook said.

Slowly Charles turned, sick with hatred. Cook had retreated to the door; over his shoulder the others craned for a better view. "Make your choice," Cook repeated, indicating the rack of knives: his voice trembled, and the girl looked back and whimpered. "Let what is in you be you. Release your potential, your power."

Charles couldn't look at the girl; if he did he'd be sick. He could feel her pleading with him. He approached the rack; his stockinged feet clung to the floor as in a nightmare. He touched a knife; its blade mutilated his reflection, its edge was razor-sharp. He clutched the handle and glanced with prickling eyes towards the door. It wouldn't work: too far to run. He struggled to remove the knife from the rack.

"Go on, Cook, help him," Smith said. The girl sobbed. Cook turned about, trembling. "Cook," Smith said.

Cook sidled toward Charles, his eyes appealing like a dog's as they linked the girl and Charles: Charles was his nightmare. Almost at the rack,

Cook stood shaking and glared towards the girl. "My God!" he cried. "You haven't—"

"My wife?" Smith called. "Not even I."

The knife slid from the rack and was at once in Cook's stomach. Yet Charles saw the blade flash on Cook's face, flayed not so much by terror as by knowledge. Cook fell on the knife. Charles closed his eyes. Blindly he wiped his hands on his jacket. At last he faced them, and almost knew what Cook had known. They were watching him with a new expression: worship.

Behind him he heard movement. He had to turn. The girl was pulling her hands free of the cords, flexing her little finger which had been hidden in her palm, wiping off the crimson paint on a cloth from the floor. As she passed Charles she stretched out her hand to touch him, but at the last moment lowered her eyes and knelt before Cook's body. Smith joined her and they linked hands. The others followed and knelt, the odd couple sinking slowly as their charge was drained. They turned up their faces to Charles, waiting.

You made this happen! he might have shouted to defeat them. You staged this, you invented it! It means nothing!

And all he'd done had been to perform their script—But his hand had held the knife, his hand still felt it plunge, his hand displayed the blade beneath which they cowered. Within him something woke and swelled, tearing him open, drawing him into itself. They saw; they knew. The girl stretched out her hands towards him, and they chorused a name.

At once it was outside his body, no longer part of him. For a moment he was filled by the innocence of oblivion. Then, finally, he knew. He felt what they had called forth sucking him out like an oyster, converting him into itself, the pain as his molecules ripped asunder as if his fingers were being wrenched loose. He cried out once. Then blood fountained from his mouth.

They moved whispering through the flat, eyes

averted. Two of them supported Cook's body to his car. "In the hills, remember," Smith whispered.

He returned to the studio, head bowed. "The river?" someone asked, pointing to the dry grey shape on the floor.

"It's nothing now," Smith said. "It won't be recognised. The front door."

They gathered up the husk and piled it into a paper carrier, where it rasped, hollow. Someone took the bag down through the pub. The candles had guttered. He threw the contents of the bag into the street beneath the gas lamps, and the dogs converged snarling to fight. Then he rejoined the others, as reverently they raised their eyes to what filled the flat, and waited for it to speak.

The Oxford Companion to English Literature describes **Ramsey Campbell** as "Britain's most respected living horror writer". He has been given more awards than any other writer in the field, including the Grand Master Award of the World Horror Convention, the Lifetime Achievement Award of the Horror Writers Association and the Living Legend Award of the International Horror Guild. Among his novels are *The Face That Must Die*, *Incarnate*, *Midnight Sun*, *The Count of Eleven*, *Silent Children*, *The Darkest Part of the Woods*, *The Overnight*, *Secret Story*, *The Grin of the Dark*, *Thieving Fear*, *Creatures of the Pool*, *The Seven Days of Cain*, *Ghosts Know* and *The Kind Folk*. *The Last Revelation of Gla'aki* and *The Pretence* are novellas. His collections include *Waking Nightmares*, *Alone with the Horrors*, *Ghosts and Grisly Things*, *Told by the Dead* and *Just Behind You*, and his non-fiction is collected as *Ramsey Campbell, Probably*. His novels *The Nameless* and *Pact of the Fathers* have been filmed in Spain. His regular columns appear in *Prism*, *All Hallows*, *Dead Reckonings* and *Video Watchdog*. He is the President of the British Fantasy Society and of the Society of Fantastic Films.

Ramsey Campbell lives on Merseyside with his wife Jenny. His pleasures include classical music, good food and wine, and whatever's in that pipe. His web site is at www.ramseycampbell.com.

I felt a great deal of trepidation being forced to live with my grandmother, unfortunately I wasn't going to have a choice until I turned eighteen, which was two long years away. When you're forty, two years is nothing more than a blink of an eye, a sunrise or a sunset, but when you're sixteen the clicking clock ticks slowly. I was going to be stuck with her because of situations far beyond my control.

I was angry at her, my situation and the world.

You see my parents had recently died in a car crash, in fact I was on my way from the funeral, which as disturbing as that was, it wasn't nearly as macabre as identifying their lifeless corpses on a pair of cold metallic slabs. Their bodies were charred and grotesquely ripped apart, resembling half devoured animals from *Wild Kingdom*.

I peeked at them through a slit in between my fingers attached to my shaking hands that were covering my face. I couldn't stop looking at their lidless eyes and how that final moment of shock and terror had become frozen on their faces like that painting *The Scream* by what's his name.

The oddest thing popped into my mind. I remembered a story my mother told me about how in ancient Greece they would put coins on dead people's eyes to pay The Underworld Ferryman as toll to get their loved ones across The Styx. I think the Ferryman's name was Charon, I'm certain it started with a C. She also told me that the true practical reason for that was to keep the deceased eyes from opening up during a viewing. I would have sold my soul to see those eyes closed, but despite my wishes, that wasn't going to happen. No matter how hard I prayed or what deal I made with God in exchange for their lives, they were going to continue looking up at me like two of those googly-eyed goldfish out of water until I looked away.

At that moment I was certain of two things. One, those two corpses were indeed my parents. And two, my life was going to be chaotically fucked from here on out.

INSIDE THE CAR:

"I just don't know what to say. All I know is that you're going to find a way to get through this," said my cousin, Wes who momentarily took his eyes off the country road to gauge my reaction.

"I mean, what other choice do you have?"

Suicide, I thought to myself.

He flipped on the car's brights and fiddled with the radio. "I forgot how piss poor the reception is out here."

I didn't acknowledge his radio comment. "Wes, I really appreciate you spending a few days with me until I get adjusted to staying here."

"Dude, you are my little cousin. I would do anything for you. Anyway it will do me some good to get away from the books for a little while. I just wish that it was under different circumstances."

I ran my fingers through my red hair. "Am I paranoid or was Grandma acting weird towards me?"

"Well, being that she's a hardcore Christian, I'm sure she is pretty steamed that you had your parents cremated, especially her only son."

"That's what they wanted; anyway what the fuck difference does it make? They were already burned. There isn't enough mortician make-up in the word that could have made Mom and Dad look normal again. "

Wes shook his head in disgust. "Jesus man, how can you say something like that? That's fucking morbid."

"I'm sorry, Wes. I'm just not myself . . . for obvious reasons."

"Well two years ago you were there for me when my dad died, and I'm going to do the same for you."

I knew he meant well, and I even believed he was telling me what he thought to be the truth, but deep down inside I knew his championing of my well-being would be short lived. How could I have ill will about that? After all, he had a life to live too.

I cleared my throat and spoke to him without looking him in the eyes. "Wes, you live four hundred miles away now, Brett lives another six hundred, no offense, but when your father died you had a mom, an older brother and sister to comfort you, not to mention my mom, dad and me. As soon as you leave town I'm gonna have no one except for that psychotic old bitch that ran my head through a pane glass window thirteen years ago, back in the good ole days when she was menopausal."

"Well, as you can imagine her lovely personality has digressed."

I cracked a smile. "Wow, look at Wes and his three dollar words. What they hell are they teaching you at that university anyway?"

"Three dollar words."

As we were driving I looked out at my surroundings. There were a plethora of trees on either side of the road and the woods were about as dense as you could get for fall in Indiana.

Wes adjusted his rearview mirror. "The leaves are starting to change and a lot of them are falling, it just looks so fucking gloomy," he said, looking at a blurred blue moon shinning behind a pre-maturing leafless tree, causing the branches to look like a skinny old man's arthritic hand pushing out of the terra, and reaching upwardly towards the heavens.

I could sense the gloom too, but perhaps it was more my demeanor. "Mom called fall the dying season."

"It makes sense."

"Yeah, a little more now than ever."

"When did Bob die again?"

"Dad died in October."

My voice cracked a bit. "Yeah, poor Betty did too."

Wes squinted one eye like he always did. "The dying season, huh?"

We were silent for the rest of the car ride; we passed acres and acres filled with stalks of dying Indian corn, until we turned into an out-of-the-way gravel road. There wasn't another house around for miles in any direction, and forget about a street lamp or even cable television. It was nineteen eighty-three, but it might as well have been nineteen fifty-three.

The only way we knew to turn into the driveway when we did was pure memory, being that there were no visible landmarks indicating any sort of turn off point. Not even a fucking mailbox.

We had spent a lot of time at that house in our youth. It was more like an old friend than an inanimate object. I heard the gravel shifting below the car tires and about a hundred yards away I could see a little blue light coming from the kitchen window. I always wanted to know the reason for that little blue light. Like why it never burnt out or why it was never turned off and centrally located in the kitchen. But like a lot of things, I never got around to asking about it.

As we reached the end of the drive, we saw Grandma's car recklessly parked, just like she drove. She had beaten us home; I wouldn't be surprised if she was the first one that left. She always was a cold, soulless cunt.

Wes popped the trunk of his nineteen seventy-six Oldsmobile Omega. When I heard its rustic thump, the realization hit me that I might not be able to get out of the car. I just didn't know how I was going to do this, how could I exist in a place worse than hell? For a moment I thought about burying my face in my hands and crying, but I was simply all out of tears. I also entertained the idea of running away, but where would I go? How would I survive? Who would hire a sixteen year old who lived in a mentally turmoil-filled abyss?

Wes knocked on the passenger side window, jarring me from my thought filled daze. "I got your bags."

I looked at him with despair so great, that I'm sure he could feel my pain radiating through him.

His breath fogged up the window a bit while smirking. "Were ya thinking about making a run for it?"

If he had only known how right he was, but eventually I removed myself. Someone once said that the hardest part about life is getting out of the car, perhaps truer words had never been spoken.

Later that night we had gotten settled in and were scouring the fridge for something to eat. Wes was leaning in and taken aback at our meager selection. "What kind of diet is she on?"

I shushed him, fearing he would wake up the old woman, yet he continued.

"Everything's low fat, skim milk, carrots, and not a single sign of meat. What the fuck? A homeless person would turn this shit down," he said in disgust.

As his rant continued I heard a controlled

rustling, which turned into footsteps followed by an aggressive sigh, and that's when I saw what I dreaded out of the corner of my eye.

"What in God's green earth are you boys doing?" she asked, with her head rattling about like Katherine Hepburn, causing the pink curlers in her hair to jostle uncontrollably.

"Oh God!" Wes screamed not knowing she was behind us.

"Sorry if we were being loud, Grandma."

She hauled off and smacked me square in the face without hesitation. "Don't 'sorry' me you little son of a bitch!"

It didn't hurt, but it did shock the piss out of me. I immediately wanted to reach out and strangle her, but I became distracted with the overwhelming scent of Ben-Gay and the creepy smile on her face so wide that her dentures became loose, clanking together in her mouth.

"Hey jack-o'-lantern, looks like someone needs a fresh coat of Polident."

Wes busted out laughing when he heard me say that. I just don't think he thought I had it in me, but I wasn't done yet. The rage and hate was building inside me.

"Let me know if you decide on not handing out candy to trick-or-treaters this year. We can stick ya on the porch, pry your mouth open and shove a lit wedding candle up your ass. If that doesn't scare them off nothing will."

"Alrighty," said Wes nonchalantly, grabbing my arm and pushing me passed her.

Wouldn't ya know it, it turned out she took acceptation to my off-the-cuff comment and the next thing we knew, Wes and I were being chased around the dining room table with the largest butcher knife I had ever seen.

"What the hell, Grandma?" asked Wes.

She held one hand on the tablecloth and the other over her head gripping the wooden handle of the knife, resembling Anthony Perkins in *Psycho*. It was nothing short of surreal.

We scrambled around the table, running a little and then stopping, trying to figure out her methodical pattern. She was gradually getting closer. The old lady was tactful, but we had one thing on our side that she didn't . . . youth.

Wes looked at me and directed his eyes to the stairs that led to three bedrooms and a half bathroom. We knew those upstairs like the back of our hands, if we could just get passed her and up those sixteen narrow wooden steps, we would be home free.

I kept on looking at Wes and the witch fringing on the brink of lunacy. I wanted to move, but I was paralyzed with fear, the fear of being stabbed by an absurdly long blade. It's funny; two hours ago I wanted to die; now all I wanted to do was live.

Wes nudged me and I finally got both feet in motion. I ran and he darted behind me to the stairs. We barely got passed the initial swing of the blade. I could feel the breeze from her stringent attempt at murder, and with that breeze came a potpourri of odors that could only be described as old person.

The stairs were narrow, even for our agile feet. Wes kept pushing me up them, driving his elbow into my lower lumbar region. Grandma started to gain ground on us, and just as Wes and I reached the summit of the stairwell, we turned around and there she stood, in all of her horrific glory. Knife raised, eyes crazed and literally throthing at the mouth.

The second that bizarre, maddening moment became singed into my mind, I realized Wes had kicked her right in the midsection. It sent her flying down the steps, head over heels. I heard every sickening thud of her skull crashing randomly into every other blunt step.

We both stood there, jaws slacked in awe.

"Holy shit! You kicked her down the stairs."

"I know."

"Did you kill her?"

Wes continued to look at the bottom of the stairs and shook his head no.

We watched her closely, and I must admit I felt a little bit of relief when I saw her body shifting and her eyes open, but it wasn't long before she tried to get back on her feet.

Wes and I looked at each other and started laughing as if we were experimenting with pot for the first time, perhaps it was nervous laughter, perhaps we were laughing at the absurdity of a knife-wielding grandma getting kicked down a flight of steps, or maybe we were laughing because it was way easier than crying.

Soon the laughter subsided as we noticed not only was she on her feet, but she was very coherent. We once again became her main focus as she skyrocketed back up the steps. I'm sure it wasn't plausible, but in my young mind it appeared as if she literally flew up the steps, and just before we could get the door closed, she stopped it with her arm.

Even though she was an old lady, at least eighty, it took everything Wes and I had to get that door shut, and when we finally did we hooked the old-fashioned chain latch, but she kept applying pressure to the door, banging up against it so hard it felt like it would break off the hinges at any second.

We pressed the flats of our backs against the door, using the full weight of our bodies to stifle her unforgiving blitzkrieg. I could see the door begin to split out of the corner of my eye and just when I thought we were losing the battle, and she was about to burst through our human barricade, the door handle stopped rattling, the hinges stop bowing, and for the moment we felt safe again.

Wes pressed his index finger over his mouth and shushed me. "Be perfectly still. She might still be at the door, just waiting for us to let our guard down."

Even though we couldn't have been standing there in silence for more than a minute, it felt like an eon. Eventually, Wes mouthed to me "She's gone," and stepped away from the door, leaving me frozen and alone still pressed against it.

I wanted to believe him, but after everything that had transpired I had to see for myself. My heart was pounding through my chest and the hair rose on the back of my neck like a black cat under a Halloween moon. I slowly bent over to look through the keyhole. What I saw I could never forget if I were to live a thousand lives. I saw her beady eye peeking back at me. It was crazed and glazed and looked as if it had murderous intent.

She adjusted her head so her other eye could get a clearer view of the goings on. She backed her head away a little, just enough where I could see the thin layer of hair on her upper lip which she obviously bleached, not to mention the brown and yellow caffeine and nicotine stains on her dentures.

Her head had horrifying birdlike movements, she looked through the keyhole one more time and as quickly as it had begun, it subsided. She made her decent down the old creaking steps, but not before screaming out one last discouraging bark. "I'm going to get you little cock suckers!"

I was stunned and looked to Wes for answers. "What the fuck dude?"

"I don't know, she was always a little crazy but she has never gone this far, even though Brett said she was really off her rocker when he stayed here during college."

"'Off her rocker'? The women needs to be heavily medicated and fucking committed! There is no way I can stay here."

"Don't worry about her, Robbie. She's leaving for her sister's house in California tomorrow, and Brett said he would be here sometime in the morning."

Brett was Wes's half-brother, seven years older than him. He watched us a lot growing up, and we always had a lot of fun with him. He gave us our first beer, not to mention my first toke. The three of us were close and shared a lot of secrets other family members didn't know, like the fact that Brett was homosexual, it wasn't that acceptable back in the nineteen eighties, so he made us promise not to tell; in fact I never gave it a second thought after he came out to us.

"Well. It will be good to see Brett again."

"Yeah, I talked to him last night on the phone, he is pretty devastated by what happened and you know how much he loved your parents."

"Yeah."

"He hated missing the funeral, but he said he couldn't wait to see you," Wes said, adjusting the rabbit ears on the old black and white ten-inch television set.

"So what's the plan?"

Wes continued to fuss with the tinfoil on the TV antenna. "I was thinking we would wait until she falls asleep and sneak out, go to the woods, start a fire and get drunk like we used to do."

"Sounds great in theory, but how are we gonna know when she falls asleep?"

Wes was still struggling to get a reception; until suddenly like magic we had an image. "Hey I forgot that it's Friday. Sammy Terry is on tonight."

Sammy Terry was a play on the word cemetery, and he was a local late night horror movie host, back in those days it seemed as if every region had one. He wore a red cape, a cowl and varied shades of poorly applied green makeup. He would pop out of a cardboard casket and introduce some third-rate horror flick. It was great.

He had been around forever, hell my mom used to watch him when she was a little girl, but Sammy Terry wasn't meaning that much to me at the moment, I guess I was just in a daze. All I wanted was for things to go back to the way that they were, where and when everything made sense. The uber reality was that there was no longer a household to get back to. My life was officially in shambles, and there was no way out of it.

That's when I realized I was in denial, not of the situation, but in the possibility of a supreme being. There was no higher power looking out for me or the people I loved. The sooner I accepted that, the sooner I could live for myself instead of false deities.

Wes laughed. "Looks like they're showing *The Hand* tonight? Remember that one?"

"You never answered my question?"

"Huh? About what?"

"How are we gonna know when the bitch is asleep?"

He looked at me mischievously. "You don't remember do you?"

"Remember what?"

Wes pushed the bed away from the wall that revealed a large heavy duty register that ceased to produce heat years ago. Once I saw the metal square vents, I remembered instantly. The register's duct pipes had been removed way back in the nineteen fifties; basically what it did was leave an overhead window to the bedroom below.

The room was now occupied by Grandma, but it wasn't always that way. It used to be Brett's room when he was in high school; we used to spy on him unmercifully.

"Look at her," said Wes.

"How long has she been sleeping down there?"

"I don't know, ever since she bought the house off Mom I guess."

I kept looking down at her. She was sitting on a bed directly beneath us, wearing a thin light blue nightgown that was flowing carelessly via the thrusting wind from a window fan across the room. She was also wearing what resembled a swimming cap on her head, with those pink rollers pushing through.

She had a small bedside lamp next to her. Its light made her flesh look like paraffin wax. The television was muted and the screen was full of white noise, which gave the illusion of a dim strobe light. I could see her rubbing some sort of lotion on her hairy, varicose vein infested legs, totally oblivious that we were watching her every move.

I became a little nervous. "What if she notices us watching her?"

"Why should she notice? She lived here ten years before buying the place and she hasn't noticed yet."

"What if she hears us?" I whispered.

"What? Hears us? Dude, she can't even hear her own farts."

I remember laughing, then catching myself in mid smile, forcing myself to stop out of guilt, wondering how the hell I could laugh when my parents' bodies were barely cold.

Wes saw that I was distraught, and he certainly knew why.

I quickly changed the subject. "Turn it up, I love this scene."

"What?"

"This is where Michael Caine gets his hand cut off," I said.

His face lit up. "This is the best part."

Wes and I sat on the edge of the bed together, and for a fleeting moment, we felt like we were boys again, a feeling that would never be replicated for either of us.

We had sat there watching the movie until well after the credits rolled and Sammy Terry was doing his intermission shtick.

"Let's go see if the old witch is out of it," said Wes, as I followed him to our secret watchtower. We both looked down the proverbial rabbit hole, fighting each other for position in an attempt to get the best view.

She was asleep all right, if I hadn't known any better I would have thought I was looking at a corpse, but over the past few days I had become somewhat of an expert on dead bodies, and despite how badly I wished she were dead, she wasn't.

Wes stood up and turned off the television. "Well, it looks like it's time to put this plan in motion. Grab the car keys while I get this window open."

The window was a bitch. For years we had struggled with it. In the summer time we just used to leave it open even during a downpour, but in the fall and winter, we had to keep it closed. If you had ever spent a winter in Indiana, then I don't have to tell you why.

With the help of a screwdriver and a wire hanger tied around the window frame's unstable handle, the window finally became ajar, letting in the brisk fresh air of an October night.

I stepped out on the awning like I had a hundred times before, watching my breath shoot out across the darkness of night, staring out into the blackness.

Wes cupped his hands together and blew into them in an attempt to warm them up. "Well chief, the beers are in the trunk and the first one down gets to pop the first top," he said scrambling towards the edge leading to a ten foot drop while jumping and hitting the ground before I even readied myself.

"Fuck!"

I looked down over the edge and saw Wes sitting on the hood of the car wincing.

"What?"

"I tweaked my fucking ankle!"

"Is it bad?"

Wes cracked a smile and slapped the hood of the car causing a slight echo. "Nothing that the first ice cold beer out of the case can't cure. Anyway, I couldn't live with myself if I'd let a pussy like you beat me."

In my teenage years my body was unbelievably durable. Even things like broken hands and noses never slowed me down. I could never jump high, but I was very astute at jumping from high places; not to mention that I seemed to always do it with incredible flare. Maybe it was the Evel Knievel in me, or my obsession with big time championship wrestling, whatever the case almost everyone found my antics nerve racking or annoying, and Wes was no exception.

I stood there perched, with my arms spread wide in a triumphant stance resembling Jimmy "Superfly" Snuka standing on a fifteen foot cage ready to pounce.

Wes craned his neck upwardly, still spouting cold smoke like a dragon. "If you put one dent in the Orange Crush, you're gonna get the beating of your short life!"

He loved that car more than life itself, it was a nineteen seventy-six orange Oldsmobile Omega given to him by his dad before he started his long dirt nap two years ago. It was a beautiful car and he had made a lot of special modifications to it. Sometimes he would park that thing in my mom and dad's garage for days and I would do whatever I could to help after school, or whatever; for the record I was never that mechanically inclined. I can tell you this about the Orange Crush, once it got those four tires in traction, nothing, and I mean nothing could catch that motherfucker.

I jumped recklessly. As I looked up at the star filled night above, it felt as if I fell forever into the everlasting nothingness. But then again, when I jumped it always felt like that, my body swirling, my mind going to unearthly places. Doing dangerous things at great heights was sort of my thing. My Zen if you will. I lofted down with my arms spread like wings, in a way that could only be described as aesthetically pleasing.

My feet hit the ground and I tumbled forward. I stained my jeans and lost a thin layer of skin here and there, it was nothing to bother with and it certainly wasn't anything that I wasn't used to.

By the time I saw the crooked smile on his face, he had the initial beer already half drunk. The outside of the bottle was frosted from the bag of ice and the eighty-nine cent Styrofoam cooler, that he bought somewhere between where he was coming from and now.

"Well there's no doubt about it, you are still one wild motherfucker."

I approached the open trunk and watched a stream of suds dribble down his chin. I adjusted my pant legs as they were askew during my tumble. He tossed me a cold, wet bottle which almost slipped through my hand.

"Jesus, be careful that shit's like gold."

I twisted the cap off with my teeth and stuck it in my pocket. It was just something I did out of habit. "Well, if you don't want me dropping it, maybe you shouldn't be throwing me things blindly in the middle of the night without warning."

"If you knew how hard it was for me to procure this you would bite your tongue."

I laughed at him. "'Procure'? They have been teaching you three dollar words."

He waved me over and we lifted the cooler together, we closed the trunk and began making our way to a little patch of woods behind the house, which was adjacent to the largest field of corn I had ever seen. It wasn't just one side, except for the house and the little bit of foliage that was about to be our camping site, we were surrounded by at least a half mile of cornfield in every direction, not to mention about fifty other random fields of corn, that I assume was at one point harvest by farmers long before I ever had a memory of the place.

It didn't take us long to get settled in. Before I knew it we were tossing fragments of downed branches and twigs to keep the fire blazing, keeping us warm from the bitter October wind.

Wes leaned in next to me and raised his beer; I clacked mine into his in the reckless attempt at a toast, as the fire slightly warmed my bottle's bottom. I felt the cool elixir coat my throat as I emptied my first bottle in about a minute. "That went down pretty smooth," I said throwing the dead soldier behind me, hearing it hit a tree and scruff some branches before making its decent to the ground.

"I wish I could wipe it all away for ya."

I popped the cap off of another beer. "I wish you could too."

Wes sipped his drink and savored it upon his palette before taking it in and speaking to me. "Well, look at it this way. The worst is over. No matter what happens to you for the rest of your life, it will never get as bad as this."

I found that ironically comforting. "You certainly have an interesting way of looking at things."

He scratched the back of his head and threw a piece of his beer label that he had been picking at into the fire. "See, they teach me more than fancy words at that college of mine."

As we continued to talk and reminisce about larkish episodes from our younger years, I heard a rustling spawning from the corn stalks that were surrounding us. "You hear that?"

"What, you forgot how loud field mice fucking could get this time of year?"

"It's funny what I remember and forget about this place, when I think back on it; I'm never sure if it's a fuzzy memory or a dream."

TWO HOURS LATER:

The fire crackled as Wes placed some overly-green twigs upon it to keep it blazing. The moon was oddly large and the stars seemed to roar past like headlights on racecars. I had a multitude of beers, my face was feeling a little numb, but my extremities were still as cold as hell.

"Jesus, Wes! I'm freezing my ass off. As lit up as I am you would think my body would be toasty. Can't you throw some bigger sticks on the fire?"

Wes carelessly discarded another bottle. "It's not my fault you're skinny. If those boney little hands of yours are feeling the freeze, you're gonna have to do the legwork and find us something decent to burn."

I stood up. "You just don't want to go because you're scarred of what might be out there . . . in the dark," I said, being halfway serious.

Wes scuffed off my comments and I made my way through the woods. As I was looking around, the realization hit me that I couldn't stay here at this house, with Grandma. Look how crazy acting she was, even with Wes here she tried to kill us for Christ's sake. Considering what I had already been through, I wasn't mentally stable enough for a traumatizing environment like this. The question was, how was I going to tell Wes? Would he tell anyone if I told him, and where would I go?

Wes yelled, "What the fuck is taking you so long?"

"Give me a second!" I recall saying with two or three fire worthy pieces of timber. I walked so far into the woods that I hit cornfield. Thinking back now, it would have been a better story if I was looking up at the star scape, remising about the past, but the truth was I had to take a shit.

When we were kids, we would spend hours upon hours roaming in the cornfields. Sometimes we would look for Indian arrowheads or artifacts; sometimes we would play *Star Trek*. When the Sun would hit the stalks just right it was like being on another planet and no one was around us for miles. We used to take eggbeaters out of the kitchen drawer and they were our communicators and tinfoil covered gourds, were our phasers.

"Come on dude."

"I'm pinching one out, you better save a beer for me!"

"You better hurry then!"

I was a city boy for most of my life, but I could still remember how free it felt to use the bathroom in a field

Wes chimed from the distance. "You coming back anytime this century?"

"Just be quiet so I can get this over with," I yelled back, not even sure if he ever heard me.

"You giving birth?" Wes asked. I never answered.

Here I was, wearing multicolored stripped tube socks and black Larry Bird Converse, squatting with my jeans pulled below my knees. Five hours ago I was burying my parents and now I was taking a crap in a cornfield. Sounds like a postcard.

Everything was silent, like it often was in the armpit of Indiana. I evacuated my bowels and shamefully pulled up my pants because I had nothing to wipe with, and as I stood up that's when I heard the sound that I'd heard before, this time only closer and louder.

What was it? I thought to myself. This wasn't field mice fucking, this was big. Big enough to give me concern. It wasn't a typical wild animal; I heard it circling me, just waiting for the right time to strike. Then again maybe I was just too drunk to take a joke; perhaps it was Wes's idea of being humorous.

"Hey asshole, you can stop fucking with me now."

I know Wes mumbled something back, but I couldn't hear it because I was too far back, which meant he couldn't hear me, which meant that it wasn't him playing games.

My heart was racing at a pace reserved for horror movies, and I jaunted back to the campfire as fast as I could where Wes had been impatiently waiting for me.

"Where's the wood?"

I was too frightened to answer. I just frigidly sat back down upon the aging stump that my ass had called home for the last several hours.

"What the hell, Robbie. You're as white as a sheet, you feeling okay? You look like you just saw a ghost."

I cleared my throat and tried to gather myself before speaking. "Wes. I saw something moving around in the cornfield and it wasn't a field mouse."

Wes's face was filled with empathy, but even more doubt. "Calm down, it was probably a raccoon or something."

I shook my head in disagreement. "This was no fucking raccoon. Whatever it was, it seemed like it was purposely keeping its distance."

"You were taking a shit, I would have kept my distance too," said Wes rolling his eyes.

I kept peering at the field behind him waiting for any kind movement or sound, hoping for any disruption that might cause Wes to take me serious.

Wes's face became slightly sad. "Robbie, you have been through a lot the last few days, all of us have, you lost your parents and on top of that you are drunk off your ass. I think this is less about something stalking you and more about your restless mind playing tricks on you."

Despite his pep talk, a few moments later we heard heavy shuffling together. This time it was followed by the sound of breaking stalks.

"That must be one giant raccoon."

Wes's eyes widened and I could tell he was searching his mind for some kind of excuse. "I know what that is," he said laughing in relief.

"What?" I asked, not too interested in his response.

"It's Sam."

I smiled; that's right I smiled. "No way! Samson can't still be alive can he? He was old ten years ago."

"Yeah, he must be seventeen or eighteen years old. Brett came up here about three months ago for whatever reason, and he said Sam came up to the porch begging for some food."

The reason I was smiling is because I fucking loved that dog. We didn't even know what breed he was; he was just a big ole one hundred and twenty pound mutt that was covered in long, gray matted hair. As far as we knew he didn't even have an owner, he would just come and go at will. The one thing that I always remember about Samson was, is how protective of us boys he was. I was hoping Wes was right, I was wishing it was Sam. I wanted to see him again; I wanted to be reminded of an easier, less chaotic time, but I knew no matter how hard I wished it to be, things were never going to be same. I knew I would always be searching to fill the void of a childhood cut short, and I also knew that until my dying day, for the rest of my nights, I wouldn't have a single haunt-less dream. That's when I decided to tell Wes.

"I'm not staying, Wes," I said with apprehension.

"What the hell are you talking about?"

I continued to spill the beans. "As soon as you and Brett leave I'm on the first bus out of here, and if I can't find a bus I will hitchhike."

Wes looked at me with disappointment. "Dude, I know it's rough, but ya just have to stick it out. In two years you'll be out of school and you can do whatever you want."

I could tell he wasn't going to be on board with my decision; so what I did, was I lied. "Yeah you're right, it's the situation talking not me," I said in an attempt to dupe him.

Moments after my bold face lie, the field began to rustle again. This time what we were about to see couldn't be explained away by one of Wes's lame ass excuses, or even by science for that matter.

I looked over at Wes and he was frozen in fear, he wasn't even blinking his widened eyes. I could hear it coming closer with each silent breath I took. Stalks were snapping and being carelessly brushed aside with ease. What was this thing? What was happening?

Finally it broke through the cornfields barrier. It was eight feet tall if it were an inch. Its mouth was open and dripping saliva from its finger-length pointed teeth, and then there were its eyes, they were the size of hard boiled eggs and they raged red, glowing in the blackness of night.

Wes only moved his eyes to look at me. "It's right behind me isn't it?"

Before I could give him a proper answer the hairy beast roared. It was so loud I could feel the vibrations rattle the bones in my body. Wes jumped up so fast that it looked as if his feet weren't even touching the ground beneath him, and before I knew it, I was right behind him, both of us racing towards anything that resembled salvation. I was praying it wasn't right behind us, but I was too scared to even dare look behind me.

"I can't find the car keys," he said patting himself everywhere frantically as if he were on fire.

I yelled at him with a mixture of fear and frustration. "You had them goddamn it."

"No shit," he said responding with equal annoyance.

My heart was pounding through my chest, my surroundings became a blur. I saw snippets of grass, shoestrings, and the moon wobbling constantly in and out of my eye line with each and every terrified, unsure step. We even passed the Orange Crush that was seemingly useless to us at the time.

After we turned the corner of the house and traveled well past the car, Wes continued to run to the old garage we used to play in when we were kids. One of the things that I remembered about the garage was that there was no lock on the side door. When we finally reached it, it was worse than I thought. It had had a bad few years; in fact, there wasn't even a doorknob to toggle.

Once inside I closed the decaying door behind me, leaning into it, expecting the creature to burst in after us. For the lack of a better solution I pulled over an old wooden cabinet that shelved old paint cans, oil rags and a bunch of other what have you. I knew it wouldn't provide any real protection, but I was simply moving off of instinct and random brain reactions at that point. The cabinet crashed to the floor leaving obnoxious fumes that we had no choice but to breathe.

Out of the corner of my eye I could see Wes frantically searching for something near the crafting table, and then after taking a deep breath I finally conjured the courage to take a gander outside, through an old dirty window that had some sort of rusted metal mesh on the outside.

I was looking for any sign of the hairy monstrosity that had pursued us into this dilapidated death trap. I was relieved that I saw nothing roaming about, but it didn't matter, we both knew what we saw, and it had to be lurking out there somewhere, patiently waiting to tear us limb from limb.

Wes didn't stop looking for whatever it was he was seeking even for a second. I was frustrated to the hilt. "There's a Bigfoot out there and we're in a papier-mâché garage that a stiff breeze could knock over."

"How do you know it's a fucking Bigfoot?"

I bent over and rested my hands on my knees trying to get my breathing back to normal. "Haven't you ever seen *In Search of…*? That thing looks just like the Patterson footage."

"It doesn't matter now," he said showing me a rifle and a handful of ammunition. "We've got this."

I looked at him almost laughing. "Wes, is that a .22 rifle?"

He nodded.

"That isn't powerful enough to kill an anorexic squirrel. If anything, you're just going to piss that thing out there off worse than it already is."

Wes started loading the rifle. "Well, for right now, it's the best protection we've got."

"Are you kidding me? A homemade slingshot and a rook from a chessboard would be more effective than that thing."

"Whatever," he said gripping the barrel tightly.

"If you use that fossil, it's probably going to blow up in your face," I said with a bit of concern and a smart-alecky type tone.

That's when I looked down and I saw that he had pissed himself. He knew I knew, and I looked up at him as if I didn't notice, but he had pissed himself bigger than shit.

The night got colder; we sat there in the dark. Wes stroked the rigid rifle's barrel, flakes and various particles broke loose and spun into the air as he held it closely, deeply believing it would protect us.

I could feel his back on mine as he rocked back and forth. There we sat in the center of the old garage floor, not knowing what time would bring. We were both hoping and praying that whatever did break into that inept decayed door I tried to barricade, would be merciful on our terrified souls.

Hours had past as I caught Wes snoring with the rifle loaded and pointing up in the air. I just knew he was going to kill one of us with that thing, and I had a very uneasy feeling that it was going to be me. I was certain that both of us were going to meet our demise, and if it wasn't from that gun going off in Wes's hand, it was going to be by way of that hairy-handed creeper.

I told myself I would close my eyes for only a second, but it wasn't for a second. Perhaps it was the exhaustion that comes from terror; maybe it was all those beers I drank or my growing indifference about it all. Whatever the reason, when my eyes opened it was day. I saw rays of light coming from everywhere that could channel a light source. Beams came in through the little mesh-covered window, the hole where the door handle used to be, and the bottom of the single car garage door that never did shut all the way, leaving a small gap between it and the concrete slab below it.

I began to rub the sleep out of my eyes and looked over at Wes and then down to the ticking hands on his wristwatch. It was half-past one in the afternoon. I couldn't believe we had slept that long, and I also couldn't believe the vicious hangover I had acquired.

Wes was resting so peacefully; I watched him slobber from the mouth down to the edge of his weak British-like chin, and just before I was about to wake him, the garage door began rolling up. The noise startled Wes; it also unfortunately caused him to pull the trigger of the rifle. Its bullet left a penny-sized hole in the ceiling.

The door struggled for a moment and then opened all the way aggressively. We saw a stunned Brett dressed to the nines, pulling off a pair of one hundred dollar shades to reveal his less than pleased facial expression.

"What in the living hell is going on?" he asked, flabbergasted.

What were we supposed to tell him, the truth? If it had been anyone else they would have locked us up and thrown away the key, but it was Brett, and if anyone was going to believe our fantastical spiel it would be him.

Wes started to tell him what had happened but Brett interrupted. "Have you guys been drinking?"

"Yeah," I answered.

His questions continued. "Did you piss yourself?"

Wes looked down at his damp crotch. "No."

"Okay knuckleheads, stand up and give me the fucking gun. You guys can tell me all about it when you get a change of clothes and some food in your stomachs."

As upset as he was, I would be lying if I said I wasn't elated to see him. Even if he didn't believe what happen to us; at least there was a semi-sensible adult around.

We followed Brett from the garage to the house where we saw Grandma's Station Wagon still parked next to the Orange Crush, which had its keys dangling from the trunk.

Brett removed them and jiggled them next to his ear. "Anyone missing a set of keys?"

I looked at Wes in disgust. "They were in the trunk the entire time you asshole."

Wes completely ignored me. "Why is Grandma's car still here? I thought she was leaving for the airport early this morning?"

Brett shrugged his shoulders. "Jesus, Wes. Maybe Aunt Freda picked her up. One of 'em can't take a shit without the other one knowing about it. Now get your assess inside and collect yourselves," he said, tossing the keys to Wes.

Wes clutched the car keys in his hands and squeezed them tightly while looking at me. I knew that look and that look meant that he believed everything that went on the night before to be true.

Wes was the first to walk in and Brett and I followed his piss-stained lead. We all took a good look around as Wes sat his keys by the door on the table the phone sat on.

As we walked through the door Brett yelled several times. "Grandma, Grandma are you here?"

There was no answer and Brett smiled while putting down a few of his belongings, letting out a breath from the weight of them all. "I told you she left; now you guys take a shower and I'm gonna crash on the couch. Tell me all about your wild outing when I wake up. I drove none stop for six hours. I'm exhausted. I'm taking the gun with me in case you little weirdo's try to shoot your own shadows and end up getting me instead."

Time drifted onward; we took our showers, we filled our bellies and flipped through old comic books until Brett had fully rested. It's funny, all of those hours went by and neither of us mentioned anything that happened. We just treated it as if there were an invisible elephant in the room.

We did anything to kill time as he slept. We reverted to what we used to do as younger innocent youths, spending our time upstairs turning wire clothes hangers into indoor basketball goals, and sinking in three pointers from behind the old Indian rug with a clumped-up fistful of tinfoil.

We never noticed the day turn into night. It could have been because we ourselves were boys and kids can become easily diverted even in the face of terrible things, but the two of us felt a huge relief when Brett woke and took the short stint up stairs to where we were. He swung the door open and stood in front of us with arms out wide. He called this his rock star pose.

"What's up kids?" he asked, even though he wasn't even ten years older than us.

Brett sat down next to Wes on the bed that was caddy-corner from the one I was sitting on. "Robbie, I'm sorry I missed the funeral; I took the week off, so I'll try to make it up to you."

Wes messed up the top of Brett's hair, which was slightly receding. "Better late than never."

"I guess."

"I'm really glad you came, Brett," I said, and I meant it sincerely. The three of us together again, helped bring some sort of semblance to the vile circumstance.

"Robbie, for you I would have walked here," he said, almost tearing up. "Why does it seem now days, we only get to see each other when someone dies?"

Wes chuckled before speaking. "Grandma can't have that much longer to live, so it won't be long before we will be seeing each other again."

Brett shook his head. "Are you kidding? That crazy old crust bag is too mean to die; she will probably outlive all of us."

"Let's hope not," I remember accidently saying out loud.

"Why did she go ape shit on you guys yesterday?"

"That's not the half of it," said Wes.

Brett leaned his head back against the wall, looked at me and his brother. "So what the fuck happened last night?"

Finally we had Brett's undivided attention. We told him about how crazy Grandma was acting, how she threatened our very lives with an unwashed kitchen utensil, and most importantly we told him of the macabre monster that seemingly came from the brink of the blackest abyss to stalk us throughout the night, toying with us like a cat pawing a half-dead mouse.

It wasn't long before I realized that Brett didn't believe, or at least didn't want to believe ninety-five percent of our story.

"Guys," he said, clasping his hands together and resting his cheek on whatever knuckle protruded the most. "You were drunk; you were watching Sammy Terry and you had just returned from a double funeral. You were then chased around by a knife-wielding Keystone Cop with poor hygiene. Isn't it possible that the combination of all of those things got your imaginations stirring, and you just imagined all of these things?"

Wes and I looked at each other not believing Brett's scenario for a second. I knew all of those things sounded like a reasonable catalyst for us to think we saw something, but despite all of those negative ingredients, what happened to us out there was real.

I stood up and approached Brett. "We know what we saw!"

Brett stood up as well and walked over to his old record player that sat in front of the highly hung window that we had sneaked out of the night before.

He didn't respond to me, he just started flipping through his eclectic vinyl collection that he had left behind from when he used to live there. He stopped at a Pink Floyd album, removed it from its sleeve and began playing *The Dark Side of the Moon* just a little too loud.

We didn't bother him as he rummaged a

Ziploc bag out of his green flak jacket, we just watched him closely as he took in his selected tune.

Brett's silence started to worry me. He reached into the aforementioned bag and pulled out more than a pinch of marijuana, proceeded to roll a joint with the assistance of a crisp one dollar bill. The old and dull needle on the record player made the song sound even creepier, and a little bit annoying; like two cats fucking on a perpetual loop. He finally stuck the joint in his mouth and lit it with a silver butane lighter.

After taking a nice long drag he finally exhaled, which was followed by a cough that sounded like a dry heave. He turned away from the window, looked at me directly and asked with no hint of cynicism: "Did it have red eyes?"

That was one of the details that we had failed to tell him during our overly excited recollection. Judging by the look on his face and the fact he knew about the eyes without us even telling him, could mean only one thing. He too at some point had seen the creature.

Just as Brett was going to tell us of his experience or experiences with the unknown beast, we heard a reckless thump against the house right outside the window which was then followed by an indescribable roar. Just like the one that Wes and I were privy to the night before.

Brett's eyes widened and his voice seemed panicked, by way of its cracking. "You two lock all the doors and turn off the lights, while I get the rifle," he said in the sternest voice I had ever heard him speak.

We knew he was panicked, and his panic caused us to rustle and bustle throughout the house. I followed Wes as we turned off every light in the house . . . except for one.

I looked on and asked. "Why is Grandma's bathroom light on?"

He looked at me, but never answered. He just shook his head in uncertainty. "We have to go in right?"

"I rather not know, maybe she didn't turn off the light because she is old and senile," I remember telling him.

"I don't care if she forgot to flush or not, we have to turn out this fucking light."

"Yeah, you're right about her not flushing; I can smell it through the door. She must have taken one righteous shit!"

Wes's face sported an unconfident expression, as we could hear Brett loading the gun, from just a few rooms away.

We kicked in the bathroom door and when it swung open the smell caught us; I don't know about him, but the first thing I noticed wasn't the aroma of feces, but the stench of death. Wes started coughing and tried to push me away, but I didn't go. I looked because I was young, fearless and a little bit stupid.

Wes and I looked in further, and that's when we saw what was left of our grandmother in front of us.

Grandma not flushing wasn't what caused the smell, it was her body. Her head was in the toilet, floating about like a fishing bobber, and surrounded by blood and other internal things that I was certain were out of place. Her wrinkled mouth was open wide and a turd was just inches away from rushing into it. Her nasty and wrinkled decapitated body was leaning against the bathtub.

I remember the distraught face on Wes; he was destroyed when he saw her wrinkled headless body flooded in blood. Her varicose veins and sagging tits fully exposed.

"Turn off the light and let's move," Brett said from down the hall.

Wes yelled, "Grandma's naked!"

"What?" he asked.

"Grandma's naked and she has a sailors anchor tattooed on her ass cheek," he repeated himself, this time adding a little more information.

Brett seemed confused. "What the hell are you talking about?"

This time I decided to explain it. "Grandma is dead, and her head is floating in the shitter next to a turd shaped like a lower case j."

For whatever reason, Brett had to see it for himself. When he reached the bathroom he pushed us out of the way so he could have an unobstructed view. His eyes soon saw what ours were trying to forget.

He turned pale and for a moment I thought he was going to vomit. I on the other hand was shocked, but had recently been in close quarters with my deceased parents' burnt remains. I don't know how, but that had given me an emotional advantage.

I looked around and everything seemed surreal. How could it not, Wes was looking at his brother as I looked at them along with Grandma who was now in multiple pieces due to an unknown evil that Wes and I had narrowly avoided the night before. The sad thing was, despite all of the blood and gore, the one thing I couldn't get over was that damn tattoo on Grandma's mud flap of an ass.

Even though Brett wanted to puke he didn't, and after he collected himself he started drilling Wes and I as to what the three of us should do.

As we followed him down the hallway we heard another disturbance emanating from outside.

"Did you guys make sure that all the lights are off, and all the doors are locked?"

We probably nodded yes in unison; all I remember is the fear and a sense of survival. The world had taken away my parents and my faith, along with almost everything else that I had believed in up to that point. There wasn't a chance in hell that I was going to let it take my life without a fight.

Wes was breathing hard, so hard I thought he was going to hyperventilate before he finally forced out his words. "What the hell are we gonna do?"

Brett looked at the rifle. "We're gonna sit in the corner of the living room, our backs against the wall with all of the lights off. If we can't see it, it can't see us," he said with confidence.

We knew that Brett didn't know what to do, but he was the adult so we listened.

The house was pitch black, and we gathered in the corner just as suggested. We had closed every door, every blind and every curtain. I even found time to turn off that strange little blue light that always illuminated from the kitchen. We huddled together in darkness, hoping that the evil that lurked outside couldn't get in.

Brett held the gun tight in his hand. I'm certain that Wes or I would have been better with it, but he was the oldest so we followed his lead. His theory worried me when he said if we couldn't see it, then it couldn't see us. If that was true then why did it have red eyes, and why did it seemingly only appear at night. If it were nocturnal, then one could only assume that it would have some sort of visual advantage.

We sat there quietly for the longest time, without any hint of incident until we heard yet another commotion coming from right outside our location; it sounded like long sharp fingernails dragging across a chalkless blackboard.

The sound would cease for a while, but every time it returned it became louder, more aggressive and closer.

"It knows we're in here," said Wes, as his teeth chattered with fear.

Brett was crying, fretting over what macabrely deviant things it had in mind for us, but I just sat there, watching the two of them break down before my eyes. They began to hold on tight to each other, and once again I was reminded of my position on the totem pole of life. They had a lot left to lose, where I on the other hand had nothing.

That's when I knew deep down inside, if it came down to it, as much as they loved me, either of them would throw me to the wolves, or in this case Bigfoot, if it meant their bond would stay intact.

While watching them reassure each other, a huge crash startled us all. It had shattered the pane glass window on the side of the room across from us; causing shards to spread out everywhere like shrapnel from a hand grenade. Its hair-covered fist was the size of an anvil.

Wes and Brett began screaming in terror as the creature peered into the window with its fire-like eyes while belting out an excited, impatient noise that sounded like a pig being stabbed with a red hot poker.

That's when I did what I never thought I

would do. I ripped the rifle out of Brett's hands. The expression on his face would have been no different if I had beaten a baby seal to death with my erect penis.

"What the fuck are you doing, Robbie?" he said in shock.

"How many slugs are in this?" I asked, trying to yell over the other worldly scream and chaos coming from the monster.

"Give it back," said Brett.

"I said, 'how many'?"

"It's got five shots."

I was full of adrenaline. I got up and stood about six feet from the window, where the creature was trying to get in. I pulled the lever, aimed the rifle in the general direction of the beast and then pulled the trigger, repeating my actions a second time. Getting off what I believed to be two solid shots.

"You're wasting our bullets," Wes rasped, practically voiceless from screaming.

"I think I hit the damn thing."

Brett unshielded his eyes. "How can you tell?"

"Because I don't hear it or see it anymore," I said, still aiming the gun at the vacant window.

I overheard Wes whispering to his brother. "Even if he didn't hit it, maybe he scared it off."

"Yeah, or maybe it's just pretending to be hurt and waiting for us to make a mistake," Brett told him.

I became overwhelmed by the silence.

The exposed window caused the cool fall breeze to force air into the old farm house, filling it as if it were an iron lung. I inhaled the fresh air that whisked through freely. I took in breaths deeply, hoping that it would assist in keeping me calm.

Wes looked over to me. "Now what are we going to do?"

"I say we get those keys on the table and get to the Orange Crush while we still have a chance."

"But what if Brett is right, what if it is just out there waiting for us?"

"I don't see what other choice we have than to go out and to get in that car. If we stay in here who's to say we won't end up like Grandma?"

"Maybe Robbie is right, Brett."

"We're losing time guys. Now, I'm gonna grab those keys and drive out of here. If you guys want to sit in that corner until morning comes, it's up to you, but that thing out there already knows you're in here, we all know its intent, and we have seen what it can do."

Wes seemed to plead with Brett. "I think he's right, once we get to the car nothing's going to be able to catch us."

Brett seemed to reluctantly agree, I could tell his heart wasn't in it. I don't think he liked the idea of a teenage kid telling him what to do.

He stood and pulled Wes up with him by the arm. "We aren't going out there unarmed," he said aggressively.

"What are we gonna use?" asked his little brother.

"Help me turn over this dinner table. We'll rip the legs off and use them as clubs."

I looked at them out of the corner of my eye, as I stood tight and perched with awareness. I was surprised about how quickly they tumbled the table and had Kubrick-like monkey weapons in their hands.

I loved them both, especially Wes, my entire childhood was built around him and the cherry tree out front. Some of my best and earliest memories involved him, but I started to get the feeling, that both he and his brother would kill me for the car keys that now lay in my uneasy hands.

They hunkered up next to me, adjacent to the door. I could feel the heat of their bodies pressing against mine, not to mention the smell of their foul breaths.

"I'm going to open this door, and walk out of it."

I was expecting more resistance, but was faced with little, probably because despite how lame my plan was, it was the only one we had. They certainly didn't have a better one.

"We're going to go on three," I said, wondering if one of them was going to bash me on the back of the head and leave me for dead as soon as I stepped outside.

When I reached the count of three and left the quasi-protection of the house, my adrenaline was in overdrive. I was looking in every direction and it took me a few seconds for my eyes to adjust.

"There's nothing out here, we're gonna be fine," said Wes, trying hard to convince himself.

"Okay guys, let's get in the car and I'll drive us the hell out of here." That's when I felt the blunt table leg striking my neck, causing me to fall and turn onto my back. Before I knew it, Brett had wrestled the gun away from me.

He stood over me with gun in hand as Wes just stood there and watched. "I'm afraid I can't let that happen, Robbie!"

"What the fuck are you doing?" I asked him as the tables were now turned.

He was breathing hard; I could see his chest heaving with emotion. "I'm not going to let some punk boss me around, I don't care who you are!"

"I can't believe you hit me."

"Give me the fucking keys."

He had the gun, but I had made up my mind that there was no way in hell that he was going to get those keys from me. The only way that car was leaving without me inside it, was going to be over my dead body, which considering the circumstances didn't seem that farfetched.

Wes continued to stand by and look on as his brother and I were fighting over the keys.

"Get over here and help me get the keys from him!"

There was still no movement even with the outcry of his brother. Wes and I had a bond that I thought could never be broken, but a monster in the woods had never entered the equation.

I was clinging onto the keys for dear life; I had my middle finger in the key chain's center. I felt it crack as Brett pulled even harder. Just like I said, no matter what I wasn't letting go.

Punches began to rain from his fist above. He kept hitting me and hitting me until my mouth was full of blood and tasted like old pennies.

The stars started to go dim and I felt consciousness slipping away, and that was the moment that the creature made itself known again, but this time at Brett's expense. It lifted him up over its head and shook him wildly, causing Brett to drop the gun.

Wes began screaming Brett's name and I got my hands on the rifle again. Brett's cries for help showed no signs of slowing. He became more hysterical with each passing moment. That's when I decided I was going to shoot that thing regardless of the consequences.

"Do something!" Wes screamed at me.

I shot the rifle and came very close to hitting it where I wanted, but at least I hit it. The Bigfoot took a few steps back which told me it did affect him despite the low caliber. It also meant I had two shots left.

Even though the creature was injured, it began to shake Brett even harder over its head, and then threw him like a dart into the side of the house where he instantly fell to the ground. There was a blood splattered indentation on the house, and a pool of blood surrounding the area in which he fell. Brett resembled a pretzel, and it looked like every bone in his body had been crushed from the impact. No question about it, Brett was dead. At least he went out easier than Grandma.

The monster looked at me and then to Wes, who was emotionally spent at this point. He wasn't even prepared to put up a fight. He was hunkered down in a fetal position ready to accept his seemingly inevitable demise.

Why it went after him, and not me I will never know. I thought it was going to kill him just like it had killed Grandma and Brett, but it soon became apparent that he had other sinister plans for Wes, as it picked him up like he was cradling a baby, and began running away with him back to the cornfield.

I fired the rifle carelessly at the beast, using my last two shots at its running, big striding body in the hopes it would panic and drop Wes, sparring him what I knew was going to be a punishment worse than death.

My attempt was in vein. Wes got taken away by that thing, and I never saw him again. No one ever saw him again.

I got in the car and began to drive away. I didn't even have a fucking driver's license, but I

CHADBOURNE

certainly couldn't stay behind. I was paranoid that the next morning newspaper headlines would read, MOURNING BOY KILLS FAMILY MEMBERS AND FLEES. I mean they certainly weren't going to pin it on Bigfoot.

So I began my lone journey on the path of the unknown, the only way I was ever going to put this pain behind me, was to get as far away from here as I possibly could. It wouldn't be easy, but I did have youth on my side.

As I drove down the driveway I was surrounded by darkness, except for the stars in the sky and the headlights spitting out illumination in front of me. I kept looking back in fear, making sure nothing was chasing me, and praying this whole thing would end.

That's when the strangest thing happened. I was looking behind me at the house in the rear view mirror. Well, remember that little blue light that I had turned off, the one that seemed to always be on for no explicable reason. It was back on again, shinning brighter than ever. Who turned on that light? What was that light? I would never know.

In a foolish decision, I put the car in park and stepped outside. I spat any remaining blood from my mouth and wiped my lacerated brow with my shirt. I took a big breath and looked around. I closed my eyes for a split second to clear my head. When I reopened them I was shocked to see something standing in front of the car. It was big and furry, and its eyes refracted the beams of the headlights. It was the one thing I thought that I would never see again.

You know what it was? It was Samson. Wes was right, that old fucking dog was still alive. I got back in the car, pulled up next to him and opened the passenger side door.

"Sam. Jump in boy," I said, thrilled to see him.

I rubbed his ears and then I floored it. It wasn't long before we were on the highway, burning up the road at well over one hundred miles an hour.

I flipped on the radio. At first there was static. I turned the knob until we achieved reception.

RADIO PERSONALTIES DISEMBODIED VOICE:

"I'm Zach Davis and you are listening to SKY 99, the only radio station that plays hits from the fifties to the eighties. Right now were going to play a tune to soothe the savage beast. Here is Elvis Presley performing 'Love Me Tender' from the '68 Comeback Special."

There we were, speeding through the night and riding the wild wind. It was just me, Samson, and The King's ghost to keep us company.

James B. Carter was born in Muncie, Indiana and was surrounded by an immediate family of prolific readers. He had a flair for drawing and writing at an early age. His youth was dominated by horror films, the writings of Robert E. Howard, and the artistic stylings of John Buscema.

He wrote several unpublished books between the ages of seventeen and nineteen. In his twenties he attended the Stan Nossett School of Fine Arts and eventually became an accomplished illustrator, professionally designing comic book characters for almost a decade, even working with comic great and two time Eisner Award nominee Troy Hickman, until he was consumed by the writing bug.

After the release of his debut novel in 2002, he became a long time guest columnist for *The Star Press*, and along the way he collected awards for his outstanding achievements in poetry.

James is now an all genres writer with a penchant for horror. He has several novels in the works including one to be edited by Paul Fry, editor of Eric Red's *Don't Stand So Close*, who also wrote the classic eighties horror films *Near Dark* and *The Hitcher*.

James is hell-bent on spending the rest of his years writing novels and shorts, fearing the only honest critic he has ever met, his three year old daughter Emma Sofia Carter.

The weight of him on top of her felt so good. *Who cared if he could never get her off?* This was much more than enough.

Heather closed her eyes and listened to her love sounds; soft and rhythmic, in perfect sync with her boyfriend's silent thrusts. He never made a sound, not even when he came and she was grateful for it. Just the weight of him, and the silence, and her moaning—the moans were always of great comfort to her, like an exotic creature, cooing in the night. It meant she wasn't alone in the world, a fear so great she momentarily tensed at the thought of it.

"No, keep going, baby. I'm close. I'm almost there," she lied, knowing it would only be another minute before he shot his load. It didn't matter that he could only last short of five minutes because his insatiable sex drive made up the difference—he wanted her several times a day. Sure, she would have preferred to go for hours at a time but sort of grew accustomed to these "mini-fucks" as she jokingly called them. And besides, she usually got laid at least every other weekend when he flew back east. She was totally hot, with legs for days and could have any guy she wanted. Men really were a sucker for blondes and big tits and hers were *au naturel*, a full C and perfectly shaped. So while he was off visiting his twin girls, she was showing off hers.

Heather started to giggle at her own sick joke when an odd tingling sensation swelled up within her, deep inside her vaginal wall. She gasped, eyes widening. "Get off me. Jacob, get off."

"What?" Jacob lifted his head from the crook of Heather's neck as she pushed at his chest. "What's wrong?"

"I can't breathe. I need air," she lied again, feeling his cock withdraw from her as he rolled over and up into a sitting position. Heather momentarily fumbled with the tent's zipper before finding a secure grasp, the plastic opening flapping outward with one upward motion of her arm.

Outside, she tiptoed around to the back of the tent as fast as possible, the dirt ground course and cool beneath her feet. *I don't fucking believe this.* Hunching over, she quickly slid her index and middle finger up into her vagina, up toward where she first felt the tingling sensation—which now felt like something else altogether. "Mike, you son of a bitch," she whispered, as her finger tips latched onto the foreign object and pulled down, freeing a shriveled, discolored latex condom.

"Heather?" Jacob called, charging around the tent, boner boomeranging against his thighs.

"Jesus!" Heather clutched her chest, condom squished firmly within one fist. "You scared the shit out of me." Jacob grabbed her by the forearms, concerned and bewildered.

"What's going on?"

Timothy McGivney

ARTWORK BY ELEANOR BENNETT

"I'm fine. It was a panic attack or something, really, but I'm okay now." Heather smiled reassuringly, relief flooding her body. *Close call.* "Just a drink of water, baby?" Jacob nodded, hesitant but compliant as usual and cupped a hand to her cheek before stepping back and disappearing around the tent.

Heather exhaled loudly, closing her eyes and shaking her head. She'd been with Mike last weekend. The condom must have come off somehow during their love making, if you could call it that—he'd taken her from behind, out on his back porch. *Why didn't he say anything?* She opened her hand and looked down at it; the condom resembled a popped, purple balloon, like it'd been fermenting within her for the past week. *And it had. It'd been inside her for almost eight days now.* "Christ almighty." She flung it to the ground, wrinkling her nose in disgust. *Way too close.*

She'd stopped using condoms with Jacob years ago. It would have been over if he had found it. She was surprised at how frightened she was at the idea of losing him. She'd been careless, really, in her affairs, almost not caring if she was caught. But now this, this overwhelming flood of emotions. *Did this mean she really loved him?*

"Fuck me."

Heather heard Jacob curse from the other side of the tent and decided she had plenty of time to debate the love question later. It was a cool night and now that she'd escaped such a messy pickle, so to speak, she started to feel the night's chill, which was lighted by a full moon worthy of the second glance she gave it as she tiptoed back around the tent to find a grimacing Jacob, holding out a bottle of water. "Stubbed my fucking toe."

"Sorry, baby." Heather winced sympathetically as she reached for the bottle but gasped when it fell between them, Jacob dropping it in midair, the water splashing against her ankles before she had time to jump back. "Jacob?"

He was standing upright, but seizing violently. His whole body shook, like he was being electrocuted, skull rocking back and forth, threatening to snap from its natural axis. Heather let out a startled cry, covering hands to mouth, but was otherwise frozen in place, stunned, as the seizures intensified. A low, buzzing sound now emanated from Jacob's throat, increasing in pitch as his eyes rolled back in their sockets and his jaw locked shut, releasing a frothy foam from the corners of his mouth.

He looked possessed, Heather thought, still unable to move but knowing she ought to do something, but what?

And then the blood came.

From his nose first, a crimson stream dripping freely from each nostril, down across his lips and over his chin, followed by his eyes and ears, the

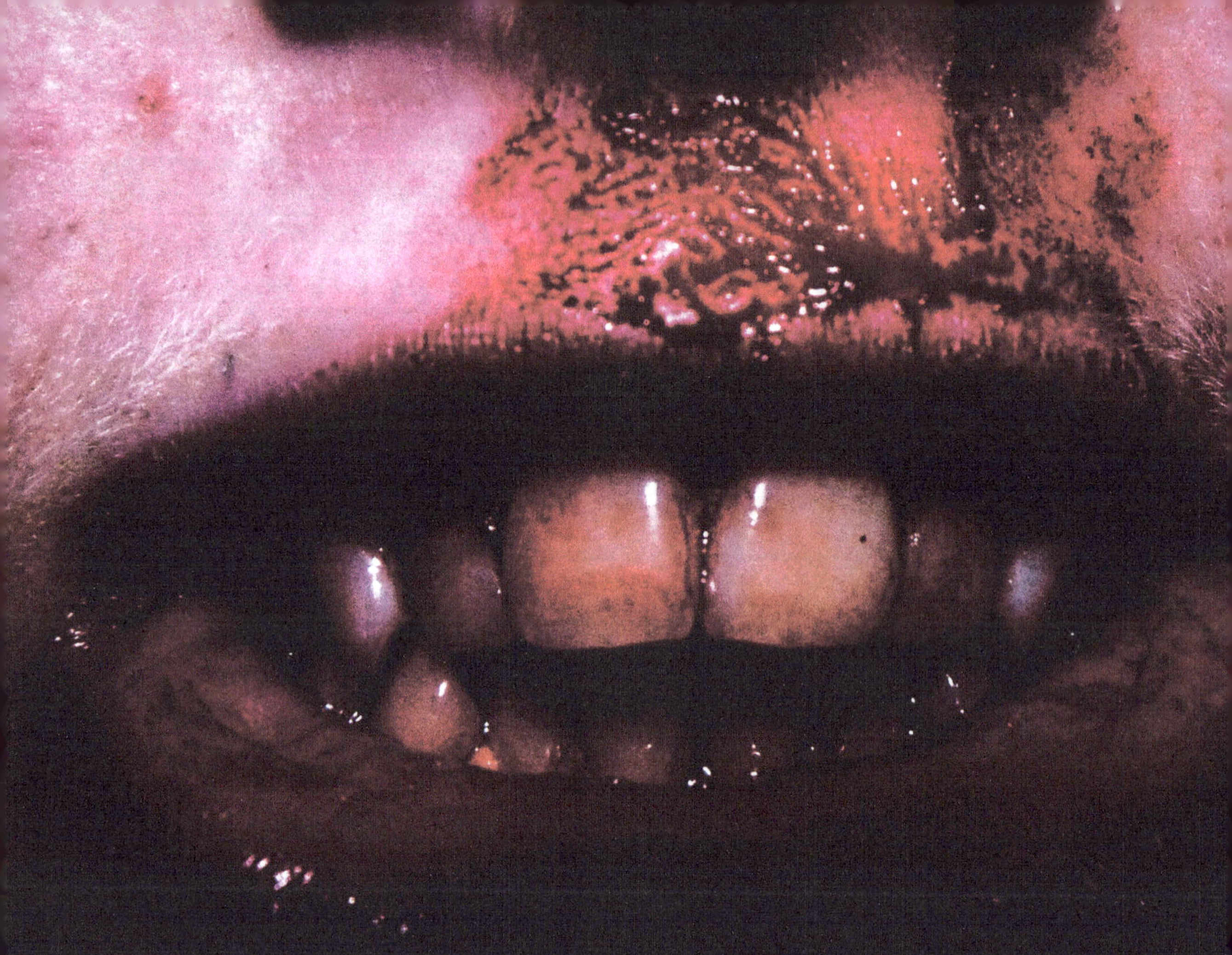

incessant blood seeping out of every facial orifice like a cracking dam.

Call 911—that's what she should do. Get her phone and call 911. *But where was it?* The buzzing sound Jacob had been making abruptly cut off with a sharp intake of breath, followed by a series of rasping, gargled hiccups, bloody bubbles spouting from his lips, his face and torso now covered in the shiny red excess, like he'd been dipped in it. *He was dying right in front of her.*

Heather took a step back and turned around, toward the tent, when she heard Jacob cough and felt her back side suddenly showered in a warm spray of what could only be blood. Tensing her back against the wetness, she pushed her way through the door flap of the tent, eyes scanning the disarray of clothing and camping gear. *Where was her purse? It'd be in her purse, damn it!* Outside. Next to the fire. Of course, she'd used her trusty hand sanitizer before dinner.

Heather barged back out of the tent, rising on tiptoes and stopping as she gasped at the sight of Jacob—face down on the ground. He wasn't moving. "Jacob?" she whispered, taking a timid step forward and reaching out a hand, but stopping. She couldn't touch him for some reason. *What was wrong with her?* "The phone. Get the fucking phone." Her eyes went straight to her purse, lying on a wooden log she'd used as a seat, on the other side of the fire pit.

Biting her index fingernail, Heather tiptoed around the blazing flames, which still burned strong after that evening's meal. Jacob always liked to have sex after eating, a full stomach and empty balls was his motto she nervously thought, as her fingers reached the phone, pulling it from her purse—but no bars. *Of course not.* Why had she expected a signal? *They were in the middle of bumfuck nowhere.*

A bone chilling, primal scream of fury jolted Heather from her thoughts and she jumped again, dropping the phone. It was Jacob, standing with hands balled into fists at his side, head thrown back, raging at the star filled night, the veins in his bloodied neck bulging, near to bursting. *What's happening to him? This isn't normal.*

As if in response to Heather's question, Jacob upped the strangeness factor by attacking himself, clawing at his face and hair, pulling chunks of it out by the root. "Stop it," Heather pleaded, voice just above a whisper. Jacob's fists were brutally pounding on his skull while his head shook side to side, like he was trying to rid himself of some unseen presence. "Stop it!" Heather shrieked, unable to take another moment of the torturous scene. And incredibly, Jacob does, eyes locking on Heather's in silent discovery, looking at her for the first time since the seizures began, his pupils dilated to black orbs, the whites of his eyes a sickly jaundice.

Unable to move, or even breathe, Heather stood trapped by a fear she's never known, riveted to the black abyss within Jacob's eyes, to the uncanny, growing hunger she saw in them but was not able to fully comprehend in that moment—that she was looking into the eyes of a predator, of death itself, come to snuff her out.

Wailing like a tortured animal, Jacob lunged at her, spewing bloody spittle through bared, gleaming pink teeth, his arms outstretched as he inexplicably dived forward, tripping over rocks encircling the camp fire and falling into it, down onto hands and knees. The copious blood dripping from him enticed the flames to rise higher, sizzling and crackling around his body—and yet, he determinedly moved straight toward her, effortlessly rising, eyes never leaving hers, the flames having no effect on him whatsoever.

This is madness. Run.

And she does.

Listening to her inner voice, Heather took off for the trail leading back to the highway. *How far was it? A mile maybe? A straight shot up the hill and then what?* She'd pass the Ford Explorer but without any keys it was useless to her. *Just get up the hill first and then see. One step at a time.*

The trail was wide and clear; soft, tiny dead leaves littered the ground, blanketing the trail but hiding the branches and rocks as well. *What I wouldn't give for a flashlight and some Goddamn clothes, and some running shoes for Christ's sake!*

"Damn it!" she cursed, stepping on an especially sharp rock, but not faltering. *No pain, no gain.* She knew she could make it to the top of the hill, she was fit and had run track in high school, but that was a long time ago and under entirely different circumstances. As long as she didn't fall . . .

She couldn't hear anyone behind her, no sounds of Jacob following, but that didn't mean he wasn't. He actually no longer looked like Jacob. It was in the eyes. His essence was missing. The Jacob she knew was no longer in there, replaced by a—

Heather slammed into something hard, felt hands on her, squeezing her shoulders. Screaming, she tried to break free but her captor held fast.

"Whoa now, lit'l lady. Where you runin' off to in your birthday suit?" Heather faintly recognized the burly bearded man, staring into his red and green checkered wool jacket, her hands pushing against the scratchy fabric. It was the perv she'd passed walking back from the lake the other day, his eyes glued to her tits. As far as she knew, he was the only other camper on this side of the highway. It was the more isolated of the two campgrounds, which was how Jacob preferred things.

"Let me go." She jerked backwards with all her might, a desperate groan escaping her throat as she threw her body weight into a twisting motion, causing the perv to slightly lose balance, shuffling around her and swapping positions on the trail.

"A sly and slippery thing, aintcha?"

Wild-eyed but alert, Heather strained her neck around the big buffoon's shoulder and peered into the darkness, back toward the way she'd come, searching for Jacob. "It's my boyfriend, asshole. Something's wrong with him."

"A lovers spat?"

"No!" Heather shouted, beyond frustrated. "I don't know how to explain it. He's—"

Jacob charged out of the night, jumped onto the perv's back with an unnatural ease and yanked down hard on a generous fistful of ginger mullet. Heather froze once again, mouth agape, watching in horror as Jacob bit into the exposed, thick bearded neck, right onto the prominent Adam's apple. A straggled rasp, passing for a scream escaped from the perv's mouth and he immediately released his hold on Heather, who'd been recoiling, her body weight leaning away from the atrocious act in such a way that she lost balance, rear end dropping straight onto the ground.

Jacob lifted his head from the perv's mutilated neck and spat out into the air, mouth already returning in search of meatier flesh as the Adam's apple plopped right onto Heather's belly button. She screamed, flicking it off her, the act of doing so propelling her to her knees and up to her feet, where she took off once again up the hill, faster this time, heart pounding against her chest.

Cannibalism? Like those ridiculous movies Jacob was always watching; something about cannibals in the hills? She only ever half paid attention, texted through most of them—when her face wasn't buried in his crotch, giving some of her "supreme Grade A head" as Jacob liked to call it . . . he did have the sweetest cum, like tapioca pud—

A shriek of fury traveled up the trail from behind her and Heather inhaled sharply, all thoughts of sugary semen vanishing from her head. *No, not cannibals. Zombies.* Like that thirtysomething days after movie—the one where the man was shrieking like a banshee, how he changed in the blink of an eye. It wasn't that far off from how Jacob was behaving now and they sounded exactly the same.

She had to sit in a movie theater for that one, watched the whole disgusting thing and then had to deal with the aftermath—Jacob jumping out from the bathroom later that night, pretending to be a spazzed out zombie and chasing her into the bedroom and onto the bed, where he jumped on top of her, tickle-torturing her and faux ravaging her neck, his cock growing hard at her squeals of protest, poking out against his boxer briefs.

He really was a tool. And to think she was falling for him.

Heather picked up her pace, lungs burning with exertion. She didn't dare look behind her, thoughts of the perv's Adam's apple hitting her like a sweet 'n sour chicken spitball pushing her on. *Faster. Faster. Faster.* And suddenly, she was at the top of the trail, coming up over an embankment and onto the empty parking grounds. She could see the perv's beat up El Camino to her left and directly across from it was Jacob's Ford Explorer. *If she only had the keys.* No time for wishful thinking.

Sailing by both vehicles, Heather passed straight through the center of the parking lot and up the narrowing dirt driveway, the ground smoother and free of rocks and other debris. *Just get to the other side.* That's what she needed to do. There'd be help at the other campsite. Families and men with guns. The hicks in this state never left home without them. If she could make it over the highway and—a loud booming sound exploded into the night and Heather gasped, only slightly slowing in stride as she came onto the main thoroughfare, the rear lights from one of those 4x4 monster trucks already beginning to fade into the distance.

"Wait! Come back!" she screamed, chasing after it, her feet hitting the paved highway with a smacking, quickening desperateness that brought a cruel and sobering reality to her circumstances as the truck vanished from sight. *This really wasn't going to be easy, was it?* "Please, come back," she breathlessly begged, coming to a stop in the middle of the road. *Jacob.*

Heather whipped around, suddenly terrified that he was behind her. But he wasn't . . . only a dark and lonely highway . . . and a cop car . . . parked a couple hundred feet up the road, right outside of some Ranger's office. And the lights were on inside, shining brightly through a large bay window. *Could there actually be someone there? Someone to help her?*

With a sudden burst of vigor, Heather took off toward the building, noticing her perspiration soaked body for the first time, the night's air cooling her slick skin as her eyes darted from the cop car to the parking ground's entrance, keeping an eye out for Jacob. *Where was that mother fucker?*

Oh, oh, what's this?

Nearing the back of the police vehicle, Heather came to a stop. The driver's side door was open. *Look inside.* She tiptoed away from the car, side stepping around the open door and peering into the front seat. *Empty.* No keys in the ignition either. She glanced nervously behind her before looking back at the lighted facility. What was she waiting for? "Get your ass in there." She forced herself to move, taking two steps toward the front of the vehicle before stopping dead in her tracks. *Sweet Jesus.*

A body lay sprawled across the pavement, shiny black boots and a tan uniform identifying him as the probable owner of the abandoned vehicle. Built like a bull dog, he was large but short and positioned on his backside, arms bent at the elbows, palms facing the sky. *Here's my knight in shining armor.* A dead cop or a forest ranger, perhaps? Whatever kind of law enforcement they had up here. A lot of good he was to her.

Heather took a reluctant step forward and gasped on closer inspection. The dead man had been shot clear through the face, his nose and mouth area completely obliterated, nothing but a sunken black hole remaining—and a pair of yellow eyeballs—somehow suspended out of the blackness, highlighted his menacing death stare. Her bowels churned at the familiarity she recognized in the corpse's eyes; they were identical to Jacob's, an acute jaundice in color and diseased . . . with hunger . . . even in death.

Ill at ease, she looked away from the disturbing sight and moved on toward the building. *What did this mean?* Up a couple cement steps. *Were there others too, like Jacob? Other people turning into these monsters?* She pushed the single glass door to the building open, noting the words *Sub Station #2* in white lettering on the door and stepped inside.

Heather saw the man locked behind bars at once; they stood staring at each other, both shocked at the other's presence. She hadn't expected to find someone in jail, hadn't even expected there to be a cell in here, which was pretty much all there was she discovered, with a quick, disappointed glance around the small, bare walled station, taking note of the clutter free desk on one side of the room and the wooden waiting bench on the other.

Returning her gaze to the prisoner, she found his eyes glued to her snatch, which she promptly covered with the palm of her hand, her other hand cupping one of her breasts, her forearm pressed against her second nipple. *Shit. Her tits were hard as rocks.*

She'd completely forgotten she was naked and now felt exposed under the florescent lights, with this Juan Valdez look-alike drooling over her. He had a black, bushy mustache that curved slightly upwards at the ends and he was glassy eyed, like maybe he was stoned. Heather coolly studied him as his eyes moved slowly up her body, lingering at her chest unapologetically before reaching her face, and then her eyes.

"Sácame de aquí." The man reached for the prison bars, gripping them firmly, his biceps bulging. Heather took a slight intake of breath, about to take a step backwards but stopped. *Spanish.* She held his gaze, squinting. He didn't look much older than her. Not exactly her type, but the grease-stained wife beater he was wearing showed off an impressive physique, she'd give him that. He *was* short though, but weren't most of the men one encountered? *Jesus, they weren't about to fuck.*

"Perfecto mundo," Heather said sarcastically, shaking her head with a sigh. "That's all you're getting from me." He was locked up for a reason—a no good one—so he could stay right where he was. She turned her back to the prisoner and moved toward the desk. *A phone.* "Please work," Heather whispered as she reached across the desk, all modesty forgotten. *Let him enjoy the view.* She picked up the receiver, but only dead air greeted her. She tried again for a dial tone but got nothing. "Damn it," she muttered through clenched teeth as she slammed it back onto its cradle.

A navy blue wind breaker was draped across the back of the desk's chair and Heather thankfully scooped it up, slipping her arms into the sleek material. Width wise, it was more than ample, but the sleeves stopped just short of her wrists and the length of it failed to reach her pubic region. At just shy of six feet, Heather was used to having to search a little harder to find the perfect fit. This must have belonged to the dead man outside, she thought, zipping it right up to her collar bone.

"Véte y agarra las llaves. Están afuera con el policía." At the sound of the prisoner's voice, Heather tensed, then looked down at her pussy and sighed. Well, at least she'd just had a Brazilian; the Colombian Coffee King would have something pretty to stare at.

"I can't help you, okay?" Not bothering to cover her nether regions, Heather turned around, moving away from the desk and closer to the prisoner. "There is noth-ing I can do for you." She raised her voice and over pronounced each syllable, like she was talking to a deaf person. He kept his eyes on her this time, never straying from her face, the slight pleading behind them instantly turning to frustrated rage.

"¡Sácame en chinga de aquí, cabrona!" he shouted. "¡Quitales las llaves al pínche cerdo ese y sácame!" Despite herself, Heather flinched and stepped back, annoyed that she showed weakness. He kept pointing past her, toward the bay window. *What did he want? Was something out there? Jacob*? Heather's heart began to race as she slowly moved toward the window, but with the light on inside, it was difficult to see out of it. She glanced back at the prisoner once again.

"¡Andale, hija de tu puta madre! ¡Córrele!" he shouted, jumping in place this time, his voice rising to an anxious shrill that Heather found hard to ignore. *Jesus, maybe she'd better take a look, just a quick peek.* She pushed the front door open and stepped outside.

The moon was still shining brightly overhead, the highway deserted and quiet, too quiet, really, for all that had just occurred. Her eyes couldn't help but look back toward the body . . . and the ring of keys she saw hanging from the officer's belt. *Why hadn't she seen them before?* She quickly tiptoed down the front steps, eyes vigilantly scanning the darkness as she made her way over to the body.

Kneeling down, she caught a slight whiff of a sickly sweet foulness she hadn't noticed before either. *Gross.* She breathed through her mouth, avoiding all eye contact with the rotting cop, the key ring easily clicking free with one twist from her thumb. *The one for the ignition had to be in here.* She stood up with a rush of adrenaline, examining the numerous keys when a gut wrenching shriek of fury erupted from out of the night.

Jacob.

Heather locked eyes with him as soon as she turned around. *Mother of God.*

From across the road, Jacob was sprinting full force, mad-hungry eyes drilling right through her.

She knew she should have gone for the car, but she was thinking *away*, and so turned around, ran back up the steps and into the building, the key ring trembling in her fingers as she pressed her body weight against the front door. She looked up just in time to see Jacob jump the steps and barrel toward the door; screamed when he ran into it, the glass structure vibrating against the assault, but not breaking. There were at least a dozen keys on the ring and she slid the first one her fingers found into the slot and turned it to the right. Miraculously, the bolt locked into place and she gasped in surprise, relief flooding her body. *But would it hold?*

Enraged, Jacob repeatedly banged his forehead into the door, shrieking with each impact as thick smears and specks of blood marked the glass in a flourish of red.

Hands out in front of her, like she'd be able to stop him if he did crash through, Heather cautiously backed away from the door. "¡Las llaves, cabrona, las llaves!" *Does he ever let up?*

"Enough already, for Christ's sake!" Heather turned around and shot the prisoner a look of death. "We're fucked, I know." With an angry scowl across her brow, she held her steely gaze on him as she moved back around the desk and took a seat behind it.

"¡Pínche cabrona loca! Nos tenemos que ir de aquí. ¡Andale, puta!"

"Shut up!" Heather screamed, swiveling in the chair so she faced him. She recognized the foul language he was spewing and had had enough. "Shut your filthy. Fucking. Trap." Spit flew from her lips and her voice went hoarse, eyes daring him to say another word.

The prisoner opened his mouth as if to reply but said nothing, the anger in his eyes dimming as he let go of the bars and stepped back.

Good. Keep it closed. Crossing her arms, Heather shut her eyes and let her head drop. *What now?* Jacob was still attacking the door. It seemed pretty solid, but who knew?

"¿Si o no?" Should she try 911 again? Heather pushed the chair back and grabbed the phone. "¿Si o no?" *Nothing.* Ignoring the prisoner's yammering, she let the phone drop from her hand; it banged against the desk with a single clack. *Was there a back way out of here?*

Keeping her eyes off the prisoner, Heather began a thorough search of the premises. There were only two doors she found on a wall opposite the prison cell, one leading to a bathroom, the other a storage closet. *How could there not be an emergency exit?* "¿Si o no?"

"What!?" Heather shouted, looking over at him in frustration, her temper getting the best of her once again.

"¿Si o no?" He whispered the words this time, rubbing his crotch with one hand; the bulge of his huge member was clearly outlined against his tan Dickies, the head of it extending down toward his right knee.

Heather's eyes widened in surprise and she gasped, the prisoner reveling at her reaction, a twisted smirk to his lips now, eyes gleeful with a smug satisfaction. He lifted his chin at her with a single nod. "¿Si o no?" he whispered again, fist now cupping what appeared to be over-sized testicles. Throat suddenly dry, Heather swallowed involuntarily, pussy twitching, betraying her. "Ahh, sí. Pínche puta." Pleased with himself, the prisoner laughed and licked his lips. Ashamed, Heather turned her back to him.

"Screw you." She'd had enough. *Where was the fucking light switch?* She was sick of his face and didn't want him drooling over her a second longer. *There it is.* She flipped the switch and the lights went out.

Holy hell.

Through the front bay window, Heather saw that a horde of those things were headed toward the station, already swarming past the police car and up the steps, their wrathful shrieks joining Jacob's, who continued his senseless charge at the door.

"¡Las llaves, cabrona!" Heather watched the first of the horde hit the bay window, a maniacal row of yellow eyes slamming against it, splintering the glass on first impact, with multiple cracking blows following in rapid succession. She was thinking how it reminded her of Alfred Hitchcock's *The Birds* when everything seemed to slow down; she felt her body go numb and the shrieking fade away.

Turning to look at the prisoner, she saw his mouth moving, but could no longer hear him. He was pointing past her. *Why was he always pointing like that?* Heather followed his index finger, turning back toward the door and found herself staring at the keys, still hanging from the key hole. *Yes, the keys. Of course.*

It was her only chance.

Heather bolted toward the door and all sound returned with a startling clarity, the smashing of glass prompting a frantic scream from her throat as she pulled the keys out of the front door. Spinning around, she felt a rush of cool air, heard the triumphant shrieks amongst the shards of breaking glass but didn't dare look back.

They've broken in. They're inside.

With eyes only on the cell before her, Heather found the biggest key on the ring—*the skeleton key.* This *had* to be the one. She grabbed its round end and easily slid the tip and then the body of the key into the slot of the cell's door. *Lefty loosey, righty tighty.* She twisted to the left and heard a click. "¡Muevele, cabrona!" The prisoner's eyes were wide with fear, but he pushed the bars to one side and as the cell's door slid open, Heather fell forward, the palms of her hands and knees smacking hard against the concrete floor.

"Lock us in, lock us in." Terrified, she scrambled to her feet, turning around in time to see the cell's door slam shut, the prisoner turning the lock, then pulling the key free.

"Esta es una pínche locura."

Heather pressed her back to the far wall, trying to put as much distance between herself and the approaching onslaught. Even with the lights out, she could still see everything quite vividly, the full moon highlighting the hellish scene. *This can't be happening.*

The horde had reached the cell and were pressing their blood-splattered faces up against the bars, trying to squeeze through, their arms reaching out, swiping at air. *They're so close. The cell was what? Maybe eight by ten at best and their arms could reach half the distance.*

And yet, still more came, so many of them, pushing and clamoring, leapfrogging their way through the shattered window, some of them falling, only to be toppled over by the ones behind. It looked like they were the campers from across the road—once grown men and women, children and teenagers, now the unthinkable: crazed man-eaters, all descending upon them, arms outstretched, mouths open . . .

Heather's arm brushed the prisoner and she looked down at him, saw that he was just as scared as she was. *Useless.* She was trapped in here with him, with this *fucking degenerate.* Pressing her hands over her ears, she tried to mute the piercing shrieks of the horde, but couldn't shut them out.

"No, please . . . make it stop, make it stop." She dropped to her knees, squeezed her eyes shut and began to rock back and forth, the shrieking only intensifying, reverberating off the concrete walls of the cell. *Get me out of here. I've got to get out.*

Heather reached out blindly and grabbed onto the prisoner's calf, her fingernails digging into his skin.

"Cuidado, cabrona. Te voy a meter unas cachetádas para que te calmas, puta estúpida." The prisoner pulled his leg free from Heather's grasp and hoisted her up by the forearms, forcibly shaking her, unruly blonde hair flapping about her face. "Agarra la onda pendeja." He grabbed her by the nape of the neck and yanked her up toward him, their faces inches apart. "O te voy a romper el pescuezo. ¿Me oiste?" Heather stared into the dark brown depths of his eyes; saw the malice and ill intent but also the sanity, the humanity.

"Si!" she cried out. "Si, si, si!" Breathless and hysterical . . . and impatient, Heather reached for his waistband and unfastened his pants, tugging them down in a feverish urgency, his boxers sliding off as well, freeing a brown, anaconda-sized cock.

"¿Ahh se te antoja la verga Mexicana, eh? ¡Mi zorra!" Semihard, it sprang upward, hitting her in the eye and she winced but reached for it anyway, grabbing it by the base with one hand while her other guided the smooth, dark head into her mouth. *My God, and she thought Jacob was packing.*

It was the largest penis she'd ever laid eyes on, her lips barely able to close around the gargantuan, mushroom-domed head. She gagged on it, eyes bulging. *It's okay, keep going.* She forced herself down on it even further, retching this time on its growing girth. *You're not cutting it.* Eyes watering, she came up for air, mouth sliding off the enormous piece of meat.

The horde was still screeching; their grasping hands visible through her peripheral vision. *Come on and give it to me, you bastard.*

"Skull-fuck me!" Heather reached up for the prisoner's hands and pulled them down onto the back of her head.

Make me forget where I am.

Spitting on the monstrosity jutting out at her, Heather wrapped her lips around it once again, determined to lose herself in the process. It'd grown even bigger, harder now she realized, amazed as it steadily began to inch down her throat, the hands on her head forcibly guiding her forward and then violently impaling her in one merciless thrust.

Heather's world exploded.

Face pressed firmly against his pelvic region, she retched, and retched some more, bile burning the back of her throat, snot running from her nostrils as she tried to inhale, nose buried deep in a moist forest of ripe pubic hair.

Unable to draw breath, panic set in and she pushed against him, screaming, the futile, guttural sound muffled by the massive appendage stuffed down her throat.

Stop fighting and let go.

A sweltering hotness swept through her body and a loud ringing sound invaded her mind.

And Heather let go.

She'd become one with the prisoner, the pulse of his cock throbbing in sync with her hammering heart as a soothing whiteness washed over her, followed by a darkness, finally, that swooped down and swallowed her whole.

Timothy McGivney is the author of the novels *Zombielicious* and its sequel, *Vampalicious*. "Si or No?" is his first short story. He resides in Palm Springs, California, is single, and currently dating (his TiVo). Check him out at TimothyMcGivney.com.

TO TURN A BLIND EYE

JEREMY TERRY

ILLUSTRATIONS BY LUKE SPOONER & ALFRED KLOSTERMAN

"The only thing necessary for the triumph of evil is for good men to do nothing."—Edmund Burke

1

Mary knew it was going to be a bad one when the sounds of shouting came floating towards her on the calm October air. It wasn't the volume of his voice that told her this, though he was already loud enough to be heard from seventy feet away through closed doors and windows. No, it was the intensity of his voice. She began to imagine what it would be like to be the target of such a thing and she shook her head violently, like a dog shaking off water. No, it would not do any good to dwell on such things. Better to mind one's own business; better to look after one's own self. She turned the kitchen faucet off and began drying her hands with a towel, thinking that there was an unfinished crossword in the Sunday paper she should wrap her mind around. And, while she was at it, maybe she would put on some Bach or Chopin. She found that classical music helped her think better, helped her concentrate on the task at hand . . .

. . . helped her drown out the outside world.

There was a crash and a scream, much higher pitched than any that had come before it. Mary instinctively spun around, pressing her hands to the window above the sink, her heart in her throat. The neighbor boy was lying in a crumpled heap in the center of his backyard, covered in dirt and crying. Was his name Michael? Or was it Marty? Mary couldn't remember. The back door burst open and the shouting man stepped out, now loud enough to rattle the windows in their frames. This one's name was John, she was sure of that. He walked over to his son and yanked him up by the collar of his shirt, ripping the fabric.

"No, Daddy! Please!"

The sound of his palm striking the boy's cheek was like a gunshot. He cried out in fear and pain, holding his hands out in a feeble attempt to stop his father from hurting him anymore.

"Shut that squealing up, you little bastard, or I'll—"

The shouting man stopped and looked towards Mary's house, as if he sensed her eyes upon him. Their eyes met and Mary's blood ran cold. She jumped away from the window as if she had been shocked and fled down the long hallway into the sitting room at the front of the house where she collapsed into her husband's old recliner. *Oh,* she thought, *oh, no! He saw me! He knows that I know! What am I going to do?* She turned her head to the side and pressed her face into the soft cushions of the chair, inhaling deeply. The smell was of salt and sawdust and dandruff shampoo. They were the smells of Richard, her husband of thirty years, dead now these past three.

"Oh, Richard, I wish you were here. You'd know what to do and I wouldn't have to be afraid."

She heard heavy footsteps on her front porch and then a hard rapping on the door. A few seconds passed and then the rapping came again, more insistent this time. She stood up and walked over to the door, "Yes, who is it?"

"Mrs. Clarendon, this is John Murphy. I'd like to talk with you for a minute."

"I'm afraid I'm a-a little busy at the moment. Could you come back later?"

"A little busy spying on your neighbors, Mrs. Clarendon? You need to open this door and talk with me."

"No," said Mary, her voice cracking. "I don't think so, Mr. Murphy. You need to go home before I call the police."

"Call the police?!" His voice rose an octave and he struck the door hard enough to crack the wood. "Listen here, you cunt. If you don't open this door right now, I'm going to kick it to splinters and then I'm going to come inside and do things to you that your husband never even dreamed of. You hear me?! Open this door!"

"Ju-just a second!" said Mary, as she fumbled at the locks with numb fingers. Murphy heard the locks click open and shoved the door, hitting Mary in the shoulder and knocking her to the foyer floor. He stepped inside and shut the door behind him.

"Now, we can talk," he said as his eyes began to scan the small room, fixating on a small bookcase against the wall.

"I-I didn't see anything, Mr. Murphy! I swear!"

"You sure?"

"Yes!"

"Are you really sure? I'd be very put out if a cop happened to show up on my doorstep tonight or tomorrow. I'd be so upset, I might have to walk back over here and pay you another visit. You wouldn't like that, Mrs. Clarendon. Not one bit."

Mary stared up at him from her spot on the floor, afraid to say anything, afraid she might set him off. Who knew? He may even be looking for an excuse to do those things he was talking about.

"Do you believe me, Mrs. Clarendon?"

Mary nodded, a silent tear running down her cheek.

"What was that? I didn't hear you."

"I believe you."

Murphy frowned. "No, I don't think you do. Not yet, anyway." He moved like water, quick and flowing and immensely strong. He placed his left foot on Mary's left wrist, pinning her hand to the floor, grabbed a large marble bookend off the bookcase and brought it down on her left hand. The pain was enormous, blotting out the world. She opened her mouth to give voice to her agony, but his rough hand clamped across her face, smothering her. He leaned down, his face only inches from hers and shushed her.

"Now," he said, smiling down at her, "you believe me. Remember, no police." He stood slowly to his feet. Mary watched him go, not daring to move until the door was shut with him on the other side of it.

2

The pain in Mary's hand was blinding. Each heartbeat felt like an explosion, making her both nauseous and light headed. She sat at her kitchen table with her head hung low and a bag of frozen peas resting on the mess that had been her hand. She was certain it was broken and she thought that she might need a few stitches on the palm. But, did she dare go to the hospital? How would she answer their questions? What if Murphy saw her go and thought that she was going to report him? Another wave of nausea struck her and she moaned, turning her head to look at the kitchen window. The shades were drawn shut, blocking out the orange-red glow of the setting sun. How did it come to this? She was locked inside her own home like a recluse, terrified of what lay right outside.

There was a soft tapping at the window. Mary sat upright, the sudden movement jarring a shriek of pain from her lips. A few seconds ticked by in silence and then the tapping repeated itself. Someone was outside, tapping at her window . . .

It's him.

Ice ran down her spine. She tried to stand up, to run and hide, but stars exploded across her field of vision and she fell back into her chair on the verge of fainting. She moaned, tears streaming down her cheeks, and spoke to the kitchen in desperation. "Please, just go away and leave me alone!"

A quiet voice spoke her name at the window.

She turned towards the sound, her terror fading into a mild sense of surprise. This was not the angry voice of a violent man, but the meek voice of a scared woman.

"Mrs. Clarendon? Please, are you there?"

Mary stood carefully, clutching the edge of the table with her good hand. The stars stayed in the sky this time, so she crossed to the sink and pulled the curtains back. Sally Murphy was standing under the window, wearing dark sunglasses and a long sleeve blouse. She wore a heavy layer of makeup on her bruised cheeks. Mary pitied the woman. She opened the window a crack and waited.

"Mrs. Clarendon, I came to apologize for my husband. He just gets so worked up sometimes, you know?"

"'Worked up'? He broke my hand."

"Oh, God," said Sally, her hand going to her mouth. "I'm so sorry. Do you need to go to the hospital?"

"Probably, but I don't know what to tell them."

"Tell them that you fell down some stairs; that works for me."

Mary was silent, deep in thought. "What if I tell the truth?"

"No! You can't!" exclaimed Sally. "He'd go to jail!"

"That's where he belongs, Sally."

"No, he's a good man. He just has a few bad days here and there." Sally frowned and took a step closer to the window. "Mrs. Clarendon . . . Mary, did he tell you he'd come back if you told anyone? He did, didn't he?"

Mary shivered and nodded.

"He meant what he said. You'd best remember that and let it go. It's better for everybody that way."

"Sally?" asked Mary, her voice quivering. "Why don't you leave him?"

She smiled in the failing light. "He loves us. He might not always show it, but I know." She turned away from the window and looked back at her home. "I have to go before he catches me. Remember what I said, Mrs. Clarendon. You fell; it's better that way." She gave Mary one last smile and walked back to her house.

3

Mary stepped inside and closed the front door behind her, locking it with her good hand. Leaning with her back against the door, she looked down at her left hand, now encased in a plaster cast. Mary took Sally's advice and lied to the attending doctor at the emergency room. He wasn't convinced with Mary's explanation of events, but in the end he had no choice but to accept what Mary told him. Her gaze drifted from the cast to the marble bookend, which still lay where Murphy had dropped it. There was a dark stain on one corner of the thing and she thought, *that's my blood.* The bookend had been a present from her husband, something she had treasured. Now, she couldn't bare the sight of the thing. She decided to throw it out with the garbage in the morning, but for now she left it alone.

She stumbled down the hallway and through the house, not taking the time to turn on the lights. She reached her bedroom and collapsed onto her bed, still fully clothed. She rolled onto her side and stared at the picture of her husband that rested on her bedside table.

"Oh, Richard, I wish you were here." She closed her eyes and dreamed of violent men.

4

Time passed by slowly for Mary as she became accustomed to her new life. She got up early, went to work, and returned home in the evenings. She found that being out in public made her nervous, so she began to make up excuses to stay home. Her only trips were to the market and the post office once a week. At night, she kept the shades drawn, her desire to view the outside world a thing of the past. She found it easy to live the life of a shut in, too easy, in fact. She began to worry, as she sat in her husband's chair with the soft sounds of a piano drifting to her from the stereo; worried that she might never recover from what had happened. The idea that she could spend the rest of her life living this way depressed and scared her. Still, wasn't it better to die an old shut in than a young and nosy meddler? She thought it was and resolved anew to mind her own business.

5

Mary was ready this time when the screaming started. She picked the remote up off of the small table that sat beside her chair and turned the stereo up. The soft notes of "Clair de Lune" drifted to her from the speakers, soothing her frayed nerves. The music had become her constant companion as of late, now she was depending on it to get her through the storm outside.

"John, no! Stop it, please!"

"Get off me, bitch!"

"He hasn't done anything, please don't hurt him anymore!"

"GET OFF!"

The song hit a crescendo, swelling and offering to take her away to someplace peaceful and kind. Yes, most of all kind. The kind of place where fathers don't hurt their children or their wives, the kind of place where people like her found the courage to do the right thing, to protect those that needed to be protected. It was a nice fantasy. Too bad it could never exist in the real world. There were too many shadows and dark places for that. Mary sighed and closed her eyes, willing herself to be carried away. To Oz, to Neverland, to Wonderland, anywhere in the world but where she was at that moment.

The sound of a slamming door brought Mary back from her reverie. She opened her eyes and sat up, listening. A few seconds later she heard the sound of someone running up onto her front porch.

"Mrs. Clarendon! Mary!"

It was Sally Murphy, although she didn't sound quite like herself. It was as if she were speaking through numb lips. Slowly, Mary stood up and walked to the door.

"What is it, Sally?" she asked, her injured hand clutched protectively against her chest.

"Please, let me in! I've got to call the police!"

"No," said Mary, shaking her head as if Sally could see the motion through the locked door. "Remember what you told me? No police. He said if I called the police he would come back and hurt me again. I don't want that to happen."

"Mary, please! He's killing my son!"

The strength drained from Mary's knees and she fell to the floor on the verge of fainting. Kill the boy? She had sat in her chair, thinking only of herself, while that monster was murdering his son?

"Oh, God no," she prayed, tears beginning to stream down her pale face. "Don't let it be true."

"Mary!"

"O-okay!" she said. Mary grabbed the doorknob and managed to get to her feet. She unlocked the door with unsteady fingers and pulled it open. Sally Murphy stood on the porch looking like something out of a horror movie. Her nose was broken, her eyes black and almost completely swollen shut. Blood ran from perhaps a dozen sources, falling to the porch and forming a pool at her feet.

"Oh, baby," said Mary, grabbing Sally's arm and helping her inside. "What did he do to you?"

"Doesn't matter," she answered through burst lips. "Call nine-one-one."

"We will, right now."

Mary pointed Sally towards the kitchen and then turned back to close and lock the front door. As she gripped the knob, Mary looked out across her yard towards the Murphy house and felt her heart skip a beat. John Murphy was standing in his front yard, covered in blood and staring at her with murder in his eyes.

"You meddlesome cunt! Send the bitch out to me or I'll come and get her!"

"No you will not, John Murphy. We've already called the police! They'll be here any minute!"

"You WHAT?!" Murphy took a step in her direction, his gore-soaked hands clenching into fists. Mary had seen enough. She stepped back inside and slammed the door, locking the deadbolt and securing the chain. Mary shuddered at the thought that those two flimsy locks were all that separated her from all of that rage. She turned and ran up the hall, praying that the door would hold.

Sally looked up, startled, as Mary ran into the kitchen and grabbed the phone. "What is it, Mary?"

"Nothing to worry about," she replied, dialing and holding the receiver to her ear.

"Nine-one-one do you have an emergency?"

"Yes," said Mary. "There's a m—"

The front door rattled in its frame as Murphy began kicking it. The two women screamed and clutched at each other in desperation.

"Ma'am? Are you there?"

"Yes, I'm here! You have to help us! He's going to kill us!"

"Okay, ma'am, I want to help you. Tell me where you are."

Mary gave the operator her address and was asked to stay on the line. Outside, a demon was roaring in the grip of an uncontrollable fury. He rained blow after blow on the door, intent on its destruction and the destruction of those it shielded.

"Sally!" screamed Murphy. "Open this door!"

"No," she whispered, tears streaming down her face and mixing with the blood that covered her cheeks and neck. "Just go away, please. Please!"

"Sally! Do as I say or it will be worse for you when I get in there! You hear me, you fucking whore?!"

He kicked the door again and again and again, tireless. Mary listened to the screams and the pounding, her blood running cold. She heard the wood of the door give with a loud crack and knew in her heart that she was going to die.

No, she thought. *You can't give up. Richard wouldn't give up. He would fight. Richard . . .*

That's it! She turned to the counter and grabbed a large butcher knife from the display rack that stood beside the sink and handed it to Sally. Sally held the knife out at arm's length as if it were a dangerous animal that might bite.

"Listen, take the phone and talk to the dispatcher. If John gets inside, use the knife."

"But, I can't!" moaned Sally.

"Yes. Yes you can," said Mary, gripping her shoulder gently. "I have to go get something from my bedroom and then I'll come right back."

"No! Don't leave me!"

"Sally, I'll be right back, I promise." There was another loud crack from the hallway and Mary winced. "Remember, if he gets inside, use the knife."

Mary turned and ran out of the kitchen, racking her brain for the location of the half-remembered object. Behind her, Sally cried out, trying to stop Mary, but she ignored her. Mary had to be swift, their lives depended on it. She entered her bedroom, heading straight to her dresser where she began yanking the drawers out one by one and dumping their contents onto the floor. It wasn't there. Where was it?

The closet.

Mary turned and threw the closet doors open, pushing aside the clothes hanging from the rod and searching the floor. Nothing.

There was a crash as the front door finally gave way and the sound of Murphy's heavy tread as he sprinted up the hallway. Sally screamed a high pitched, hopeless scream that was cut short when her husband reached her.

Out of time! Goddamn it, where is it!

Mary looked up and finally saw what she was looking for. She reached up and gripped the small metal box, lifting it from the shelf and placing it on the closet floor. Mary opened the box and removed the revolver. The .38 had belonged to Richard and hadn't been touched since he had passed away. Still, Richard had taken good care of the gun and Mary knew that it would fire. She took the gun and held it in her hand, loading it with fumbling fingers and then snapping the cylinder closed. The gun felt too big for her hands and surprisingly heavy. The weight calmed her. It was a mean thing, something that she hated. Now, she would use it on the only person that she had ever hated. She stood up and ran for the kitchen.

When she entered, Murphy was standing over Sally with his bloody hands around her throat, roaring obscenities into her red face. Mary yelled his name and raised the revolver, thumbing back the hammer. Murphy turned and stared down the muzzle of the gun, dropping Sally to the floor.

"Cunt," he said, and charged.

Mary flinched as she pulled the trigger, the round taking Murphy high on his right shoulder. He stumbled and fell, knocking Mary to the floor and yanking the gun out of her hands. Mary screamed and thrust her hands up, trying to shield herself from the coming blows and managed to get a finger in the gaping wound on his chest. Murphy roared in pain and slapped her hand away. He held the gun high over his head and brought it down on the center of Mary's face. Mary cried out in agony as she felt her nose shatter. He brought the gun down again, breaking her jaw and knocking out several teeth.

This is it, she thought. *I'm going to die, beat to death by a madman in my own kitchen.*

He pulled the gun back, tensed for another blow, and then his body went ridged as if he had been electrocuted and he reached around behind his back. Mary turned her foggy vision up and saw Sally standing over her husband with the bloody butcher knife in her hand.

"Get off her, you fuck," croaked Sally.

"Sally . . . you . . ."

Murphy reached for Sally, intent on disarming her and then finishing the both of them. Sally was ready. She dodged backwards out of his reach and then dove forward, plunging the blade up to the hilt in his chest and pushing him off of Mary. Sally yanked with all of her might and pulled the knife free of her husband's ribcage. Then, she brought it down again and again, screaming out her pain and rage, relentless. She was still thrusting the blade when the fog thickened and carried Mary away.

*

6

Mary heard the hospital room door and opened her eyes as much as her swollen lids would allow. Sally was standing in the doorway, a single white rose clutched in her small hands.

"Mary?" she whispered, taking a step closer. "May I come in?"

Mary nodded, immediately regretting it, as waves of pain spread from the center of her face outwards, making her feel a little nauseous. Sally closed the door and walked to the bed, taking a seat in the chair that sat nearby. She stared at her feet for a moment, as if she was at a loss for words, and then she held the rose out to Mary. Mary took the flower and tried to smile, even though it hurt her broken jaw to do so. "Thank you, Sally."

"No, Mary," said Sally, tears streaming down her bruised cheeks. "Thank you. If it hadn't been for you, I'd be dead right now. My son would be too. You saved our lives."

"How is he?"

Sally paused and took a deep breath, trying to calm herself. *It's bad then,* thought Mary. "He . . . he has some swelling in his brain and several broken bones. The doctors performed an operation to relieve some of the pressure, but . . . he hasn't woken up yet. The doctor says that he's in a coma. He might wake up tomorrow . . . or he might never wake up." Sally shook as a silent sob wracked her body. Mary lay quiet, waiting for it to pass.

"Mary, do you believe in prayer?"

It was a complicated question. Mary gave her a simple answer, "Yes, I do."

"So do I," she said, giving Mary a weak smile. "I'm going to pray every day for God to bring my son back to me and I'm going to thank Him for you. He will make everything all right, just you wait and see."

Mary nodded, wishing with all of her heart

for it to be so. They talked for a few more minutes and then said their goodbyes. Sally kissed Mary on her forehead and then left, closing the door behind her. Mary lay still for a long time after she was gone, staring at the rose with tears of her own brimming in her eyes. Sally treated her like a hero, but she didn't feel like one. Heroes were supposed to be strong and selfless, putting others before themselves. Heroes were supposed to be brave. They always did the right thing no matter what the cost might be. Heroes were everything that she hadn't been for Sally and her little boy. What if she had stood up to John Murphy the first time the yelling had started? What if she had called the police the day he broke her hand and destroyed the peace of her home? How might things have turned out different? It didn't matter.

Things happened the way that they did and there was nothing, no matter how much she might want too, that could change that. Mary closed her eyes, feeling a soul-crushing shame deep within her heart of hearts. After a time, she slept and had bad dreams.

Jeremy Terry is the author of *Mirror, Mirror*, the second title in the Novelette Series from SST Publications, and *Dreams of the Dead* available from Damnation Books. His short stories "The Farm House" and "Obsession" appeared in *Peep Show, Volume 2* and *Tales of Obscenity #1*. He lives in Florida with his wife, three kids, and Great Dane named Max. You can connect with him on the web at www.facebook.com/jeremyterrywrites/.

JACK

TWINS

For June and me since our earliest rememberings and except for our years in New York City the world's always been a hostile place.

So this is nothing new, really.

We were born fraternal twins at three minutes past midnight and ten past midnight respectively on October 30, 1956 in the first windy minutes of Halloween. Mischief Night as it was called then. While we two were screaming our first tiny outrage at being thrust out of someplace wholly warm and secure—that single place on earth I believe in which there's never any need or any good reason to scream—much older kids were out soaping windows or letting air out of tires or setting fire to brown paper sacks full of dogshit on their neighbors' porches.

There's a Scots belief that when a woman bares a boy-child and girl-child together she'll never have another. Our mother never did.

But that was okay with both our parents. My mother Hanna didn't care much for sex in the first place. She had us and that was all she wanted. Sex was kids. Period. The act itself was ugly, slippery and revolting. Hanna's feeling was that enough was enough. And now that my father Willie had satisfied her in the only way she was capable of being satisfied he was happy too. He could fuck around all he wanted on the side. He had a sporting-goods store right down by the lake. A prime location both for business and for poaching because there were more and more tourists coming in every year and all those ladies in sundresses needed all that good advice on bait and rod and tackle.

I suspect my father died happy.

That summer we were six years old. For some reason unknown to us Hanna decided to visit my

KETCHUM

ILLUSTRATION BY STEPHEN COONEY

father at the shop around lunchtime and brought along June and me and I remember seeing a big ruddy-faced man in a cowboy hat standing at the counter with Pete Miller the hired help, the big man sighting down an over-and-under shotgun while Pete placed upon the counter a yellow box of shells, Pete looking worried at my mother as we passed through the store and saying something to her and she just waving back at him and marching us down the aisle to the back storage room where my father would be taking his lunch. Which he sort of was.

She was a long lean brunette with the biggest breasts I've seen in all the years since and my father Willie had one of them in his mouth, or a part of one, his face buried in her flesh and her legs wrapped around his butt which was naked and slamming her back against the wall with the *Playboy* calendar hung from it and the drapes pulled to and my mother and June and I just stopped and stood there looking, June and I thinking it was funny, smiling, because there was my father naked with this strange naked woman doing *something* to one another, the two of us starting to giggle and I don't know what my mother would have done if she'd had the time but whatever it might have been she didn't because the big man in the cowboy hat pushed past her striding into the room, little Pete behind him pulling on his arm and the big man just shrugging him off and raising the shotgun and I remember my father turning at the sudden commotion and the scared open-mouthed look the brunette was wearing like she'd seen a view of the world that was intolerable just before the man screamed *son-of-a-BITCH* and fired. One barrel was all it took at that range and both their heads were blood and bone and scrap against the wall.

COONEY

The man later said that he wished he'd aimed slightly to the left.

She was a whore but he'd known worse.

My mother took over the store and kept it running well enough to put us both through college but she was never the same after that.

Neither were we.

We'd always been special, June and I. Somehow we were aware of that from the beginning. Like old married people we'd finish each others' sentences. Even before we were old enough to fully *form* decent sentences. We'd be out playing in the woods by the lake. *Henry*, she'd say, *I wanna . . .*

. . . go pee, I'd say. *Me first*, I'd say and we would.

There's another belief that twins possess such uncommon bonds of sympathy that each will know immediately when danger or misfortune threatens the other even when separated over long distances. Likewise that any particularly special state of happiness or well-being in the one will be reflected in the other. Until college we were separated for hardly moments but both beliefs were certainly true of us as kids. My mother said that as infants we would quit squalling and fall asleep in our cribs at exactly the same moment, then wake together mornings and begin wailing for the breast as though our internal clocks were precisely one. We learned to walk the same day. June's first word was *mama* and mine was *papa* but they came out of our mouths within fifteen minutes of one another one Sunday afternoon while we were playing on the living room floor, my father in front of the TV set and my mother ironing and my mother's somewhat sexist explanation for why the words were not the very *same* word was that it was natural each gender should gravitate toward its own and her reasoning on the order of the words was that like a good boy I was just being polite.

Until the hour my father was shot naked in the back room we had little curiosity about our bodies. We bathed together of course and knew full well we weren't made the same. It wasn't a problem for us. In most other ways we felt *exactly* the same.

We've discussed it over the years.

We've come to the conclusion that it was as though we lived in two worlds at once back then. There was the world of June and Henry along with everybody and everything else. Then there was the world of June and Henry. The first world was by turns fun and new and confusing and it needed to be learned. The second was known from the start.

Before my father died our bodies belonged to the second world. Known and completely accepted. But each of us had seen something else that afternoon beyond the sudden splash of blood and death that lingered. Something *linked* to the dying but not directly of it.

Because when my father was shot he was still inside her.

We saw that clearly as he turned at the noise behind him from where we stood to one side in the doorway. The thick pole of his cock half in and half out of her and how that was possible we had no idea but when he fell our attention was still there, on his cock and not on the gore spewed across the wall and ceiling, on his swollen glistening flesh dwindling and falling to his thigh like a flower parched and dying.

Only then did we even seem to *hear* Hanna screaming beside us or truly see the ruin wreaked upon the bodies or become aware of the big man shouldering Pete aside and headed for the front door.

It was only when the flower died.

And after that, alone in the woods down by the lake or at home in the bath or the bedroom, we were pretty curious indeed.

A few times Hanna caught us. And that was a problem bigger than it might have been because once the fact that my father had gone to his Maker with his pants down got to be common knowledge around town my mother developed a sudden Baptist streak which went not only to churchgoing but to pamphleteering and preaching to anybody who'd bother to listen. It also went to severe punishments for little boys and little girls who *said* they were just playing doctor while the Lord knew and *she* knew that what they were really doing was carnal and sinful and damned.

We were locked in closets—separate ones—for hours at a time. We were spanked, pinched and knuckle-jabbed where it wouldn't show, denied dinner or breakfast or lunch or sometimes all three of them together. There was a braided knotted rope left hanging on the door to the attic at all times to remind us of those other times when she'd used it. We were raved at, sermonized, forced to pray. We *would* be taught a lesson.

We never did learn.

We wanted to see the flower rise. The only problem was the *when and how*. We knew it would eventually.

We wanted to see just what would go inside her and how far.

I remember her first orgasm as well as I do my own. I think I might've even shared it in a way. It was the summer of 1967 and we were eleven. The Summer of Flowers was what the hippies were calling it. The day was sunny and we were down by the lake, a fairly secluded spot you could only reach by boat since the woods were still thick for acres behind it. The owner believed in rabbit and deer hunting, not real estate and was considered a goddamn lunatic by most everyone else in town as a result.

We'd go skinny-dipping. Almost always we were the only ones around.

That day as we lay naked in the sun on an old beat-up checkered quilt I had two fingers inside her and she was wet and slippery of her own accord which was new over the past year and fascinating to us and she showed me how to guide the fingers on the outside too, in and out and up with what must for her have been final a understanding, a final access to expertise in her own nature. When she began to shake I withdrew, frightened that I was hurting her but she said *no no no* and pressed my fingers back to her and shut her eyes and worked the fingers as though they were her own.

She arched her back and moaned and I could feel her shudder all the way up my arm and began to shake myself as though some sudden breath of December had moved across the lake.

She fell back laughing, trying to catch her breath and then I was laughing too.

"My god," she said. "What *was* that? I want to *die* like that, Hank! God I do. And mama thinks there's something *wrong* with this? Hanna's crazy!"

We laughed some more and she reached up to tickle me, she was apt to do that all of a sudden and I squirmed over on top of her and tickled her back and we rolled around that way off the quilt and on again. We lay down exhausted.

"Put your fingers back in me," she said. "Leave your hand there. I want us to fall asleep that way. Okay?"

"Okay."

It was nearly noon and the blue sky unbroken by any cloud anywhere and we slept in no time at all.

We woke to somebody saying *shit,* look *at that!* and laughing and somebody else saying *jesus, that's Hank and June!* and we saw Danny Beach and Phil Auton heading toward shore in Danny's old rowboat, two kids in our class at school for godsakes, both of them laughing and yelling our names now that we were awake and sitting up staring at them, June with one hand between her legs to that spot mine had just deserted and the forearm of her other arm across the wide pale nipples and her breasts only just beginning to show.

Perverts! Fuckin' queers! they drifted toward us shouting, the last of which of course made no sense at all. I scrambled into my jeans and tossed June hers along with her teeshirt and she stood with her back to them while they yelled *nice ass, Juney! turn around, babe!* and pulled them on. We slipped on our U.S. Keds and I grabbed my shirt and the blanket and we ran off into the woods. It was the only thing we could think to do. Just to get away from them there.

We were shaken. Now everybody'd know. We walked along the deer-paths June in the lead going nowhere in particular, just moving deeper into the woods. After a while she turned.

"D'you think they'd sink the rowboat on us?"

"Wouldn't dare," I said.

"Do you think they saw where your hand was?"

"I dunno."

But I did know. I'd seen Danny Beach staring directly at it. Staring between her wide-open legs. And it was as though she read my thoughts again, was completing yet another of my sentences.

"But you're pretty sure they did, huh."

"Yeah. I guess. Pretty sure."

"Okay. Then we're screwed," she said.

We walked a while in silence.

"I don't care," she said finally. "Let them tell their parents. Let them tell the whole goddamn school, the whole goddamn town. What we did was nice. And we're doing it again, aren't we."

She looked back at me for an answer and I had to laugh and shake my head, it was so much June.

"Sure we are," I said.

My own first orgasm was inside her. The following summer.

We were twelve.

Hanna was in church where lately we had refused to go and we were big enough by then and Hanna sufficiently small beside us so that rage hell and damnation though she might she had no choice but to accept our decision. Besides, she now knew what the whole town knew. I suspect she was secretly glad we stayed away.

We were on my bed. We had made the flower grow.

I slipped into her as easily as a finger into a jar of jam and just as sweetly and began to spasm within only a few thrusts, June bucking up to meet me. It seemed I'd never stop coming—for a terrifying moment I thought I was hemorrhaging, pumping out blood inside her—these rhythmic pulses so blinding and electric and soon she was rising from a pool of me.

We lay side by side in each other's arms, not caring a damn about the glistening sheets beside us. Each of us smiling, the curtain behind us fluttering in the cut-grass-smelling summer breeze.

"If Willie'd been that fast," she whispered, *"he might be alive today."*

"You *bitch!*" I grabbed her and started to tickle. "You just goddamn *wait* 'till next time!"

Then we both looked at one another and howled *"WHEN!"*

In September of our junior year in high school they tried to get her.

I was working the counter nights at Silverman's Drugstore and Soda Shop and it was nearly closing time and June always came by to walk me home. Her habit was to stop in at 9:45, just enough time to have a chocolate egg cream with me before I locked up and not enough time so that it was likely she'd run into classmates.

We had friends among them but not many. Other outcasts like us. We used to call them the Halt, the Lame and the Blind. Actually they were more like the Exceptionally Gifted or Bright, the Ill-Favored and the Meek. But outcasts all the same. June and I were exceptions, being none of these exactly—I having grown up fairly good-looking in a dark-eyed, hooded way and June having captured full womanly beauty at the ripe old age of seventeen. We were smart enough but not brilliant. And neither of us was meek.

On this cool September evening she was late. Only five minutes late but that was enough to make me close down early at some vague undeterminate urging and as I turned off the lights and locked the doors my pulse was racing. I could hardly breathe. Our house was just five blocks away, two down Main and three along West Cedar which was one of the perks of working at Silverman's in the first place. You would walk there. But this night I took it at a run and I found them in a little stretch of wooded area a block short of our house. I saw them only as moving shapes in the moonlight through the scrub and birch and bramble but I saw them from the street as though I knew exactly where they'd be.

Danny Beach was one of them and the other three were seniors and we knew them well. She'd not gone easy. When I got close enough I saw that one of the seniors had a long thin bleeding gash along his cheekbone and the other was bleeding from the head from what must have been a rock and that was the one who had his pants down kneeling in front of her while Danny held her arms and the other two her legs. So it was that one I went for, the one with the head-wound, kneeling.

I don't know where the rotten log came from but it was big enough in my hands and I took him exactly where the rock-wound glistened in the moonlight, rotten bark flying and when he went down Danny got scared and let go of her arms which was a mistake so that by the time I cracked the ribs of the biggest of them, the one whose face she'd scratched, the other was off and running and June had Danny in a headlock and was pummelling his face in fury. I let her hit him a while and then said *hey, sis, don't kill him for godsakes*, though it was certainly possible *I'd* concussed the other guy into oblivion. He sure didn't move.

But my voice seemed to calm her somehow. She let Danny off with a bloody nose and lip and he and the guy with the cracked ribs hobbled off through the woods yelling that that they were going to fuck us up, *you hear that? you fucking perverts are gonna get yours!* but by then the guy on the ground was stirring so just we picked June's panties and purse up off the wet leaves and left him there and walked away. The panties were torn. She stuffed them in her purse.

"They hurt you?"

"Bruises. Bastards."

"You want to tell somebody about this? The police?"

"Jesus, no. That's all we need. I don't think they'll try it again, do you?"

"No. I doubt it."

"Then let's just leave it. Want to have that egg cream now?"

"Good idea."

The night the dead began to rise we'd been living in New York City for eighteen years. Neither of us was particularly well-equipped to deal with Manhattan at first, armed with nothing more than B.A.s in English against an already Masters-in-Finance world. I worked as a reader and then as an agent in a literary agency while June tried her hand at acting under her new name, Celia Night. Over the years she'd done a few print ads, a non-union commercial, a lot of off-off-Broadway, a few seasons of summer stock and a walk-on in ONE LIFE TO LIVE. Like most actors in New York she got by waiting tables. She kept her eyes open though and she wasn't stupid. When I went out on my own as an agent and started to make some good money we went in with a friend and bought a restaurant, stole an excellent tex-mex chef from a rival and kept the price down on the tequila. We did fine.

We were happy. We lived together as husband and wife. Boyfriend and girlfriend. Significant Others. Whatever you wanted to call it.

It was Manhattan. There was nobody to question us. Nobody to care.

The highrise on West 68th was built like a bunker against fires, all concrete walls and steel doors. So we were in no real danger at all that night. We just sat in the condo bedroom watching the news coverage on CNN, phoning friends when it was possible to get through to them and twice listening at the door to sounds of mayhem in the hall or else gazing out our sixth-floor window to the dead wandering through the eerie empty streets or being shot down by police. Tiny cracklings far below.

The homeless got the worst of it that night and over the days that followed. Dead or alive they were easy targets, half of them with senses already dulled by drugs or booze or mania and their population plummeted. But Manhattan never shut down the way more rural areas had done. Closed off to bridge-and-tunnel traffic the City's dead proved almost manageable. For how long that would continue we didn't know. But by the time we ran out of food a week later our walk across the street to the Food Emporium was no more eventful than usual, though the shelves looked skeletal. Deliveries were going to be a problem.

Then the city legislature reversed a decades-old policy about the right to bear arms in public and we picked out a brand-new Ladysmith for June and a used Colt Python for me. We practiced at the crowded new firing range a few blocks down on Broadway at what used to be the World Gym.

Don't worry. You'll get better at this, June said.

I never did.

Another week or so passed and I worked at home by computer, e-mail, fax and phone and June left the restaurant to the manager. Business was way off anyway and supplies were hard to come by.

We spent a lot of time in bed.

Then the day before yesterday our Aunt Joan called, Hanna's sister. Our mother had died that morning and risen and died again. Both times shot by a Remington double-barrel shotgun, the first wielded by a dead-panicked thief who hadn't the cash to pay for it but was scared to be without it and the second in the hands of old Pete Miller, who'd moved into the apartment over the store when his wife died god only knows how long ago and who'd heard the blast and perhaps remembering my father got downstairs just in time to see her struggling to rise off the floor, shooting her down his final act as hired help.

Were we coming to the funeral? my Aunt Joan wanted to know.

Neither of us liked the idea at all. Our mother had been religion-crazed for years, grown more and more fervent as she got older. She'd helped us only grudgingly through college. Mostly we'd lived on scholarships. It was possible the only reason she did as much for us as she did was to get us out of town.

We embarrassed her and she embarrassed us.

It wasn't as though we loved her. June and I loved only each other.

"I'll go," I said. "Somebody ought to."

"You don't want to go."

"Neither do you. I'll go."

"Are we going to keep the shop?"

"Hell no. She should have sold it years ago. I bet Pete'll buy it. He hasn't spent his first dime yet."

So this morning I picked up a rental car at Hertz a few blocks away and headed for the Lincoln Tunnel. Traffic was light. At the entrance to the Tunnel a grim faced balding man with a .38 police special on his hip handed me a pass which I'd have to present on the way back along with the usual toll.

Three hours later I was at the lake.

The turnout this afternoon was small. A handful of fellow-traveller Baptists toting rifles and shotguns. Aunt Joan, unarmed but for the fierce set to her jaw. Me, the pastor and old Pete all wearing sidearms under our jackets. I pled June out to ill-health to those few who bothered asking. The day was mild and the cemetery was old and there was so much recently turned earth it looked like we were holding services in the midst of an ant colony. June had wired flowers and so had the church and so had my Aunt and Pete.

Pete seemed to be taking it the worst.

Hanna had been a difficult woman but probably it was difficult too for Pete to shoot her.

I didn't get to ask him about the store.

I didn't get through the service.

Halfway into the Lord's Prayer I felt a buzzing in my head like a television tuned to nothing but loud static and knew that June was gone.

It was good that as family I was seated on a folding chair because in those first few moments I couldn't have trusted my legs to do anything but buckle. I must have said something because my Aunt gave me a look and a deeper frown than usual but then I saw reflected in her eyes a grave concern and tentatively at first she touched my shoulder and then pulled me over and wrapped her arms around me while I sobbed and stopped the service howling my grief for what reason neither she nor any other could begin to understand.

I drove back knowing exactly where to find her.

Under what circumstance or where it had happened to her I would never discover but once it was over she'd gone home to our apartment, the same sort of instinct that took some of the dead to Times Square or their favorite bar or restaurant or back to their office buildings or shopping malls or homeless haunts beneath the stairs.

So that I found her where I expected her to be, at home in our bed, June naked and waiting for me, her little brother by seven minutes only, the world a hostile place once again for both of us in which there is need and very good reason to scream, the bright eyes empty and the gash in her neck ugly as badly butchered meat but waiting there in our bed for all that, waiting for the flower to rise one final time maybe or waiting for nothing at all but that other part of her which lived.

There's another Scots belief that when one twin dies the other will not as a rule live long, but that if he does somehow survive the vitality and strength of the dead twin passes on to him, even sometimes to the point of giving him strange new healing powers like the power to cure thrush by breathing down the throat of the sufferer. I have no use for healing powers even if that were true. And I don't particularly care to breathe down anyone's throat but June's.

I've closed our bedroom door and propped a chair against the doorknob in order to sit in the living room and write this down. I've half expected pounding, growling, sounds of that raging hunger they all seem to have turned toward me now but there have been no sounds, nothing at all.

She's waiting in our bed. When I last saw her, her hand rested gently between her legs.

I've given a lot of thought to it and there's only one thing I can really think to do. Lie down beside her and let her create in me a wound which is in some way twin to her own and then before I pass into wherever it is they go, turn the Colt on her and then on me. I won't let the two of us be damned even today, when half the world is.

We were born on Mischief Night, June and I. The first windy moments of Halloween.

We've done nothing wrong.

Jack Ketchum has published twenty-seven books to date and is shooting for thirty. Five of his novels have been filmed—*The Lost*, *Red*, *Offspring*, *The Girl Next Door* and *The Woman*. He is the four-time recipient of the Bram Stoker Award from the HWA and was elected Grand Master at the World Horror Convention in 2011. His latest book is *I'm Not Sam*, written with film maker Lucky McKee.

Asleep with the Black Goat

PIERCED NIPPLE

Aaron J. French

Illustration by Luke Spooner

As I approached her, gazing down at curvaceous hips curled in a U-shape, the backs of thighs, her bare stomach and chest, auburn hair descending in waves and a face like a cat, the eyes of a hawk, the smells of sex hung in the room, recalling memories I could not place, memories like dreams . . .

Days, hours, and minutes had blurred together since meeting her two weeks previous. The ecstasy, anguish, and bliss. Ashley had made a mold of them, fitting me into it.

I stood before her divan, room drenched in candlelight. I could practically feel the waxy glow on my skin. Ashley reached her arms around my waist, the fingers of the goddess sinking into my flesh as she took me in her mouth.

I shut my eyes. The sensations rose up through my body, finally reaching my head, where they exploded in my black mind like fireworks. I tingled all over, equal parts fear and excitement.

Somewhere in the midst of it I heard the door to the room open and someone walk in. She seized me tighter when I tried to turn and look, urging me to stay in the moment, in the feeling, the volcano of passion in my groin. I heard the muttering behind me and knew the Black Goat was with us. I was afraid, but I didn't have a choice. I let them lead me into the darkest corners of my soul.

Pierced Nipple was the name of the bar on 9th and Kessington. I had driven by countless times as I commuted to and from my downtown job, wondering at its secrets, a passion stirring in my jeans, knowing ultimately that I was too much of a coward to venture inside. I was afraid of such places. Afraid of the desires they stirred in me.

But there was no mistaking that charcoal façade, almost graffiti smudged, darkly frosted windows, and a front entrance made of stainless steel. Orange neon perpetually blinked above it, whether night or day, displaying the pair of words:

Pierced Nipple

Finally, drunk one night, I cultivated enough potency to go wait in line with the rest of the gloomy freaks. I felt nauseated by their hair products and cigarette smoke. Pulsating techno-goth music rumbled within, and a few fishnet girls swayed their voluptuous hips.

I was the only one not wearing heavy boots or black leather. I didn't smoke, and I twitched as we waited to move forward. It's a good thing I was drunk or I never would've survived the thirty minutes it took to gain admittance. My fear was strong, but it was somewhere in the back of me, like a shadow. The gigantic bald man wearing a Danzig T-shirt checked my ID at the entrance and let me in.

I moved through the sea of gyrating bodies under a fusion of blinking strobe colors, music blaring into my ears. Their bodies felt almost sick and squirmish as they buffeted against me. The women eyed me, plenty of them bare-breasted, with piercings dangling and multi-colored tattoos.

My passions swelled drunkenly. Somehow I found my way to the bar, where I ordered a drink from a razor-thin redhead in stilettos. The countertop and liquor rack were made of glass, making a mandala of the dizzy strobe lights.

Drink in hand I plopped down on a stool. The room had begun to spin. Music cut into my ears, sounding like nails on a chalkboard. I had never really listened to techno music; it had always been outside my realm of experience.

I looked around at the interior of the building I'd thought of entering so many times. It had papier-mâché rock walls embedded with skulls and ghostly cobwebs festooning the ceiling. Lights, disco balls, mock alters; even crucifixes lined the dance floor where several buxom women danced in cages.

A sudden rush of wind and a half-naked male wearing roller-skates whizzed past, handing me a flier. It felt vaguely morose in my fingertips, slightly fecal. I squinted down at the image on the front, which showed a man and woman having doggy style sex on top of a pile of raccoon hats, like the kind Davy Crockett used to wear. I couldn't help but chuckle, grotesque though it was, and I slipped it into my pants pocket. I had to show it to the guys at work.

"Smoke," said a female voice.

"No, thanks," I said without looking.

"Wasn't a question."

Like that a hand with black fingernails seized my thigh, so tightly that I cried out and my body reflexively contracted. "Jesus Christ!" I wailed.

She let go, as a pluming cigarette waved before my face. "That was a command," she said.

I rubbed away my thigh's itching pain, then took the cigarette and turned to her. I was all geared up to let her have it—to call her a trifling slut and ask what her problem was—but when I saw her beauteous catlike face, horn-rimmed, and her lush, flowing auburn hair, I stopped. It was like looking at the face of an angel. I would've done anything she asked.

I brought the cigarette to my lips, as she watched approvingly, and inhaled from the filter, drawing smoke into my lungs. The tar-thick goop burned my throat, and I vomited.

"Good," she said, reclaiming the cigarette. She waited until I'd recovered then hopped off the stool, helping me to stand. I couldn't remember the last time I'd been sick. I was embarrassed, but she didn't seem to mind. *No one* seemed to mind, not even the bartender.

"Ashley," she said, shaking my limp hand.

I choked on a dry throat, but managed: "Mark."

"Wanna fuck, Mark?"

I froze, contracting with fear and excitement. I thought I must've misheard what she said, but instead of inquiring about it, I merely nodded and replied, "You know it."

"Nice." She smiled. "Follow me."

She led me out the back entrance into the alleyway, which we crossed swiftly like a dream of moonlight, then through another doorway, which led into some abandoned-looking warehouse.

I clutched her hand as we crossed uttermost blackness and a rubble-strewn floor. I could smell oil and auto-parts—a garage? But then we were going through yet another door, which she shut behind her and locked, before flaring a match and candle and revealing her lair. Florid linens of lace and bead strings hung everywhere, around many paintings on the walls, mirrors and strange pieces of iron artwork. There was a dresser with makeup and other feminine products, and a shiny green chair next to an unmade mattress. Clothes lay in piles, with plenty of other dresses and things on hangers in the small, doorless closet.

I'd grown up an only child—*enfant unique*—nothing but a lonely, fastidious mother in the house. But I imagined if I did have a sister, her room might look something like the one in which I presently stood.

"It's not my real house," she said, as if picking up on my thoughts. "Just a crash pad." Yet something about this made me think she was lying.

She lit additional candles, and then, stepping over a pile of shoes and fabric, plopped down on the bed. On her back, with her legs slightly spread, auburn hair fanning out, her breasts melting in their black halter top. Her orange skirt rode up her creamy white thighs. She kicked off her heels and wiggled her toes at me. "Come on in, the water's fine."

I stayed where I was. I wanted to move toward the bed, and certainly my cock did as well, but I was overcome with fear and God knew what else. My heartbeat rang in my ears; tumultuous butterflies darted through my stomach; my skin felt like it was on fire.

Ashley frowned. "Is there a problem?"

I couldn't make the words come out, and this made me angry. Wasn't this what I wanted, the reason I had come? Yes it was, but now I was chickening out. *I hate you!* I screamed at myself. *Come on, move it!*

Ashley grinned and rose from the mattress, as if through water. "I see you are afraid," she said, striding toward me. As she came she somehow managed to drop her skirt, stepping out of it. Underneath, she wore red satin panties.

We embraced and she seemed to draw me inward, into an ocean of warm sensations which smothered my fears and insecurities. Her caresses covered them like bandages. I could again move my arms and legs, and at last I was able to wrap myself around her, drinking her in.

She breathed into my ear, "*How long has it been since you fucked someone*?"

My hands slowed across her body. "Why?" I asked. "Is it obvious?"

She chortled. "Hey, don't be so uptight. I was only curious. I'll answer first. The last time I had sex was almost a year ago."

I held her away. "You're kidding me. I'll bet you do this every night. Hell, I never even met you before and you propositioned me. Is this some kind of joke?"

I could feel my erection dwindling, but at least the fear had been replaced by something a bit more powerful—something I knew was hateful.

Ashley looked hurt. "It's no game," she said. Then she brightened. "Christ, you are uptight. I'll have you know that I was raped last year by some muscle-bound asshole and I'm still working to feel okay with my sexuality. When I saw you tonight something happened; it clicked. You don't look like the other fleabags at the Nipple. You're different."

"Jesus, I'm sorry. I had no idea. I thought—"

She silenced me with her fingertip. "Don't sweat it. I get stereotyped as a slut all the time. I've gotten used to it. You answer now."

I hesitated a moment, her sudden confession awakening my guilt. Finally, I said, "About a year."

She smiled, clasped my hands, and led me to the mattress. "It appears we're twins, then," she said. "That would explain your fear. But I have fear too. Fucking can be scary sometimes."

You have no idea, I felt like saying. And there was no goddamned way I would tell her the truth—that I hadn't had pussy since pussy had me. A grotesque, schoolyard expression, but it was going on eight years.

I moved with her, my heart rate accelerating again. I went to my knees as she pulled off my shirt; within a second she was after my pants. Armies of excited gremlins jumped about within me, and my whole body sung like a struck tuning fork.

She tasted of the sweetest honey. Piece by piece we removed the last of our clothing. Then we performed oral sex on each other. Her immaculate pussy was the prettiest thing I had ever seen, formed by God with the utmost precision and care, using the finest hair, the finest tissues. I dove into her with everything I had, and it felt divine.

She eased me onto my back, relaxing me, and spent the better part of ten minutes coaxing me to full erection. I saw her exquisite naked form hovering over me, leg to either side, and then she descended as if out of heaven, guiding me into her and grinding her hips.

Not since childhood—not since I was a boy and the world appeared devoid of suffering and heartache—had I experienced such pleasure. My hands clutched her buttocks, helping to guide her as she rocked back and forth. I saw her pitching above, eyes closed in wanton abandon, thrusting with all her might. I knew then that I loved her, that I would do anything for her, even rip out my own heart at her request.

It felt good to have a reason to live again.

Afterward she lay in my arms, head on my chest, dozing. But I was awake, staring up at the ceiling. That's when I saw it moving along the wood and plaster. At first I thought I was seeing things. It looked like a face, a goat head actually, complete

with hooking nose, beady eyes, and two curving horns. It drew down almost to the mattress, bringing the white plaster with it like stretchy gauze. It stared into my face, paralyzing me. My heart raced and I started to get very hot, even though the air in the room was cool.

The face was studying me, tilting its head from side to side in careful inspection. It turned its attention to sleeping Ashley and mouthed four words that sent a shiver down my spine. *Her soul is mine . . .*

All at once the face turned black, along with the ceiling, and then, like a creeping vine, it spread across the walls and floor, blackening everything in its wake. Soon the furniture and even the candles grew dark.

In my terror I tried waking Ashley, shaking her shoulders and calling her name, but it was no use. She seemed in a trance, as if she'd fucked herself into a coma.

The room became a black abyss, and out of that emptiness a sound like clopping hooves emerged. The Black Goat appeared right where the door had once stood, his dark obsidian body rippling with muscles and covered in coarse hair. He approached where we lay and glared down at us, his hard, hating eyes regarding me with a fiery intensity; yet when he looked at Ashley his gaze softened and turned almost melancholic. He raised a hand and traced a strange symbol in the air, which hovered in the dark like tracer flames.

The symbol became my name.

She is linked to me by fate, he whispered. *Her soul was written into the* Book of Names. *It forever goes with me, through all its incarnations.*

"I didn't mean to . . ." I stammered, unable to find the words.

Now that you have linked yourself to her through this material ritual, your soul is thereby placed into my book as well. She has acted as a medium in order to reckon this change. You too will travel with me until the end of the age.

As rapidly as the darkness had descended, it lifted. The Black Goat vanished along with it. The room restored itself to its original condition. Candles flickered, and I heard faint sounds of the old building settling in the night. I took a deep, quivering breath. It was a while before I fell asleep.

We began meeting every weekend. Our routine was the same: meet at the Pierced Nipple and have a few drinks, maybe a spastic dance or two, and then retire to her warehouse abode for a night of ecstasy.

Always, post coitus, my mind would wander, refusing me sleep. Ashley, on the other hand, couldn't keep her eyes open another minute after we'd finished. Without fail the strange goat being would make his appearance. Sometimes he'd be standing off in shadows, half visible, watching us. Other times various pieces of him materialized in the walls and woodwork, even in the mirror, in rows of books and table legs.

I never completely overcame my fear of him, but eventually I got used to the phenomenon. It never once tried to harm Ashley or myself. It seemed to be keeping an eye on us like a concerned father.

When I finally decided to broach the subject with Ashley, I was afraid she'd call me crazy. But I was surprised to find her very open. She listened to what I had to say, my various accounts of seeing the fragmentary demonic being in her room at night. She remained quiet and allowed me to finish.

Then, licking her lips as she smoked, she said, "Well, what you're describing is not all that uncommon. Ever heard of night terrors?"

I had, so I nodded. But: "I don't think you're understanding me. I've never seen this Black Goat before. Not until after I met you and we started sleeping together."

"You're blaming me?"

"It's not that, either. It's just . . . well . . . I do think it has something to do with you. Fuck it . . . maybe I am crazy."

"Here's a thought. What if it's got something to do with fucking?"

"What?"

We were in her room in the old warehouse, the door closed, candles flickering. A Sisters of Mercy CD played quietly in the background, and we were drinking a cheap Cabernet.

"I've lived here off and on for almost five years," she said. "And I was raped in this room, you know. Before that I did have sex with other guys, lots of times. And *we've* had sex lots of times in here."

"I don't see your point." There was an edge to my voice because I was fighting jealousy.

She stamped out her cigarette. "Sex has a great many symbols and meanings attached to it, wouldn't you say? People feel invested in it, so whether they realize it or not, they pour as much of themselves and their emotions into the act as they can, hoping it will reward them. With an orgasm, a lover, a husband or wife, love—whatever. These expectations cycle above their bed like an auric cloud."

"That's intense. But what's it got to do with seeing a hallucinatory goat?"

"Imagine if all that stuff—which no one is aware of, but which nonetheless is there—had a breath of life blown into it. Imagine if it took form and coalesced into a creature of the spirit world, the world of archetypal forms. What would it look like? A satyr, perhaps?"

I shook my head, still not sure what she was getting at.

"What if that creature chose to haunt the particular area in which it had been brought to life, the room where all this fucking and feeling had taken place? The expression, in an artistic sense, of the thoughts, fears, and expectations surrounding sex, carved out in the physical world and granted form . . . perhaps that's what you're seeing?"

Her words left me speechless. For the first time, sad as it seemed, I had actually *listened* to what Ashley said, instead of just ogling her body parts. And I was blown away. "You speak like a writer," I said.

"I did work for the school newspaper at my community college before I dropped out. Nice to know I haven't lost my touch. What do you think of my hypothesis?"

I shrugged, hesitating. I felt nervous about answering her, fearing I might sound stupid, like I didn't understand what she'd told me—which was half true.

"I'm not quite sure," was my final, soaring response. "The Black Goat seems so real when it's happening."

"A projection of your own fear," she said calmly. Then, rolling over nakedly on the bed to display the bottoms of her buttocks escaping from the miniskirt, she added, "If you're not careful the Black Goat will draw more and more force from the depths of your subconscious, until it then reaches an independent existence, and ultimately the ability to destroy you . . ."

But I had already stopped listening. My hands were crawling up the backs of her thighs.

The first night she didn't show up at the Pierced Nipple, I thought I was going to have a heart attack.

The second night I felt faintly on the verge of passing out. Sitting on my barstool, I scanned the sea of dancing, leather-clad bodies, feeling sick to my stomach. None of the painted-up faces matched Ashley's.

On the third night, I got extra drunk and stumbled across the dance floor, shouldering into people. One of the megalithic bouncers quickly spotted me and threw me out on my ass. I offered him my middle finger as I landed in a puddle of water.

I built up the courage and crept around the alley to Ashley's derelict abode. Three nights of no Ashley was enough to drive me crazy. I told myself I didn't care if I found her with some other guy. I just wanted to know if she was avoiding me.

Illuminating the darkness with my cell phone light, I opened the door to her room. It was empty. All the furniture had been removed, and the room smelled faintly of mildew and old dust.

I stood looking into the doorway for several minutes, confused and afraid, hand quivering as it clutched the cell phone. It didn't make sense. Where would she have gone? What about her things?

I curled into a ball on the vacant floor and

passed out. My sleep was dreamless. In the morning I found two beetles locked in passionate coitus, struggling together on the bare wood.

Stumbling out into the bleary light of day, the Pierced Nipple looked much less exotic: more trashy and rundown. The outside air reeked of burnt motor oil and fast food.

Ashley was gone.

As I shrank to my knees in the alleyway, tears starting to come, I saw the familiar figure of the Black Goat swirling into form in the back walls of the Pierced Nipple. The goat, with its long snout and horns, grinning at me. *You are mine now,* it seemed to say. *Your soul belongs to me.*

I didn't know if I'd ever stop screaming.

What dirt and darkness the world was . . . especially like this, without her. When I was alone. When she had left me.

Was I not good enough? Didn't she love me, as I loved her? Would she ever be in touch?

Good enough for the goddess Ashley? No such thing. My treasured promiscuous Gothic idol, my tiny black queen. She lived for the night, for the clubs, the drugs, and the boys. She never loved me, for there was no love in her. Passion and rage alone. And besides I was unworthy. I was a worm.

Sure, I'd been dumped before, plenty of times. But Ashley cleaved a greater wound. She had been the best: best lover, best nurturer, best friend. All I desired, she had provided. She had shown me untold pleasures, from which my body still reeled with shock.

But of course like any vengeful goddess she had taken it away, and I was left in the dark, in the confused storm of my thoughts. I felt so pathetic.

I could hardly get out of bed. The room smelled of my defeat. The apartment too smelled of tears and booze, grime and smoke. Would I ever emerge from this cloistered hell? Hard to know. Especially when the only thing that could save me was Ashley, Ashley, *Ashley* . . .

I'd been left with my inner anguish and the face staring at me as I lay in bed, constructed in the walls, the curtains, the glass, the ceiling. The angry hooked nose in the folds of my bed sheets. The blackened horns and beady eyes. The demonic Black Goat was my tormenter. My sentence for lying with Ashley and imbibing her intoxicant pleasures. And now he would never let me be. He would haunt me for the rest of time.

Days, weeks, (months?), passed in a wave of melancholy submission, as I confined myself to my home, refusing even to go to work. I was certain this decision would see me unemployed but I didn't give a shit anymore. Without Ashley in my life, nothing mattered, and every minute that passed without her was an excruciating eternity.

On a Friday afternoon I left my house unshowered and unkempt, reeking of alcohol, and purchased a length of heavy rope from a Walmart around the corner. The clerk looked at me with suspicion, but seeing as how we were at Walmart, he passed me off as just another freak.

I returned home and tied the rope to the highest beam in the building, fashioning a noose to the frayed end. It took several tries, but with the help of a Google search I was able to manage. I lay back in bed, staring at the dangling noose through the open bedroom door.

It was only matter of time.

I slept and drank so much that my reality began to blur until it blossomed into a full-blown fantasy. I spent so much time in bed nursing an alcohol bottle—slipping in and out of dreams—that I forgot what was real. I wondered if Ashley had been real.

Sometimes I stared out the window, observing with disinterest the dim gray world passing along. I couldn't access my fears or emotions. I felt numb. I felt done in. I felt myself moving in and out of strange mental pictures bound up with memories of Ashley. Suicide was sounding more and more appealing.

Finally I awoke in the darkness to find a slumping shadowy form—not myself—strung up in the noose, dangling beyond my bedroom door. The sight of it sent jolts of panic all through me, the first sensations I'd felt in weeks. I stared at the

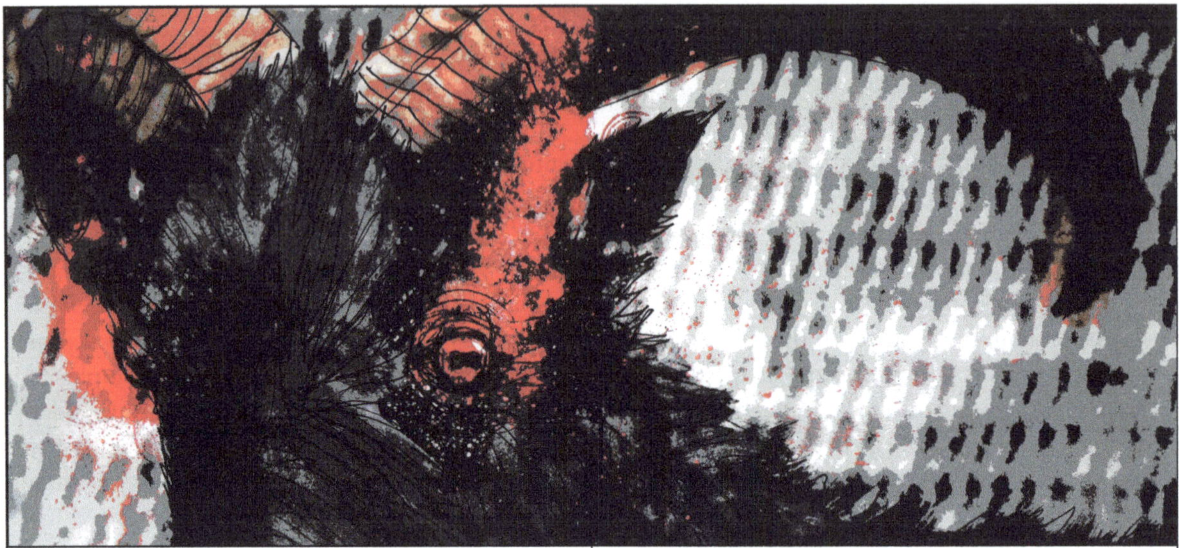

shape, wondering if I was dreaming it. I'd been having so many dreams lately that it was hard to tell.

The face of the Black Goat, now a constant companion to me, glared back from the walls and ceiling.

I forced myself out of bed, moving toward the door. The room smelled faintly of rot and feces. I wrinkled my nose as gooseflesh usurped every surface on my body. I could almost hear the Black Goat breathing, his stinging exhalations stinging the air. I moved into the living room, where I had attached the noose to the high arched beam. That was supposed to be me dangling from that frayed, coiled end. Not her. It wasn't meant to be like this.

"*No*," I whispered to the darkness. "*No, no, no, no, no*—"

But the body wouldn't go away. And the face . . . oh *god* her face . . . looked blankly into that unknown world beyond this world, and I could see how lost, how forsaken she was, and all at once I burst into tears.

"*No, Ashley, no*!"

Teary salt drained into my mouth, mucus bubbled in my nose, and I reached out to run my fingers along her cold, waxen skin. She was nude, but that grand body, which I had once lived for, now appeared stiff and grotesque. Decay was setting in. Soon she'd be gone. There was no chance of us being together again. Ever.

The truth hit me like a bucking steed, and half crawling, half stumbling, I staggered into the kitchen and grabbed a large knife. My knees felt like jelly, and a bitter taste coated my throat. I stood on a chair and cut down the noose, letting her fall into my arms. She was heavier than I'd expected, and I lost my balance and we both toppled over. Sharp pains ignited in my lower back, like biting insects, and I screamed, still sobbing. But the physical pain was nothing compared to the thought of losing her, of never being able to lie with her again—that what I had treasured so fervently was becoming a feast for maggots.

The Black Goat ran out of the walls, ceiling, and furniture, coalescing into the center of the room. In a moment he stood before me, fully material. I looked over as it stalked within inches of where I lay on the floor. Ashley's corpse was sprawled on top of me.

Her soul has been added to my book. She will go with me through all the cycles of time, and I will accompany her through every succeeding incarnation. I'll make sure she suffers sufficiently.

Hearing his harsh words jarred my emotions. I looked into his aquiline face: flat black nostrils, eyes like inkwells, ram horns curling back over his shoulders. He was so close that I could smell the fecal, animal scent of his woolly legs, fibrous muscles, and cartilaginous hooves.

"Why?" I managed to groan.

These are cosmic laws, to which you humans tend to remain ignorant. Which is why you do not think before you act, why you consign yourselves to fates unwished for without realizing it. But everything is natural. I exist for a purpose: to carry out karmic sentences. But there is something unique about your case . . .

With every second Ashley's corpse grew heavier. The oppressive terror of the Black Goat seemed to smother me, constricting my thoughts and breath like a viscous gauze. I managed again, "Why?"

At once he turned slick, vicious, and darkly transparent. His eyes shone intensely with red hellfire. The fecal smell wafted ripely as he raised his right hoof—and I saw that, inexplicably, the goddamned thing was bladed.

This time your human love has taken me. I shan't allow two souls united so decadently to fall away from each other. I'd rather hasten you after her through the Gates of Death. So perhaps it is true what they say about me: that I am just a hopeless romantic after all.

With a lurch his hoof came down on my neck, slicing. In the final seconds I attempted to struggle but Ashley's corpse kept me rooted in place. I felt a horrible feeling of strangulation then I was being pressed down into the earth . . .

. . . falling deeper and deeper . . .

. . . falling away . . .

Aaron J. French (a.k.a. A. J. French) is a member of the Horror Writers Association. He edited *Monk Punk*, an anthology of monk-themed speculative fiction, as well as *The Shadow of the Unknown*, an anthology of nü-Lovecraftian fiction. His latest anthology *Songs of the Satyrs* will be published in 2013-14. Aaron's article on Thomas Ligotti appeared in issue #20 of *Dark Discoveries*, where he is an associate editor. Aaron's fiction has appeared in many publications including *Dark Discoveries*, *Black Ink Horror*, *Something Wicked*, *After Death*, *Bedlam*, *Beware the Dark*, and *The Lovecraft eZine*. Look for his zombie collection *Up From Soil Fresh* from Hazardous Press, his metaphysical horror story collection *Aberrations of Reality* from Hydra Publications, and his novella *The Order* in the *Dreaming in Darkness* collection about a Lovecraftian secret society. He is the Reviews Coordinator for Hellnotes.

CROSS MY HEART, HOPE TO DIE

SHERI WHITE

Artwork by Allen Koszowski

Stephanie hated eyeballs. The look of them, the mention of them, and the mere *thought* of them.

They rolled around in her hand, squishy and warm, like . . .

Stephanie's stomach lurched; she threw her hard-boiled egg in the trash by her desk. *Great, something else I can't eat anymore*, she thought. She had recently given up grapes after unwittingly putting her hand in a covered box filled with peeled ones at a Halloween party. She imagined eyeballs felt like that. And now the hard-boiled egg grossed her out. What was next? Why couldn't she keep such horrible images from invading her thoughts?

She knew she had a phobia and that it wasn't a very common one. But not many people witnessed a friend tripping with scissors in the second grade. Stephanie would never forget the scissors' blade jutting from Amy's eyeball, blood and fluid oozing down her face. Amy's scream played in Stephanie's dreams frequently.

Her lunch break was over, so she turned to her files and began to work. Gradually, the mundane task of proofreading distracted her from the eyeball images.

"Hey, Stephanie—"

Stephanie jumped in her chair, startled by her boss's voice behind her.

He laughed. "Didn't mean to scare you. I guess you were pretty involved in that stuff."

"It's okay, Trevor. I just wanted to get it done before I left tonight."

"You know, you've been doing a great job here. How long have you been working for me now, six months?"

"Yes, sir. I've enjoyed my time here very much."

"Well, you're almost up for review, and I think it's going to be a good one. You're going places in this company. I'm going to keep my eye on you."

He pointed at her, winked, and walked away, leaving Stephanie staring at his back with a look of horror on her face.

Stephanie tossed and turned in her bed, unable to get Trevor's words out of her head. She would finally doze off, only to feel eyeballs sticking to her body. Then she'd jolt awake, trying not to scream.

This is ridiculous. She grabbed the remote from her nightstand and turned on the TV. *A Clockwork Orange* came into focus on the screen, with protagonist Alex's eyes mechanically held open as he was forced to watch violent films.

"You've got to be fucking kidding me!" Stephanie cried. She threw the remote at the TV and ran into the living room. Her Ambien was sitting on the coffee table. She took one and swallowed it dry. She collapsed on the couch, breathing hard. She turned on the TV and let the CNN newscaster drone while the Ambien lulled her to sleep.

Stephanie woke several hours later, refreshed and determined not to let anything spoil her day. The eye thing was silly, really. Who was scared of eyes?

She went into the bedroom to get ready for work. The TV was still on, but thankfully another movie was playing. She turned it off, and then headed for the shower.

The hot water helped Stephanie calm down. She washed her hair, but then as she rinsed it, some shampoo dripped into her left eye, and she gasped. She turned to the water and let it wash out her eye; she couldn't stand the thought of rubbing it out with her fingers.

She looked in the mirror after she got out of the shower. Her eye was bright red. There was nothing she could do about it; no way was she putting drops in her eye. She figured it would heal on its own soon enough.

"What's wrong with your eye? You don't have pinkeye, do you? That's contagious; you shouldn't be here."

"No, Trevor—I got soap in my eye this morning. Nothing for you to worry about." Her eye burned, but she tried to ignore it.

"You should get some eye drops," he suggested. "Go to the drugstore downstairs and pick some up. You'll feel better."

Stephanie shuddered. "No, it's fine. It'll clear up soon." She turned to her computer and began her work for the day.

Stephanie's eye twitched while she worked. It annoyed her a great deal, but she couldn't wipe at it with her finger. Finally, tired of looking like she was flirting with her colleagues, she took a little mirror out of her purse and checked out the eye. It seemed redder, swollen. The white of her eye was red, with tendrils of darker red snaking out from the iris.

Gross.

She decided to go home early; maybe take a warm shower to help her eye. She packed up her things and stopped at Trevor's door. She knocked lightly and he looked up.

"Hey, Trevor . . ."

"Holy crap, Stephanie! Your eye looks awful! You should really go to the doctor, or it might get even worse."

"Yeah, maybe I will. I'm heading home to take care of it, if that's okay."

"Sure, go ahead. I'm sure you'll be fine. Just looks a little infected or something."

Stephanie let the warm shower water rinse her eye, hoping it would alleviate some of the redness and itching. Instead, the water stung, and she cried out, backing away from the stream. She got out of the shower and grabbed a towel, dabbing carefully at her eye. She looked in the mirror, recoiling at her reflection.

The eye was practically popping out of her skull. It was red, inflamed; the pupil and iris couldn't be seen. Red rivulets ran from the eye down Stephanie's cheek.

"What the hell?" she cried. She started to cry, but her eye burned from the salty tears. She dabbed her face with the towel again. Red streaks stained the white towel. Stephanie dared a peek at the mirror once more, and immediately regretted it. Not only was her eye swollen out of its socket, it now had white pustules dotting it. Stephanie screamed and ran out of the bathroom.

She grabbed the phone by her bed, but hung up. Who would she call? An eye doctor? Out of the question—what if he wanted to *touch* her eye? Same with 911. Stephanie sat on the bed, her arms around her knees, and rocked back and forth. Finally she went to the linen closet, grabbed a hand towel, and headed back to the bathroom. Careful not to look in the mirror, she folded the towel and wet it with warm water. Gently she put it to her eye, hoping at least the swelling would go down.

Stephanie sighed. The warm towel felt good against the inflamed eyeball. After a few minutes she looked in the mirror. The swelling had gone down considerably, much to her relief. Now she could blink, but her eyelid brushed against the pustules. She shuddered. She leaned into the mirror to see the nodes close up. They were mostly a creamy white, but with a pinhead-sized bit of gray in the center. To Stephanie's horror, the gray spots moved slightly.

"What the fuck?" she whispered.

Now she *felt* the movement; the gray spots grew a little larger. Stephanie felt some pressure against her eye, and then . . . *pop*. A tiny worm undulated out of one of the pustules, floating along in a thick fluid. Stephanie screamed as the other nodes popped as well. Worms slithered onto her cheek, falling onto the bathroom counter. Viscous fluid oozed and dripped on top of the worms. The eye deflated like a balloon, falling out of its socket and flattening against her cheek.

Stephanie stared at her reflection, unable to scream or talk. She shook her head in denial. The eyeball flopped around on her face. Her mind snapped.

"Well, this isn't right," she said to her reflection. "You certainly can't go out in public looking like that!"

She grabbed the scissors from the vanity drawer. She lifted up the flattened wet eyeball and held it out from her face. Then she took the scissors and cut through the muscles and veins holding the eyeball to her skull. It fell with a wet splat on the counter. She screamed from the pain, and then smiled serenely.

"That's better."

Blood flowed from the empty eye socket. The muscles lay limply against her cheek. The white of her right eye was now taking on a red tinge. Spots dotted the redness.

"Something's just not right, though," she mused. "But what?" Then a verse from her childhood Bible study classes came to mind.

And if your right eye offend you, pluck it out, and cast it from you . . .

Stephanie nodded as if a voice had spoken to her and picked up the scissors once again.

Sheri White lives in Maryland with her family. She has had a love of horror since she was two years old and watched *The Wizard of Oz* for the first time. She is a mom to three girls, ages 24, 17, and 15, and has instilled a love of all things scary in them as well.

In addition to reading and writing horror, Sheri also proofreads, edits, and reviews for many horror sites both online and in print.

She has been published in many small press magazines and anthologies, and will have a collection published soon by Necon E-books.

Friend her on Facebook at https://www.facebook.com/sheriw1965.

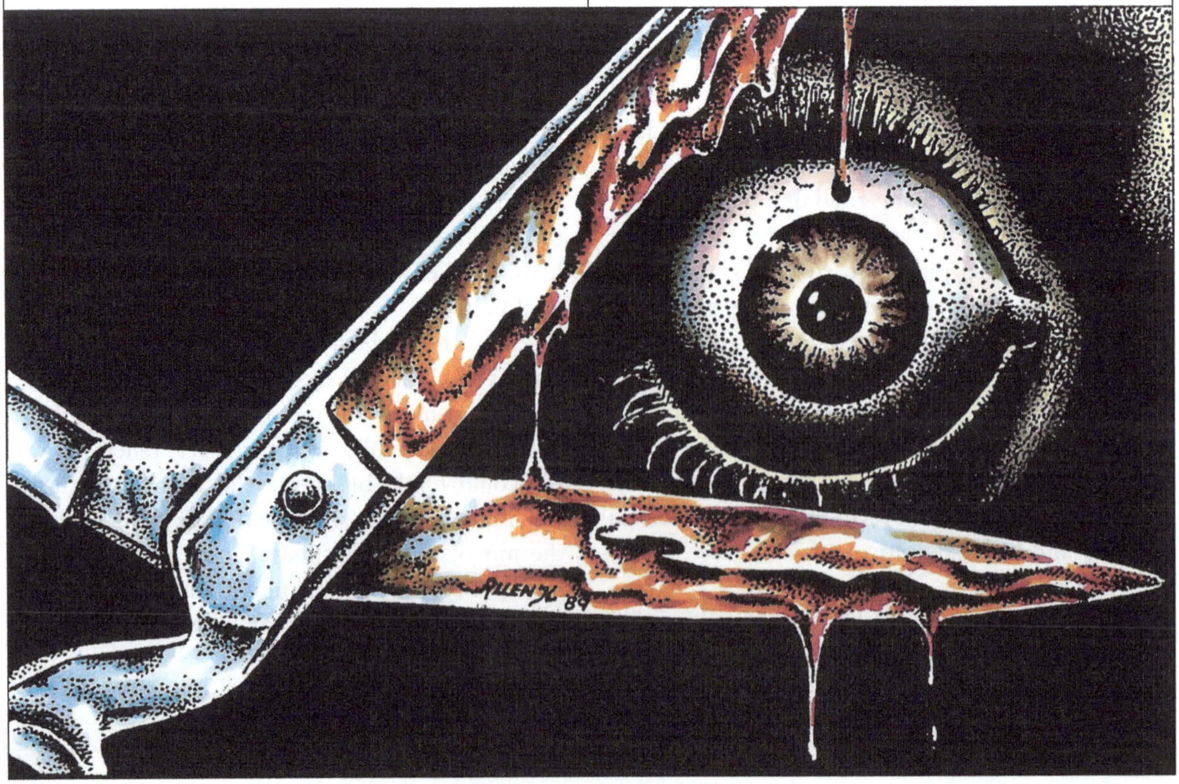

Pool Days

Russell C. Connor

Illustration by Daniele Serra

The water was cool and refreshing, filtered and chlorinated to the perfect shade of clear aqua. Rick swam below the surface, moving his lithe body through the water with his arms, and emerged to take a long breath and revel in the exhilaration of such luxury. It was a perfect summer day, cloudless and heated to a blistering hundred degrees. A pool day if ever there was one, and Rick loved pool days.

The woman he was living with was away at work, making money for him while he stayed at home, supposedly on the hunt for jobs he was always turned down for because of some inane reason: his longish hair, his lack of degree, his over-qualifications, like flipping the meat at McDonalds was tantamount to rocket science. Rick had found that when you were good looking, women believed whatever you told them.

Unfortunately, just because he was free didn't mean the rest of the world was. He was used to being the center of attention, but as he turned a slow circle in the water the only things staring were rows of empty deck chairs. The pool was vacant of even the thirty-something mothers that brought their kids to swim. That meant there was no one to admire him, which was bad, and no one to try to fuck, which was worse. However, it also meant . . .

He took another nonchalant look around the apartment pool, squinting at the tinted windows of the office to make sure no one watching. When he was sure he had reasonable privacy, he sidled to the edge of the pool and positioned his dick against one of the high-pressure jets that pushed in new water after it had gone through the electric pump.

Rick had had sex with many women in more positions, places, and orifices than most porn actors, had pleasured himself countless times, had anything that would fit shoved up his ass and performed every bit of kink he could dream up, but there was nothing on this earth that made him come harder than a powerful stream of water passing over his cock on a warm summer pool day. It was absolute nirvana.

He crossed his muscular arms on the concrete lip of the pool, laid his head on them, and closed his eyes, pretending to sunbathe while he conjured a mental image of the blonde who worked at the donut shop that he had been flirting with. He was pretty sure she was married; like that mattered. He just wanted to fuck her, not start a life with her, just pin her down and shove it in with her panties still around her ankles.

As he daydreamed he pumped his hips gently, teasing his cock by moving it in and out of the water stream. He opened his eyes, took one more cautious look around, and slipped it out over the top of his swimsuit, allowing the jet to hit him without the interruption of fabric. He gasped from the shock.

God, it was good! The water flowed fast around the tip of his dick, more efficient and unrelenting than any blowjob could ever be, tighter and more encompassing than any piece of pussy he'd ever had. He became very still, holding in the perfect position for the water to hit that pleasure spot on the underside of his penis, so close to orgasm. It felt like a million hands caressing him, working in tandem to bring him to climax . . .

In fact, it felt *exactly* like a hand caressing him, and he looked down into the water in time to see a tiny, green hand emerging from the jet nozzle, its fingers wrapped around his dick, before it retracted, yanking him toward the side of the pool and pulling his penis into the hub of the nozzle with a wet *thunk*.

He experienced a moment of raw panic in which he thrashed, trying to free himself, but he was stuck good, far too large for the hole (*not the first time for that*, he would ordinarily have joked) to back out. The effort brought only a shooting pain from the shaft of his penis. He carefully bent back at the waist and looked down to check out the situation. He was married to the tile wall at the hips, his thatch of pubic hair undulating in the trickle of water still able to squeeze out of the blocked pipe.

And he could still feel that hand in there, encircling his penis and tugging on it like a cow's udder.

Rick looked around. There was still no one

within shouting distance, and he wasn't sure he would call out even if they were. For Christ's sake, they were going to have to dismantle the pump system to get him out of here, drain the water and rip into the side of the pool, and that was not an ordeal he was ready to commit to quite yet.

And he might not have to. There was a simple solution to this. All he had to do was lose his erection and he would be small enough to slide back out again.

That was easy to say, of course, but how was one supposed to go about getting rid of an erection? Men were trained from birth to get them, attended seminars on how to keep them, and developed drugs to continue having them long past the point nature intended them to. He had no problems whatsoever in this department, but he had never been in a time crunch to lose one before.

And it wasn't going to be easy with that damn hand still jacking him off inside the jet nozzle.

What the hell was in there anyway? He had been so concerned with getting out of this mess he hadn't stopped to consider the nature of the thing that had gotten him into it. Was it some kind of reptile or water insect that had taken shelter in the pump system? He didn't think they had hands and he wasn't sure such a creature would have been able to withstand the pressure. Besides, there was something entirely too sentient, too tender, too . . . *affectionate* . . . about the thing giving him a hand job.

It did feel good, he had to admit. Whatever it was, it had more expertise pleasing a cock than most women. And, he knew, the easiest way to lose an erection was by coming. Not that he couldn't go four times an hour when the occasion demanded, but he would have an easier time wilting the flower after a good sperm evacuation.

So he leaned against the side of the pool and let the green hand do its business while he did his.

They were a minute into it—and it was so mind-blowing he was ready to buy the hand an engagement ring and propose—when he heard the rusted squeal of a gate hinge. He looked up to see one of the moms bringing three kids into the pool area. They did not look at him, were heading around the far side of the pool, but Rick still felt a moment of shamed alarm, like being caught masturbating, and now his penis did die a bit, and he tried to pull away from the wall again.

The hand yanked.

This time there was nothing loving about it; the hand was angry. He felt an excruciating crack of pain rocket up from his crotch, accompanied by an odd ripping sensation, and looked down to see that the skin of his penis had torn just a bit on the right side where it met his body, allowing a thread of blood to seep into the pool water.

Rick knew he should call for help now—bring on the ambulance and all the rescuers like Baby Jessica down the well, this was his fucking COCK we were talking about here, his life, his sunshine, his reason for being, and it was injured and throbbing like a rotten tooth—but he still did not want the embarrassment yet, to become the ending segment on the evening news that the anchors always delivered with those big shit-eating grins. So he ignored the pain, bit down on a scream, and glanced to make sure the mom and her kids did not see while he stirred the bit of blood until it dissipated in the water.

The hand was still trying to get him to come, moving fast and hard on his shaft, but there was no joy in it now, only searing pain as the outer skin was torn loose like the vacuum-sealed wrapper of a Slim Jim. He was losing his erection quickly, the sides of the jet nozzle becoming less constricting, and he tried to break free again. And again the hand pulled back, tug-of-warring with his tool.

Only this time it did not stop.

He felt as though his whole body was being sucked into the nozzle, as though he were being turned inside out and funneled through a hole the size of a fifty-cent piece, but that was not true, the laws of physics had not changed, it was just that the pain was that . . . fucking . . . BAD. He screamed now, heedless of the mommy and children at the pool, and another one of those terrible ripping sensations occurred. He was scared to look down, scared that he had been Bobbitt-ed.

And even though it was horrible, more pain than he had ever thought the universe could hold, he realized there was still a certain underlying pleasure in it.

All of the other nozzles around the inside of the pool began to squirt red into the clear blue of the pool, injecting his blood into the perfectly pH-balanced water. Rick felt a last tug and another unexpected sensation as his precious dick was torn off and he was suddenly free in the water.

He had come.

Russell C. Connor has been writing about demons, serial killers, and the end of the world since he was five years old. His short work has appeared in *Black Petals Magazine*, *AlienSkin*, and *Sanitarium*, among others. He currently has seven novels available, including the supernatural crime-noir *Finding Misery*, and *Whitney*, about hurricane survivors facing a deadly plague and a ravenous beast. His newest, a Bermuda Triangle horror novel called *Sargasso*, was released in March of 2013. He lives in Grand Prairie, TX with his mistress of the dark, rabid dogs, and extensive movie collection, and has been a member of the DFW Writers' Workshop for 7 years.

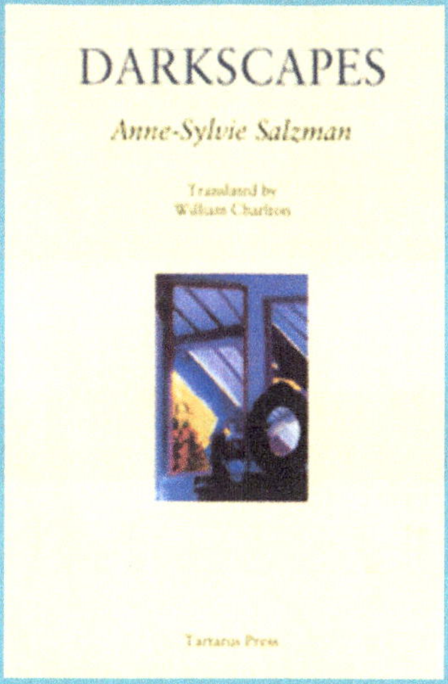

DARKSCAPES
Anne-Sylvie Salzman
Tartarus Press

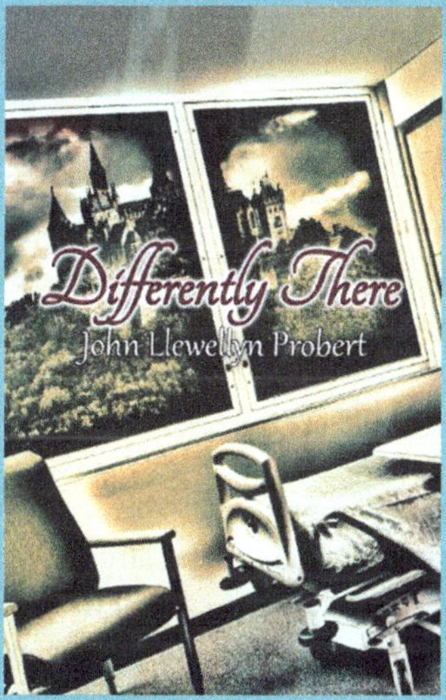

Differently There
John Llewellyn Probert

interzone
247

Company at the Lavoisier

A Novelette

Aubrey was shouting so loud she became worried she might damage her vocal cords if she didn't stop. Her brother's moped scooter was deafening—even though she was wearing his helmet—as it steered and hitched along a private road.

With her hands behind her back, fingers tightly curled around the bar above the rear trunk, she cried, "Gary, do you know where you're going?"

"Yeah!" he hollered back over his shoulder.

Her troubled eyes reached out to the greenwood, searching for a familiar spot.

"How much farther?" she asked, this time shifting forwards and grabbing his shoulders.

Annoyed, he looked at her. "Not far. So just let me drive."

Where they were the peaceful, summery night air carried a wild lavender fragrance. Sweet and soothing. But she disliked the feeling of being lost.

Ignoring the scratchiness in her throat, she cried out, "How do you know this is the right way?"

She heard him let out an angered groan.

She sat back and found her hold on the bar again.

A few minutes later, the striking view of a European Gothic style mansion appeared.

"The Lavoisier estate!" she exclaimed.

Gary followed the paved path leading up to the large luxurious house's main entrance.

Right beside the first level of the decorative stone steps, he braked and shut off the motor.

Her body rocked when he swiveled off the bike and bent over to hold it steady while dropping the center stand. She yelped and desperately grabbed onto the seat afraid she might fall.

When the bike went still she took off the helmet and fiddled with her hair.

"You could've let me get off first," she said, upset.

He shrugged and helped her climb off. The helmet was left on the seat.

Together they stared up at the mansion and saw a good number of its great windows filled with soft light.

"I heard this place was empty," she said,

Terry 'Horns' Erwin

Illustration by Luke Spooner

double-eyeing the impressive architecture.

He shrugged again. "This is where she said they'd be."

"No, I don't believe it." She shook her head with a distrustful smirk.

He turned to her. "Aub, please don't blow this. You promised."

"I know what I promised you."

He smiled at her, applying a skeptical look, then they moved up the extravagant stairs together.

"They're so . . . wide. White granite, I think," she said as they came to the flat going to the next short set of steps, then the door.

"I guess they just moved in," he said, more curious than before after getting closer to the grandness of the house.

"This girl, *Terri*, did she say what university she attends?"

He shook his head.

"Gee whiz, you sure let your little head do the thinking for you on this one," she grumbled.

He was embarrassed. "Wait, no, she said because they travel so much, she has to do online classes."

"Pff."

"Please, you *promised*."

"Yeah, yeah. I do want to see the inside of this place, though."

"*And* . . . you'll be nice to everyone. The guy I told you about?"

She chuckled. "If he thinks I'm letting him put his filthy hands anywhere on my body, well, he can just think again."

They walked up the last set of steps.

"I told you," he said, "you won't have to worry about that kind of thing."

"You could have at least told me where we were going and I could've dressed smart."

He smiled at her queerly.

They laughed.

"My sis the fashionista," he joked. He couldn't even remember the last time Aubrey had used makeup. But he wasn't one to talk, for he never followed the trends.

He stepped into a baroque recess for a moment and used a large decorative door knocker to announce their presence. Then he stood back beside his sister.

"For the life of me, I don't know why I agreed to this," she said nervously.

"Woody," he spoke softly out of the side of his mouth.

"Ah, yes, and you'd better take good care of him while I'm away."

"I told you—"

The big door opened.

Light flashed and the shapely figure of a female slipped into view. She was holding a can of beer.

"Hey, Gary!"

Gary smiled and stood like a rock.

Aubrey knew he was anxious but trying to look cool and less nerdy. Part of her wanted to laugh, and the other part needed to comfort. Her brother, like her, didn't often get attention from the opposite sex. She knew what being a social leper was like. Whoever this chick was, one thing Gary hadn't gotten wrong was she was hot.

But why did she like Gary?

"Is this your sister then?"

Aubrey smiled and stepped forward, holding her hand out.

The female held it lightly and they shook.

"Hi," Aubrey said.

"Hi, I'm Terri."

"Aubrey."

Terri had beautiful eyes, the makeup perfect. And Aubrey wished she knew how to make hers look as good. From what she could tell, Aubrey guessed they were about the same age.

Terri touched Gary on his chest. "C'mon you guys. Let's get better acquainted."

Aubrey saw her brother's on-pins-and-needles look when Terri turned her back. She wanted to assure him she wasn't going to do anything to ruin his chance with the beautiful female who'd invited him to an evening. She squeezed his arm for a second and whispered, "She likes you."

He flushed.

They went inside and Gary closed the door.

Terri turned and said, "We've set up a comfy circle in the parlor." She grinned and showed them the way.

As was expected the interior was breathtaking, and Aubrey soaked in every lavish detail as they crossed through the rooms. It wasn't until they entered the parlor she became suddenly tense remembering again what she had agreed to. A date with a stranger. Some guy she'd never even seen before.

He stood up from a chair when they came in.

"Zyler, this is Gary and Aubrey."

Aubrey right away felt better about herself when she saw what he was wearing. In fact it then occurred to her how Terri was dressed. Both were wearing casual. Zyler looked a bit older, maybe by five years or so, but he was very good-looking.

"Gary and Aubrey, this is Zyler," Terri said. "He's a childhood friend."

Zyler walked confidently across the rich carpeting, also holding a beer.

Aubrey thought he looked like a movie star, handsome with his hair styled neatly, and she feared what he might think of her. But her concern only lasted a moment before she cast aside the idea, clearing her mind of such nonsense, convincing herself she didn't care nor wanted any such affection. She knew Gary on the other hand had his hopes up high he'd find romance. Nevertheless, she flinched with insecurity when he introduced himself only to her. Her brother was given a curt nod.

"Nice to meet you, Aubrey," he said, taking one of her hands in his and holding it without asking first.

She drew back her hand, breaking contact, but she was fast to flash him a frail smile.

Terri called for them to all be seated.

Someone had pulled together four lovely designer armchairs and arranged them in a circle near an open fireplace. Naturally, it was unlit.

"Gary, you come sit here next to me," she said sweetly.

Aubrey followed her brother and took the chair on his opposite side.

Zyler returned to the one he'd risen from before.

Before Terri sat down, she stopped suddenly and said, "How rude of me. Would either of you like a drink? A beer? Water? Soda?"

Aubrey looked at her brother and found him looking back. Both of them shook their heads.

"No thanks," he said.

Terri smiled and plopped her bottom on the chair. She leaned over one side and set her beer can on the floor.

"So tell me, Gary," Terri said, "how long have the two of you been sibs?"

Aubrey thought she'd heard her wrong. Her brother was apparently confused as well.

Zyler coughed then chuckled.

Terri laughed. "Just joking. Feel free to ignore my weird sense of humor."

"*Bizarre*," Zyler added.

"Shut up!" Terri laughed and moved out of her seat a bit to try and playfully slap him.

Seeing her brother clam up, Aubrey asked, "Does your family own this property?"

Terri fell back into her chair, still struck with giggles. "Hell no. I wish, though, huh."

Aubrey and Gary exchanged glances, confused.

Terri explained, "My dad's *people* set him up here for a month. Do you ever read books on the paranormal?"

"No," Aubrey said.

Terri looked to Gary for his answer.

Aubrey spoke for him. "No, he doesn't either."

"Of course they don't," Zyler blurted out. "They seem like intelligent people."

Terri made a face at him.

"Anyway, my dad's kind of a big-name author slash investigator slash lecturer . . . who knows."

"He's a cool guy who happens to believe in ghosts and things like that," Zyler threw in.

Terri said, "He might be speaking at your college later this month."

Aubrey and her brother stared back clueless.

Obviously aware of their ignorance, Terri slouched in her chair, arms loosely resting over the sides.

Aubrey looked down at the can for a moment and wondered how many beers she might have consumed before they'd arrived. The beautiful girl's face did seem a tad red, and so did her brother's when she glanced over at him. The reason his was rosy was more easily explained. From her angle, Aubrey could see the girl's blouse was somewhat unbuttoned, open in a way one could see a lot of her naked breast and flash of nipple when she moved the right way. If she could see it, so could her brother.

"So what are your majors?" Zyler asked, directing his focus mostly on Aubrey.

"Teacher education. Multiple subject teaching," Aubrey answered.

Gary answered for himself. "Nuclear engineering."

In the middle of taking a drink, Zyler incautiously pulled the can away from his lips, catching some of the spill in the cup of his hand. "Wow, now isn't that some heavy shit!"

Aubrey noticed the boredom glazing over Terri's eyes. And she thought this is where her dear brother strikes out. There was nothing she could think of to say or do.

"What do you think about that?" Zyler asked Terri.

Terri slowly sat up, crossed her legs and gripped the arms of the chair. She looked at Gary with desire.

Aubrey was finding it hard to figure her out.

"I think Gary is wonderful, bright, and super handsome," Terri said, looking fixedly at Gary with a suggestive smile and spirit in her eyes. "What any woman would want in a man."

Aubrey let a short laugh slip. She looked at her brother and without hesitation expressed her apology. Though it didn't matter because he was intensely aiming his attention on his "admirer," and hers to him. Aubrey shied when she saw Zyler doing the same thing to her, his smile almost too charming to endure.

Terri continued, "Which is why when I met him I wanted to get to know him better." She slipped to the edge of her seat, angled more towards Gary. "Traveling with my dad this past year I've ran into a lot of interesting people."

"You've moved around a lot?" Aubrey asked, nervously mindful Zyler was eyeballing her. So much for her brother's prior assurance.

"No," Terri replied. "He didn't raise me. I've only recently reconnected with him."

Gary, stammering at first, asked Terri, "It's slipped my mind, but what did you tell me you were studying?"

"I didn't," she said impolitely. "So enough with all this boring small talk. Let's have some fun." She slapped the arms of her chair and jumped up.

Aubrey was offended by the way Terri had cut her brother off. She noticed Gary didn't seem to have taken it as critically. Of course why would he with such a sexy babe stroking his otherwise deflated ego?

Terri walked over and lifted a book off the mantle. She waved it as she returned to her chair.

Zyler put his can down on the floor.

"This is my dad's stuff." She opened the book and leafed through the pages.

All eyes were on her.

"Did you know the Lavoisier mansion is rumored to be haunted?" she asked, not bringing up her eyes. "That's why my dad's here." She stopped glancing at the book and looked up. "Well, not right this minute. He's back in New York for a few days but his equipment is set up in the east side of the house." She unintentionally looked over at Zyler then said, "I was excited when Daddy said we could have Zyler in for the month with us."

"So was I," Zyler said, expressing his wonderment of the stunning building in which they were all sitting in by gazing up at the high ceiling and around the room.

She turned the book over and laid it on her lap.

"We . . ." She glanced at Zyler. ". . . I haven't gotten to hang out with my friends in a long time. So I wanted to . . ."

"Just cut to the chase," Zyler chimed in.

She gave him the finger.

"Let's have fun, okay? Let's have a séance," she said.

Aubrey looked cynically at her brother.

He raised his brows at her.

"I know, I know," Terri said, laughing. "You both are too academic for such clowning, but that's why it'll be amazing."

"Amazing?" Aubrey questioned grouchily.

"More valid," Zyler explained, pitching forwards in his chair.

"Because we're so narrow-minded, you mean," Aubrey said. She couldn't help it.

Gary shot her a frustrated look but she suddenly didn't care. She was starting to not like these people. Though, the male was unquestionably pleasing to look at.

"Sure, it could be fun," Gary said, holding his eyes away from his sister.

"Yay!" Terri cried softly. She clapped then fixed the book in her hand. "Okay, everyone, pull our chairs closer together." Excitedly she jumped up and grabbed her chair and scooted it forward.

Aubrey was the last one to do so. She'd resigned herself to playing along with the attitude the night would soon be over and they could leave, her promise to her brother satisfied.

"Now I'm not a medium like my dad—or at least that I know of yet—but I've read up and have a good base to start from."

Aubrey was trying her best to hide her lack of interest but she could plainly see her brother was once again thinking with his small head.

Terri continued on as she consulted the book. "My dad describes the Lavoisier as a place where terrible acts of brutality and murder once occurred."

"Typical," Zyler joked.

He smiled at Aubrey but she didn't return it. And then she subsequently caught herself eyeing the lewd big bulge straining the crotch of his tight jeans.

"Nineteen thirty." Terri searched the pages. "Here it is! An Austrian surgeon named Anton Von Hacker. He was educated at the University of Vienna. And in nineteen twenty-nine he came to the United States. In less than one year he's said to have murdered his wife and four young women right here in the mansion." She turned a page and studied it for a second. "An American surgeon who'd met with Von Hacker briefly depicted him as a religious fanatic and a mental case."

"Nice." Zyler chuckled.

Aubrey fought the impulse to stare at his junk again.

"How did he do it?" Aubrey stolidly asked.

"Huh, wha?" Terri looked up at her, then she skimmed a few pages.

Everyone waited.

"*Gross*," Terri said. "It's reported he splayed out his victims, slicing and surgically removing their female genitalia while they were alive . . ."

"Ugh, that's just fucking nasty," Zyler said. He looked at Aubrey and quickly apologized for his crassness.

Aubrey glanced at her brother and found his eyes were locked on Terri, he was clinging to her every word.

"I'd forgotten about that part," Terri said.

"The little details. . . ." Zyler teased her.

"All Von Hacker ever told the authorities was *Ich sehe Gott*." She read a bit more. "In English it means *I see God*."

Everyone was silent for a moment.

"Enough about this," Terri said and hung the book, supported by its spine, on an arm of the chair. "Okay." She sat with good posture. "Each of us hold hands and form a joined circle."

Everyone clasped hands.

Aubrey felt the clamminess of her brother's hand and the strong, dry warmness of Zyler's. This time she'd given him a humble smile just as he'd taken her hand in his. Maybe she wasn't being reasonable, a tad too defensive.

"The lights?" Zyler asked.

"No, leave them." Terri shook her head.

Zyler shrugged and smiled at Aubrey.

"Everyone shut their eyes and don't open them again until I tell you to," Terri said.

Everyone did.

Terri began to speak to the beyond. "Spirits of this house, we call upon you to hear our words of goodwill, and we welcome you to enter this circle we've made for you . . . a portal into the realm of the living . . ."

Not able to get into it, Aubrey cheated and peeked out more than once. The guys were peeking too, so only Terri was manifestly serious about what they were doing.

". . . Come before us at your desire. Speak to us who will listen. . . ."

Aubrey had her eyes shut when she heard the metal crunching noise.

After Terri had gasped, everyone opened their eyes. Only Terri and Gary still held hands after standing up.

Zyler, standing, bent down and picked up both beer cans that were completely flattened.

"Good thing they were empty," he joked, inspecting them.

Crossing her arms, Aubrey frowned, thinking to herself, What adolescent games are we playing here?

For the first time tonight, Gary made a joke. "Guess the spirits thought this was an AA meeting."

Terri laughed and squeezed his hand flirtatiously.

It was obvious to Aubrey the girl wasn't being one hundred percent genuine with her brother. Poor Gary if he really was expecting to find love.

Zyler tossed the cans over to Terri who released Gary.

"This is crazy," she said, turning the cans this way and that.

"So you didn't step on them?" Aubrey asked, unexcited.

"Nope," Terri said. And she must have seen Aubrey's doubtful look because she asked both Gary and Zyler the same question. "Did you feel me twist or move at all before?"

Both guys shook their heads.

Aubrey hadn't felt Zyler twist or turn.

After a long pause of silence, Terri exhaled with a laugh and suggested they do something more physically exciting. "Zyler, please help me in the other room for a minute."

Terri discarded the cans on her chair and she and her friend excused themselves, pledging they wouldn't be long and that they had something fun in store.

When she was certain they were gone, Aubrey went over to the chair and picked up the cans. She checked them.

"Are we having a good time yet?" she asked her brother.

He shrugged.

And Aubrey didn't need for him to say a word because she could tell he was still hot for the beautiful female whose sense of fun was a mystery right up there with the worst of them. She sighed with pity.

In the entrance hall Terri grabbed Zyler under his shoulders and pressed hard up against him.

They kissed passionately, tongues twirling together.

Then they quickly broke apart.

"That was silly and unfulfilling," she said. "They didn't buy the crushed cans, sorry."

He hesitated, an instance of confusion, then nodded. "I'm going to fuck that Ms. Snooty in there so hard and fast she'll beg me not to stop."

She grinned and toyed with his collar. "Oh, I can't wait to suck off her nerdy, Einstein of a brother and make him service me just however I want."

He chuckled, "Innocence is so delicious."

"Mmm. I agree." She ran a finger up his groin causing him to moan. "Especially ones with such scholarly attitudes."

He kissed her forehead.

"Sis seems frigid, yeah?" she said.

"Virgins," he said.

"Did you and Mark get the room set up?" she asked.

"Yes."

She glanced behind her to make sure no one was listening. "A brother and a sister. This is hot!"

"Yes." He chuckled.

She patted his rear end. "Hurry up and check the room then come back to us and we'll separate the guests."

Dashing off, he took the grand staircase up two steps at a time.

Aubrey and Gary were checking out the room's décor when Terri strolled in.

"Hey guys," she said.

Gary set down a giant glass ashtray he was looking at.

Slinking towards him, Terri came up next to him and laced her arm around his.

Aubrey could see beads of sweat popping up on his forehead. He was, in every sense of the word, smitten.

"So, Aubrey," she asked. "What do you normally like to do for fun?"

Fidgeting, Aubrey touched one of the chairs and passed her hand over its shape. "I don't really have time to goof off. Neither does Gary."

Terri tightened her arm around Gary's and smiled seductively at him.

He grinned.

"Well that's too bad," Terri said. "Everybody needs an outlet. Don't you agree, Gary?"

"Yeah," he said.

Aubrey stopped and stared at them. She hated the effect Terri was having on her brother, making him speak like such a goon. "I guess so," Aubrey said. "So what's your outlet? Séances?"

Laughing, Terri said, "No, that's Dad's. My mom taught me a whole different lifestyle of fun and pleasure."

"Are your parents still married? I know you said you recently connected with your dad."

"Divorced."

"How long?"

Before Terri answered, Gary felt her arm slip away and then suddenly her hand was touching his bottom. Her fingers caressed a cheek. "My dad stepped out before I was a year old."

Just as Aubrey was about to ask another question, Zyler walked in. She noticed he was breathing heavy at first.

"Are we having fun yet?" Zyler asked, directing his eyes at Aubrey.

Aubrey saw Terri whisper something in her brother's ear. And he nodded, smiling like a kid in a candy store.

Moving in such a way to block them from her view, Zyler thrust himself on Aubrey.

She instinctively leaned to the side to look past him.

"I think your brother wants to spend a little exclusive time with her," he said.

Aubrey understood. But she didn't like it, and she wasn't completely sure why.

She nodded and partially smiled.

"I could show you around the house, if you want?"

She liked that idea. "Yes."

"Okay, follow me."

Before leaving the parlor, she looked back at her brother. He was happy. She told herself again the night would be over soon and then they could get on with their lives.

From one spacious, hardly furnished room to the next, through a series of look-alike hallways, Zyler walked her around the first floor of the mansion. Aubrey found him to be a gentleman but she still knew nothing about him. And he did have an unlearned side to him below the surface, which presented itself in small doses.

"So as you can tell," he said, "I'm not a top-dollar tour guide."

She smiled kindly.

"Truth is, I haven't seen half the place myself," he added.

"And yet you offered to be my guide."

"Got me." He chuckled.

They moved to a large window with no curtain or shade.

She looked outside and saw a dark landscape and a spate of tall bushes.

He came uncomfortably close.

Shy, she turned her back to the window instead of facing him directly and stared out at the room.

"A person could get lost in a place like this," she said.

Grinning, he followed her eyes. "I agree."

"Is this a ballroom?"

"Do you want to dance?"

Her eyes flickered at him with surprise and self-consciousness. She impulsively turned towards him. No guy had ever asked her something like that. She hadn't even gone to her high-school prom. His attractive face was all but a few inches away from hers now, and she trembled with emotion. Romantic thoughts caught her off her guard. And she began to give in to the passions of her body, picturing the bulge she'd seen between his legs, feeling a thirsty, carnal heat rush through her.

As he drew even closer, she lost herself further in the fantasy, knowing she'd always wanted a moment like this. And when his soft yet lively lips touched her mouth, she suddenly awakened and pushed him back. Her rational mind was appalled. She criticized herself, blaming hormones for her lack of discretion even though it was just a kiss.

"I'm sorry," he said low. "I shouldn't have tried . . ."

She shook her head. "It's fine. No, it's okay."

She walked away.

Following near, he said, "You're just really nice."

She slowed and turned her head. "Thanks."

"Really smart . . ."

She smiled.

". . . and really pretty."

The last word caused her to halt. She didn't glance back but she blushed and smiled brighter. Then after a few seconds she began to walk again as he quickened his pace to be beside her. She forced her mind to preserve what he'd called her, despite how strongly she suspected he was being insincere.

When Aubrey stepped into the parlor it was empty.

Zyler walked around her and said, "Ah, they've gone up to the playroom."

She looked at him curiously. "Like table games and video games?"

He laughed softly. "Kinda."

"Gary likes chess." She shrugged.

"Let's go join them."

She nodded and followed.

They stopped in the entrance hall and he motioned at the beautiful winding staircase with its artistic hand railing.

She smiled and without any objection let him lead.

On the level above they passed through a darkened hallway with lots of doors. He brought her over to one of them about midway down. Like the many around it, the door was of a quality better than average.

It opened without warning and Terri nimbly slipped out, hastily pulling it shut with her.

"Good, you're here." She smiled.

Aubrey looked to Zyler for an expression but Terri's voice stopped her.

"Gary and I have created a little surprise for you two." Terri reached into a hip pocket and brought out two small silk scarves. She handed one to each of them. "Tie them over your eyes."

Aubrey watched Zyler go at it without delay.

"Here, turn around," Terri told her. "Let me help you. You won't wear them long, only for a minute. It'll be fun. I promise. It'll be a thrill!"

She felt Terri's body move against her backside, and she put the scarf over her eyes slowly.

Terri tied it firmly in place.

"Okay, are you ready?"

Aubrey wasn't but she nodded anyway. She assumed Zyler indicated he was because she heard the door open. She felt Terri take her hand and direct her forward. The door was then closed.

"Don't worry, I've got you," Terri said, excitement almost audibly crackling off her tongue.

Aubrey was steered around for much longer than she'd expected. "All right, I think I'm done now." She started to reach for the blindfold but felt it suddenly taken off for her.

Terri was holding it now.

The first thing Aubrey noticed was the room was dimly lit. She tried to focus on so many things at once. A few burning candles along the wall added a peaceful mood. She saw a large bed and presumed they were in a bedchamber, probably one of many. Before fully giving her attention to the special structure a few feet in front of her, she noticed Zyler had disappeared. She glanced back and saw a single scarf lying on the floor.

"Where's—?" Her eyes questioned what she was seeing.

Someone had made a high wall out of, what looked like, cardboard. Long as well as tall, it was tri-folded, reminding her at first of a dressing screen.

She carefully stepped closer.

"Go on," Terri encouraged her, moving forward herself.

Aubrey's breath was instantly taken away when her eyes discovered the holes. Three of them at waist level, one in each section of the stand. What was sticking out of them shocked her so greatly it made her throw her hands up over her mouth to block her cry.

She watched overwhelmed with disbelief and disgust as Terri kneeled down before the flaccid penis on the far left and began playing with it. At once it started to grow. Aubrey could see a snippet of a pubic mound when whomever the cock belonged to pressed eagerly forward. They were clearly shaven smooth.

"Go for it, honey," Terri said, grinning up at Aubrey for a second. "Just let go of your inhibitions and free your desires." Like a ravenous animal, Terri turned to the cock, which had grown stiff, and put it in her mouth. Her fingers massaged the balls.

Aubrey faltered backwards a few steps. She glimpsed the cock sticking out of the middle hole and one to the right of it. One was erect and one was semi-hard. The one plump; the other slim. She wanted to look away but could only stare. It was both obscene and fascinating.

Terri twisted so she could see her, still bobbing her head, the cock stretching her cheek. She wobbled over on her knees, reached, and took the closest cock in her hand and began jerking it. Someone behind the screen moaned with pleasure. Speaking with her mouth full at first, she mumbled, "Don't leave." She pulled her head back and let the wet, hard cock pop out of her mouth. It rebounded like a springboard. "Go lie down on the bed . . . relax. I can handle this part alone." Now she was stroking two at the same time.

With her heart thumping and her breaths sharp, heading spinning, Aubrey couldn't take anymore. She cried out, "No!" And she ran to the door. Frantically trying again and again, but it wouldn't open.

All of a sudden, someone grabbed her shoulder.

She spun around, releasing a scream.

"Aubrey! Aubrey!" Gary shouted. "It's okay. Calm down. Calm down. You're all right."

She stopped panicking. Her flustered wide eyes adjusted to seeing her brother. Terri was coming towards them.

"You don't have to do anything," he said.

Seeing he was standing there in only his boxer shorts and holding a scarf in his hand, Aubrey suddenly felt betrayed. Tears formed in her eyes.

"It takes time to understand and accept this lifestyle," Terri said.

Gary snapped his head around. "She'll be okay. She'll be fine."

"*No!*" Aubrey cried out. She pounded his chest with her fists then pushed him away. "You're sick! *God*, I can't believe you! You'd have let me . . . suck your *dick!* My own brother!"

His face filled with confusion and a little shame. "No, no, it wasn't like that." He looked to Terri for support.

She placed a hand on his back. "Aubrey, you're taking this too hard. Blowing it way out of proportion. You're being a drag, actually."

Gary raised his eyebrows, certain her less than sympathetic words hadn't helped.

"Aubrey, please let me explain," he said.

Shaking her head, she pulled hard on the door, and this time it opened.

He tried to stop her but she got away.

"Come back!" he yelled, seeing her dash down the hallway.

"Go on, Gary, take care of Sis," Terri said, rubbing his back.

He turned to her with a down look. "I didn't think you were going to involve her."

"But I want you to come back here to me, because I want to fuck you all night, in every position," she said. She kissed him while playing with his cock through the fly of his shorts.

He took one of her breasts in his hand and gently squeezed it.

She moaned, letting her head fall back.

When he tried to free her breast from the shirt, she stopped him and said, "When you get back. Now go make things better with your sister."

She watched him hurry back to the glory hole wall and quickly climb into his pants and whip his shirt over a shoulder. Then like a fireman racing to the emergency alarm, he rushed out of the room.

A flood of emotions had caused Aubrey to run the wrong way, opposite of the main stairs. When the hallway turned, she followed it without concentrating on a sense of direction. She just wanted to cower in a dark corner and cry. She felt completely vulnerable and humiliated.

The hallway came to a dead end and, without a clear head, she opened the nearest door and lunged inside. The only thing that mattered was her need to hide.

In the darkness she felt her way around the room. She tripped at one point and knocked her knee on something solid, but she didn't care. The brief pain was slight. Her mind was too troubled to concern itself with any minor physical discomfort. She found a small table by the wall. Searching its surface her fingers crawled up the rod shape of a lamp. The shade moved and tapped her wrist when she reached under and up to switch on the bulb. Faint light afforded her just enough vision to figure out she was standing in a private den. Across the way there was an empty wall-length bookshelf and on the floor in front of it stood a huge, elegant double-pedestal desk that her knee had already been introduced to.

She glanced at the door.

Her tears started to flow freely.

On the lamp table beside her, she now noticed two crushed aluminum cans.

She picked one of them up. Her mind was blank.

With her back up against the wall, she slowly dropped until her bottom smacked the carpet. She brought her knees up to her chest and sat there curled up, thinking and crying.

Not long after, a strange scratching noise made her look to the ceiling. It seemed to be coming from more than one place at the same time. Looking intently, she found nothing. She gasped when it started directly above her.

Staring up, she set the can down on the

floor next to her. The scratching continued, and the thought of rats scurrying between the walls entered her mind.

She was beginning to get up when the lamp suddenly when dark, its bulb shattering for no known reason.

She screamed and started to go towards the door when something shoved her hard enough to make her tumble backwards and strike the wall. Her frightened eyes searched blindly in the dark, afraid to move again. Then all at once, it felt like a dozen invisible hands were violently molesting her body. Severe pressure stabbed her private parts. Raspy whisperings raided her ears. A voice speaking in a foreign tongue. She fought to but couldn't open her mouth. Pinned to the wall, terror swept over her when she felt the top of her skull being ripped apart then something, an inexplicable evil, forced its way inside her.

She fell unconscious and collapsed.

Gary slowed down at the turn and called out to his sister. He stretched into his shirt. Even with the inadequate lighting he could still see where the hallway ended and knew she had to be in one of the rooms. He was thinking about how terrible he was feeling when from far down he heard a scream.

He ran and when he got almost to the end of the hallway he spotted a slat of faint light bleeding out from under one of the doors.

"Aubrey?" he called, walking up to the door. He tried to open it but it was locked. "Aubrey, hey, listen to me, please, will ya?" He paused to think of what words he wanted to say.

The room was silent.

"You've got to believe me when I tell you this wasn't my idea. You've got to." He tapped on the door, hoping she would at least say something. "Terri told me her friend would keep you company while she and me and some guy named Mark . . . well, it just kind of happened." He looked down at his feet disgusted with himself as his own words made an impact on him, recognizing how foolish he'd been behaving, no better than the disorderly, oversexed and brainless frat boys he despised. Sure, Terri was the sexiest female he'd ever had a chance with, but this just wasn't who he was. Or at least he wanted to believe that was true. He stared at the door. "Terri has a different lifestyle. I just wanted to be with her . . . I-I never thought somebody as hot as her would give me the time of day." He listened a moment for a sound. "I'm ugly. I'm not cool. I'm not anything." He hung his head low. "I'm sorry."

He started to touch the door when it unexpectedly opened.

Aubrey slipped out and he moved back to give her room.

Clearly she had been crying.

"I shouldn't have pressured you into coming with me. I just didn't know any other female I could bring when Terri asked me to get a date for her friend. I was afraid she'd write me off. I would watch Woody for free; you know that, without a favor. I know you can't trust your roommate with your cat."

She looked up at him with steely eyes. "I forgive you, Gary."

He started to smile but was hesitant. "You really do?"

She nodded.

He hugged her and, looking over her shoulder, saw the light under the door flick off.

She seemed to hug him back mechanically, barely lifting her arms.

"We can leave right now," he suggested.

She nodded. "Go to the bike and wait for me. I want to finish using the toilet first."

"I'll wait here."

She shook her head. "No. Get the bike started. You owe me."

The last part got to him. "Okay," he said, not crazy about the idea of leaving her alone with the others. "Do you have your cell phone?"

She nodded.

"Call me if anything happens," he said, for the first time remembering he had his too but had left it in a pouch on the bike. He quickly added, "Like if you have trouble finding the front door."

A thin smile lifted on her face.

He left and when he got to the turn in the

hallway, he looked back at her. He heard the door close.

One of the guys was close to coming—she was practiced at knowing—so Terri stopped pleasuring him through the hole. She pulled herself off his cock until it was all the way out of her pussy. After Gary left, she'd asked the two of them to switch to any of the glory holes they wanted and, without peeking, she'd stripped off all her clothes and walked backwards to the wall, using her fingers to find them. The cock she really wanted to try out was Gary's. He was such a beginner and she'd loved, from what she had seen, the way his shaft curved sharply to the left. And any new cock was always the most arousing for her.

She stood straight and said, "Guys, let's take it to the bed."

She saw their cocks pull back from the holes and disappear.

Just as she was turning to go over to the bed, someone knocked on the hallway door a few times. Thinking it was Gary, she jogged to the door and answered it. When it swung open, nobody was there. She leaned out and quickly scanned the hallway both ways. An annoyed expression rose on her face, but then she looked down and saw a pile of clothes on the floor. She could tell immediately whose they were. The plaid slacks belonged to Aubrey. She squatted down and sorted through the rest: a woman's polo shirt, a simple white cotton bra, granny panties, socks and sneakers.

Intrigued, she watched the hallway and when she stood up, she caught a glimpse of Aubrey's nude body stepping into one of the rooms down the way, a quick flash of her pale ass and she was out of sight.

"Hmm, a little game," Terri said softly. "The shy girl is coming out of her shell."

She thought about it—how she would like to have her first before the boys got to her—and she leaned back inside the room and said, "I'll be right back, guys. You two have fun for a sec but don't finish."

"Hurry up," Zyler said.

She closed the door after herself, dropped the bra she was still holding on top of the pile, and walked in the direction she'd seen Aubrey go. As she strolled past the rooms, she wondered where Gary was.

When she stopped at the door, she heard a noise inside the room, like something had fallen.

She turned the knob, pushed the door open, and stuck her head inside.

The room was dark.

She walked in and closed the door. Staying close to the wall, she felt for the light switch and flipped it.

Soft light spread out over the room from the bronze pendant fixture hanging on the ceiling.

"Aubrey, dear?" She walked away from the wall and searched.

The guestroom was less decorated than the master bedroom, of course. There was a smaller bed, an ornate mahogany highboy, a dressing table, and a black butterfly decor style dressing screen standing up in the far corner, which would have been too narrow to have used for the glory holes. Instantly she noticed one of the closet's sliding door panels had come down. A perfect place for her shy little virgin to hide.

"I will find you," she said in a frisky voice, as she crossed over to the closet. "And I know you'll like it when I do." Playfully she jumped into the open space, her boobs jiggling freely, and looked inside the closet. "Hi!" she said and was disappointed when she saw that it was totally empty. She carefully stepped back over the fallen panel.

"So you're going to make this harder, huh." She stared at the bed.

Slowly walking towards it, she said in a less playful tone, "Speaking of *hard* . . . there're two hard dicks I could be playing with right now, so I'd hope you know how to skip to the end of the game. Besides, we'll both be winners." She giggled.

She thought Gary's sister had to be underneath the bed or on the other side of it or behind the screen. There was no other place to hide. At least that was until she heard Aubrey's faint laughter coming from the next room.

As she stopped beside the bed, her eyes, filled with frustration, shot over to the door connecting them.

Zyler was pumping Mark's asshole faster when he heard the lube bottle fall off the side of the bed, which, in turn, caused him to slow down.

"Your shaved cock feels amazing tonight," Mark grunted.

"I know," Zyler proudly said and rammed one last time deeper on purpose.

Mark cried out and fell flat on the bed. Then he flipped over onto his back laughing.

Zyler, still on his knees, with a slick boner poking the air, looked down with a grin at the guy he'd fucked at least ten times already in the past week, about as long as he'd known him.

"Maybe it's because your sister sucked you off especially good tonight, eh?" Mark said with a derisive tone of voice.

"Fuck you," Zyler said, half serious. He dropped down face first on the bed.

"You just did." Mark chuckled.

Zyler put his hand on Mark's chest.

Both men heard the door open up.

Someone walked across the floor.

"Well, well . . ." Mark said, lifting up on his elbows.

Zyler saw the spicy look on his face and shifted over onto his side.

They watched Aubrey, in her birthday suit, stride confidently over to them.

Zyler sat up and scooched to the edge of the bed.

Her hair was tussled. Her look was emotionless.

Zyler eyed the untrimmed thatch of hair between her thighs.

"Your sister could talk a fish out of water," Mark said, sitting up next to him.

Without a word, she came up and placed a hand on both their shoulders.

Mark lifted his hand and idly held onto her forearm.

"Hi, sweetie," Zyler said. He reached out and hooked an arm around her hip, pulling her forwards gently, fingers caressing her ass. "Would you like to join us?"

When she didn't resist, he guided her up with him on the bed. He glanced at the door and was curious where his sister might be. Probably getting her muffin licked clean by Gary.

Mark stood down off the bed and waited for them to get into a position, stroking himself calmly.

Getting her straddled on top of him, Zyler lay back and said, "You don't have to speak, just feel. Don't be afraid." He was decidedly thrilled with the idea of being inside her—this pristine, stuck-up bitch. He reached down between them and managed his cock inside her vagina. The tight warmth made him flex and arch and moan with pleasure, but he didn't start thrusting, not just yet. He was surprised when she hadn't reacted.

Mark climbed on the bed and walked on it until he was behind her. He'd decided not to fuck with using the lube. This chick could bolt at any moment. He licked his hand with a good amount of saliva and quickly glazed his erect penis with it. Squatting, with one hand on her hip supporting his balance, he forced himself into her anus. It took a few hard tries, but penetration was achieved. He cried out with satisfaction.

Zyler jerked when he felt the sensation of Mark's stiff shaft putting pressure on his own through her walls. Again he was struck when she didn't react or at least make a sound. She was most likely scared and overwhelmed to the point of freezing up. Although her body seemed willing. You could never predict beginners, they always acted different.

They began to fuck her in a working rhythm. This was one of Terri's favorite sex positions.

Zyler couldn't see the look on her face because she was keeping her head up. He played with her breasts, which were much smaller than his sister's. While he was gingerly rubbing the nipples between his fingertips, he fantasized about the others, with Mark out of the picture. Gary would be in Mark's place and Terri would be riding his own face and she'd be turned towards Aubrey. A perfect sibling chain fuck.

Suddenly he noticed she was staring at him, locks of her hair hanging down, concealing her features, brushing his chest. He felt he was going to come soon because Mark's thrusts were escalating his climax.

As a wave of pleasurable tingles flowed out from his lower region, just to the point of ejaculation, she said something he couldn't quite understand—a foreign word. Then she sprang off him like a cat lunging at its prey and quickly crawled to the side of the bed and jumped down on the floor.

Not able to control it now, his come pumped out of his cock and flowed in repeated streams upon his own stomach.

"Damn it!" Mark complained. "I knew she would." When he saw what had happened to his friend, he reached down and touched Zyler's semen, spreading it all over Zyler's own stomach and chest. "Look who made a mess."

Zyler didn't fight it; he was in the lull of being spent.

"Hey, girl, come back here and finish me, too," Mark called out.

She walked all the way over to the darker side of the room and started messing with the fireplace.

"What on earth is she doing?" Mark asked, falling onto his butt. He slapped his friend on the leg.

Zyler sat up.

"Aubrey," Zyler said. "What are you doing?"

She didn't answer.

They watched her get down and mess around in the hearth. A brick was moved, then another.

Both guys watched curiously and waited.

They saw her stand back up. She turned around and walked towards them, and now she was holding something in both her hands—a large case of some kind.

She went to the bottom of the bed and set it down on top of the mattress.

Mark glanced at Zyler and said with a smile, "Man, you shouldn't've busted your nut. Looks like Terri planned a little surprise she didn't tell us about."

Zyler wasn't so sure.

She unfastened the case's belt locks.

Mark got down and went over to see what she had.

"Oh goodie, you brought toys," he said, coming up beside her.

The case looked old . . . antiquated.

He watched her unfold coverings of some kind of fabric.

When she lay bare what was inside, his eyes bulged with horror.

She grabbed one of the strange-looking surgical tools and, before he could get away, slashed him across the neck with it. The curved amputation knife opened his flesh with perverse ease.

Zyler wasn't exactly sure what had just happened, until he saw his friend swing around, clutching at his throat, and he heard his short blood-filled scream, and then the gurgling. There was a shocking amount of blood. One whole side of her was spattered with it.

Before he jumped off the bed and bounded for the door, he saw Mark fall limply to the floor. An instinctive awareness told him something wasn't right, she wasn't normal; a sense of evil, and it propelled him to run instead of fight.

He looked back and saw her searching inside the case.

When he tried, the door wouldn't open. He frantically shook the knob and kicked the door, hoping it would jar the lock. His sister knew where all the keys were.

His heart flagged with dread when he saw her coming towards him with a tool whose blade was in the shape of a number four. At once he ran for the other side of the room, his mind set on finding anything he could use to defend himself with, maybe a brick from the fireplace.

Like her feet were on rollers, she wondrously glided across the floor, so fast she met him halfway, cutting off his path.

He gasped and lurched to the side.

He drew back and then punched her, delivering a quick blow to her face.

He saw her eyes slate over with a solid silver

color and not a muscle in her face twitch when she attacked.

Terri, at first frustrated but now mad, put her hands on her bare hips and stared down at the floor in front of the master bedroom door where Gary's sister's clothes had been. They were now mysteriously gone. Apparently the little goody-goody bitch thought she was getting her back for—for what? . . . offering her the best orgasm of her boring, bookworm life?

She glanced down the hallway both ways. Still no Aubrey . . . no Gary.

She growled.

She pushed open the door and went into the room intent on getting her brother to help her find and then throw out both ungrateful nerd fools who'd spoiled the party for her.

Initially it appeared as though the bedchamber was empty. A baffled expression rumpled her pretty face when she discovered the bed vacant.

"Zyler?" she called. "Mark?"

She expected them to come out of some dark corner like two mischievous young boys doing things they never wanted their parents find out about—sweaty, laughing, perhaps kissing each other, maybe even with creamy facials. She knew how much her brother loved to get, and give, those.

The glory hole wall they'd built caught her eye when it shook with force.

Suddenly two limp cocks poked out of the holes.

"Ah, I see," she said. "You two finally took me seriously when I said not to finish without me." She moved slowly towards the wall. "Zyler, our two guests have decided to play head games, and not the fun kind, so I want them gone. And I want you and Mark to come help me."

The guys didn't answer.

Just a few short steps away, she saw both cocks wiggle.

"Okay, I get it." She got down on her knees in front of the wall. "I'll drink you both dry first. But right after they're banished, you both have to reciprocate, and I mean good and long." She chuckled.

When she took one in each hand, she made a gross face. "Eww, you boys have been sticking your willies in ice! How'd you get so small?"

With her fingertips she started to jerk them both. She held one still and came up under it, tilting her head just right to start flicking it with her tongue. Realizing neither cock was swelling, she closed her eyes and clamped her lips around the one she was licking. When she started to suck, it didn't feel right. She threw her hands against the wall and simultaneously spit it out, reacting to her first thought one of them had tripped and the wall was coming down with them . . . on top of her. But when she opened her eyes, the horrific image in front of her struck to shatter her sanity. Both cocks lay on the floor. She saw the raw points where each had been severed.

Two hands shot out of the holes.

The screams that were trapped in her chest escaped and she fell back onto her rear end.

She saw wet red hands clawing at the air—sticky blood covering the spread fingers, the palms, the wrists.

With extreme fright, she scrambled across the floor, driving herself to clumsily rise on her feet.

The glory hole wall crashed down with a faint smack.

Racing to get there she could see the door was opened how she'd left it, when it abruptly slammed shut.

After a few wild failed tries to get it to open, she whirled around and pressed her back up against the door.

Terror gripped her as she watched someone—naked and drenched in blood—stalk towards her. When they were close, they suddenly stopped.

Breaking into tears and shaking her head, Terri whimpered, "Get away from me . . . Leave me alone . . ."

Aubrey got into a sumo stance.

Now clearly realizing who it was, Terri found a small moment of strength. A furious cry flew from her lips. "You sick, twisted bitch! What have you done to them? I'll kill you, do you hear me! I'll kill you!"

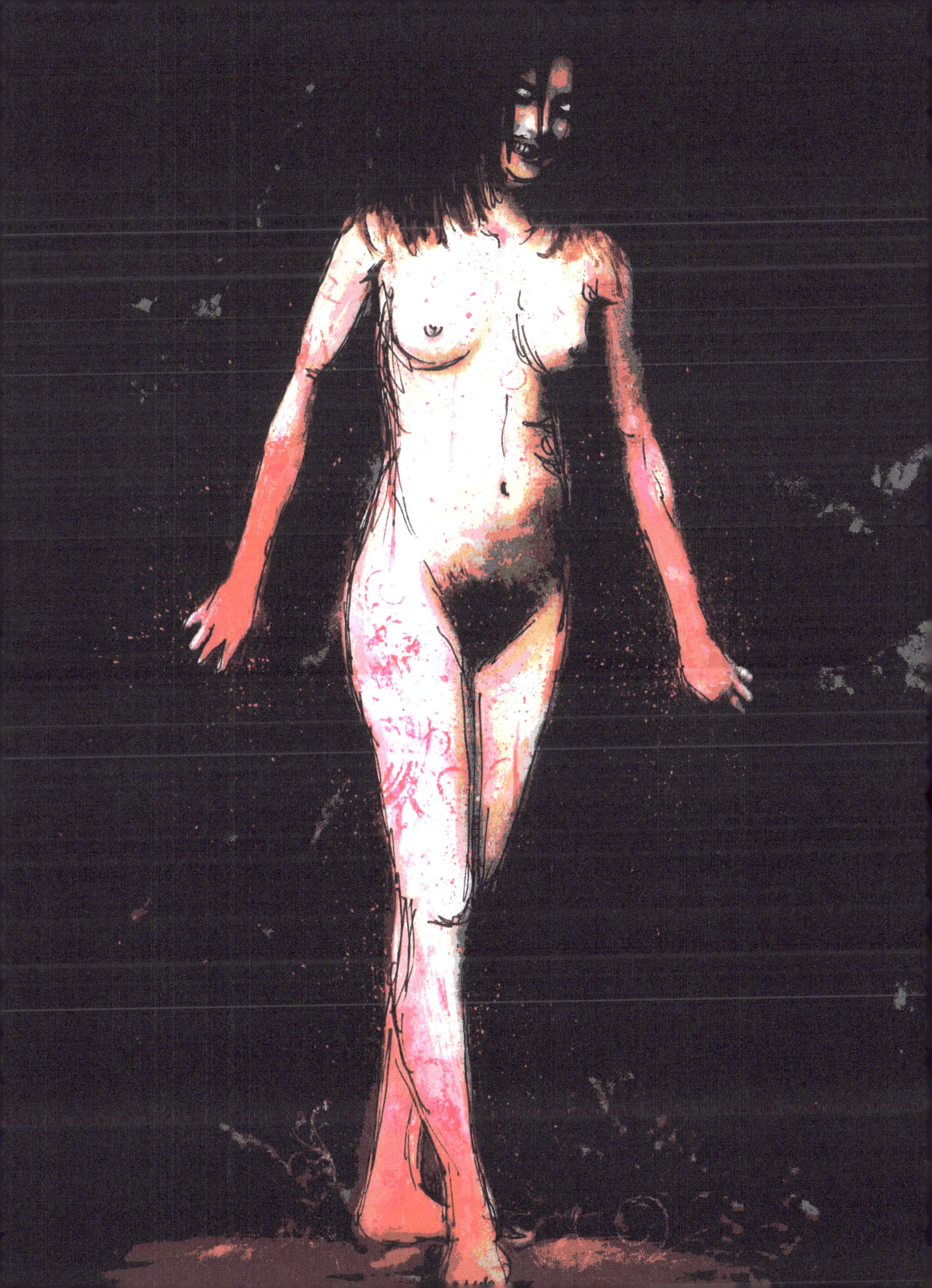

With her legs far apart, Aubrey reached down and touched her vulva.

Terri thought she was masturbating at first and started to charge at her with her hands balled into fists. She stopped dead when she saw the girl's strange eyes and caught the madness of what she was doing.

Aubrey fingered herself, stuffing them deep inside her pussy, and gradually pulled out of it a long, nasty-looking metal object. Some kind of instrument Terri had never seen before. It had a shovel-shaped bladed end.

Aubrey stood up straight and held the terrifying object out in front of her, with clumpy soupy shades of crimson fluid spilling off it.

Terri recoiled and took sluggish steps backwards.

Aubrey, slowly coming forward, began to speak with rage. Her voice was not one but two.

Terri heard the unearthly sound of a male speaking in German occurring at the same time.

"You wretched whore!" Aubrey spewed, she jabbed the cervix slicer at Terri. "Do you think your sins will go unpunished? Like my adulteress wife, you will come to learn the penalty of sin!"

Terri clasped her face with shock. She shook her head uncontrollably. "Anton Von Hacker . . . No . . . No . . . *It can't be!*" She began to sob and stagger to the door. In a weakened, lost state she pulled on the door, expecting it would not open. She felt slippery warm fingers touch her back then pull her hair. Breaking down, she slipped to the floor.

Gary was becoming more worried. With the bike vibrating between his thighs, he touched his cell phone and tried to call his sister again. Thoughts and emotions were flooding his brain. Tonight had been one big mistake. And as much as he still wanted to have sex with Terri, the thought of what could have happened to his sister was (there was no other way to put it) unacceptable. How could these people have been so crude, so deceptive? Aubrey should have never been tricked into such an ordeal.

Her phone went to voice mail.

After shoving his phone in his pocket, he suddenly realized he wasn't wearing his shoes.

He snickered and said aloud, "If the professor could see me now."

He shut down the bike, hopped off the seat, and jogged back inside the Lavoisier mansion. A nervous feeling came over him as he hurried up the staircase to the second floor. He didn't want to have to face Terri.

The hallway was silent and empty.

He wondered what could be taking his sister so long and tried to ignore the bad idea that any of them had forced her to do something she didn't want to do. He'd never be able to forgive himself.

Before the master bedroom door he hesitated and took a breath for courage and for willpower should he see anything, for instance Terri naked, that would make him give in to his lust.

He opened the door and walked in.

A weird air touched the room. It was unplayfully quiet. As he walked over the shadowed floor both his socks got wet. He jerked and lifted them up slightly afraid of what might have caused it. But he continued on. The glory hole wall had been knocked down. He didn't see anyone around until he noticed the bed. Someone was there, though he couldn't see who because they were underneath the covers. He crept towards the bed, seeing the covers raised in a mound, detecting a trace of movement.

Sex?

For a brief moment he thought about just grabbing his shoes lying over by the toppled wall then sneaking out. But what if his sister was under the covers? Being raped?

He stood at the bedside with both fear and a pinch of excitement in him, trying to prepare his reaction to what he would see and what he might say.

He reached out and took hold of the top edge of the blanket.

He yanked it back.

With sudden surprise he let go and moved away from the bed, trying to grasp what he was seeing.

Terri lay on her back with her head tilted up,

mouth agape, eyes frozen on the ceiling, arms in a crucifix position, her tits hanging naturally to either side shaking lightly. Someone, another female, was kneeling down between Terri's legs with their face buried hard in her crotch.

His eyes widened as the fear began to rise up inside him. The anxiety of finding out the truth of who he believed he was seeing but so desperately wanting to be wrong.

By accident he kicked something spongy on the floor. He glanced down, confused as to what it was. A gross hairy blob.

All of a sudden the female down on all fours rose up.

She turned her face sharply towards him.

He began to choke on revulsion when he recognized her.

Aubrey was soaked in blood, her bare breasts washed in crimson, dark fluid dripping off the tips of her jutting nipples onto Terri's thighs and the sheets and into the dark, sickening hole left from where Terri's sex organs had been removed.

Aubrey's face was obscured with sopping gore, hair slick with more.

Her shiny silver eyes from out of the thick, bloody mask stared dead at him.

He reeled back in horror, the reality he trusted becoming undone.

She jumped easily on her feet.

"*Ich sehe Gott!*" she snapped and leaped at him from the bed.

Terry 'Horns' Erwin lives in Norwood, Ohio. He is a member of the Horror Writers Association and a Black Bed Sheet Books author who has written three novels—*Stationhouse No. 1*, *Chophouse* and *Chophouse 2*. His stories have appeared in caboodles of books and magazines and Internet sites. He's an avid horror collector of books, films, posters, memorabilia, and anything else connected with the genre. At times he can be one of those pesky horror trivia guys who knows things that make some scratch their heads and roll their eyes. He is an animal rights enthusiast. Currently he's hard at work on a screenplay. Visit him at www.hornsthewriter.com.

Kealan Patrick Burke

Empathy

A Novelette

Illustration by Stephen Cooney

Will Chambers heard the muffled thump in the upstairs bedroom and sighed. He'd hoped his absence wouldn't wake Melanie but here she came now, trudging down the stairs, eyes narrowed at the light, auburn hair tousled, dressed in nothing but an old LAPD T-shirt and a pair of black silk panties embossed with roses. Ordinarily the sight of her—long pale slim legs, unhindered breasts pushing against the material of the shirt—would have been enough to arouse him and force the worries from the forefront of his mind. But not now.

Dear God, not now.

He watched her shuffle to the table and yawn as she withdrew a chair and plopped down into it. "What's wrong?" she asked, stifling another yawn.

He shrugged, offered her a feeble smile. "Couldn't sleep."

"Me neither."

He suppressed a laugh at that. When he'd left her in bed, she'd been snoring softly. As always, his absence had roused her, like a silent alarm.

"You must be working too hard," he said, and took another drag on his cigarette.

Smoke threaded its way upward, only to be shredded by the frantic whirl of the fan. He followed the nicotine with a slurp of coffee and sighed.

"Maybe, but what's your excuse?" Melanie asked again, crossing her legs and playing with a lock of her hair, her eyes filled with the memory of sleep. He knew she hadn't meant her words to sound as snide and accusatory as he took them. He'd lost his job at *The Delaware Gazette* almost a month ago now, replaced by some hotshot young kid who'd come straight from Penn State armed with 'fresh and innovative ideas,' as Will's editor had put it. So far, Melanie hadn't confronted him about his prolonged unemployment, or when he might start taking steps to rectify the matter. In truth, he was afraid to tell her his plan. Writing was all he was good at, and the thought of working as a salesman or security guard disturbed him—not because of the work involved, but because of how stifling it would be to his creativity. What he wanted to do was write a novel, but he had not yet summoned the requisite courage to announce to Melanie that she would have to support them while he tried his hand at it.

"I couldn't stop thinking, that's all. You know how it is sometimes. Stupid brain won't shut down long enough for me to get to sleep."

She nodded in sympathy. "Yeah, I know. Did you try reading for a while?"

"Yeah. I grabbed that horror novel you'd left on the nightstand. Talk about the absolutely worst possible book to choose on a sleepless night."

She grinned, exhaustion still clinging to her face like a well-worn mask, and spoke as if addressing a child. "Aw, did it scare you, honey?"

No, I was scared to begin with, he almost said, but returned her smile instead. "It was a little on the violent side."

"It's a horror novel. What do you expect?"

He stubbed out his cigarette, clucked his tongue when the air from the fan encouraged it to stay alight and mashed it until tobacco erupted from the filter.

"I think it's out," Melanie said. Her hand slid across the table to rest on his forearm. "What's the matter? Tell me." He offered her another shrug, but she squeezed his arm.

"You've been walking around with a frown all week. Even when I say something funny enough to get a laugh out of you, it sounds like you're doing it to keep me satisfied. Something's bothering you and you know I'll plague you until you tell me what it is."

He slid another cigarette from the gaping box by his left hand. "It's the video."

"The one you watched on the Internet?"

He grimaced around the cigarette and nodded.

"I can't understand why this is staying with you," Melanie said, rubbing her fingertips along his wrist and across his palm. It tickled, but Will was afraid if he told her so she'd take her hand away, and right now he desperately needed her touch, needed to feel the blood, the life, ever so softly pulsating beneath her skin. "I mean, it was a terrible thing to see, but in fifteen years of reporting for the *Gazette*, I'm sure you've seen worse—"

"No I haven't," he said, with a bitter smile. "I've seen accident victims, murder victims, all the awful aftermaths. This wasn't an aftermath. I've never seen anything even remotely like that."

She sighed, leaned forward so her elbows were on the table. "It'll go away eventually," she said softly. "You just need to get it out of your system."

"Maybe, but what I saw on that screen isn't the worst of it."

Melanie said nothing, but waited for him to continue.

He swallowed the fear that seemed to force the words out of him and cleared his throat. "Those people . . . that woman who died . . . who they killed."

Melanie nodded somberly.

"When they . . . when I close my eyes, I see what they did to her, in more detail than they showed on that tape."

Stop now, he thought in one dazzling, desperate moment of panic. *Don't go any further with this. You'll scare her.*

Melanie's hand found his fingers, squeezed them tight.

Will lowered his gaze to the tip of the cigarette. "I see every minute detail, from the blade touching skin, to the blood pooling around her head as they begin to cut. It won't go away."

"Honey, don't—"

"I hear her screaming and . . ." He swallowed again, but this time it was bile he was forced to restrain, just like the first time he'd seen what his mind now replayed in vivid detail. "Tonight, in bed, it sounded so clear it could have been playing at a low volume on the radio." He gestured emptily. "The sound changes when they saw through her vocal chords."

Melanie's face had lost all color. Her free hand now covered her mouth. "Jesus, Will. Stop, please," she mumbled.

"She whimpers." He gasped for breath as the panic that came with remembering seized him. The cigarette began to tremble in his fingers at the realization that talking about it—something he had hoped would help—only served to make them clearer, more vivid. "She sounds so child-like, as if . . . as if the pain is so incomprehensible it reduces her to an infant . . . oh God . . . that sound . . . and . . . and when it's over . . . when it ended, up here, tonight," he whispered, tapping an index finger against his temple, ". . . they take her head and raise it to face the camera . . . but . . . it's not her face."

"Will . . ."

When he looked up, there were tears in his eyes. ". . . It's yours."

She stayed with him until dawn's sepia-toned fingers parted the blinds and painted bars of fire on the wall. They'd moved to the sofa, where he lay on his back staring at the ceiling, Melanie nestled against him, her hand on his chest. He stroked her cool skin while she slept, occasionally squeezing her closer to him, though they could be no closer, smiling now and then at the pleasurable moan she gave when he drew his fingers down her spine. He felt as if the only way to smother the horror that seethed within him was to pull her inside him, so perhaps she could fight the terror with him. So he wouldn't have to fight it alone. For now, she was a slender, sleeping figure, oblivious to the nightmare that danced across her husband's eyes with every breath, every blink.

He was scared, and it was a preposterous fear. But knowing the foolishness of it didn't lessen its severity and now he felt as if the simple act of watching an execution, something not meant to be seen, had broken something inside him; that a rudimentary shield, essential to the sanity of man, had ruptured under the weight of his shock, and now the world had shriveled and dimmed, become a dank dark cell.

As he watched the sunlight crawl across the walls, he squeezed his eyes shut, praying nothing but dark awaited him there.

A knife grinding through muscle . . . a gurgled moan . . . Blood plumes, squirting upward and blinding him . . .

His eyes flew open, blinking in time with the stuttering thud of his heart.

"Oh fuck," he whispered shakily. "Oh fuck, God, why won't this stop?"

A sob so loud it frightened him burst from his mouth and Melanie jerked awake, startled, her eyes searching the room before she blinked once, twice and looked at him.

"Will?"

Tell her it's all right.

But he couldn't. He could not tell her it was a dream, a nightmare, something that hurt and frightened him for a while only to flee with the realization that his imagination was to blame.

Instead he said nothing, but covered his face with his hands and wept.

"Will?"

But even in the darkness behind his hands, he saw shredded skin.

"I could stay home," Melanie said, standing behind him and massaging the concrete tension from his shoulders. Will shook his head, and stared at his hands, at the faint trembling there. He was coming apart.

"No, you go. It won't do you any good to sit around here looking at me feeling sorry for myself."

She was already dressed for work, and looking more beautiful than ever. In truth, he did want her to stay—the thought of being alone filled him with cold panic—but he knew it really wouldn't help. She couldn't chase away the shadows that capered behind his eyes no matter how much light her company brought with it.

She gave his shoulders a squeeze and went to

fetch her purse from the kitchen counter. "Okay, but you call me if you need me and I'll come home."

He nodded. "I'll be fine. Don't worry."

She turned and watched him for a moment. "You'll get over this, Will. I promise."

He wanted desperately to believe her, but the fact remained that she hadn't the slightest inclination of what he was going through, of how much his world had changed in so short a time. If he could only let her see the nightmare that had corrupted his thoughts, if he could, just for a moment, share the images that relentlessly invaded his sleep, only then might her words mean something. As it stood, her attempts to make him feel better sounded trite and absurd in the face of his overwhelming fear.

Alone.

Melanie was a mere whisper of light in a roomful of shadow. "Call me," she said and kissed his cheek, her lips cool against his skin.

"I will," he replied, and did not look at her as she waved goodbye from the door, afraid if he did, he might see a thin red line forming around the base of her throat.

She left and silence took her place in the kitchen.

Exhausted, frightened and already beginning to feel the dark creeping back to the forefront of his mind, Will stood and hurried to the phone.

He would not watch the news.

He would not watch a movie.

He tried to watch cartoons but even the animated violence quickly brought to mind the echo of what he had seen.

He switched to *M*A*S*H*, and quickly changed the channel when one of the characters, a surgeon, got blinded by a fount of arterial spray.

He settled on a vapid sitcom—surely a safe choice—but soon even the wisecracking characters clustered around the bar began to lose their heads and bleed into their drinks.

The audience laughed.

In the end, he stabbed the OFF button on the remote so hard his fingernail cracked.

He lay on the sofa, finger throbbing, struggling to fill his mind with benign images: a sunny beach, the gentle hush of waves, a parade filled with grinning clowns and people in animal costumes; then a carnival, a place taken from a box marked 'safe' in his memory: dour-looking barkers plying their trades, starry eyed children clutching prizes, spinning lights, the scent of sawdust and cotton candy, and the deafening sound of screams of screams

of screams

Until the scream was his and the room grew silver teeth.

"Is this going to cost me?" Will said.

Don dropped his considerable weight into the armchair across from Will, and smiled. "Relax. You're one of the most together people I've ever met. I doubt this is going to have me running to write you up for *Psychiatric Times*." He shrugged off his sport coat and scowled as he draped it over the arm of the chair. "I need a new suit."

"Heal thy friend and I'll buy you one."

"You couldn't afford the type of suits I wear," Don said. "Even I can't afford the type of suits I wear, but I have an image to maintain, you know?"

"What kind of image is that? Overweight, balding forty-something on the verge of a midlife crisis, too fond of Scotch and not fond enough of his second wife?"

"People like you negate the need for an autobiography."

They shared a smile, then Will sat back and sighed. "Thanks for coming over. I couldn't think of anyone else to call. I need your help."

"So you said on the phone. What's the problem? Nightmares?"

"It's a little more than that. Actually, it's a lot more than that."

Don relaxed into his chair and clasped his hands over his large paunch. "Tell me about it."

Will gave him a tired grin. "Now you sound like a doctor."

The big man shrugged. "I've been impersonating one for over twenty years now, my friend. Sooner or later it starts to come naturally. But, as I say to all my paying patients, don't think of me as a shrink, think of me as someone who owes a small fortune in alimony and has nowhere better to be right now."

"Comforting."

"Works every time."

There was a moment of companionable silence, then Will cleared his throat. "Someone sent me an e-mail a week or so ago. In it was a link to a web site called Noble Sacrifice dot com."

"Doesn't sound like porn," Don said.

"No. It was a website of banned movies and images."

Don frowned. "Movies and images of what?"

"People being killed. Accidents filmed by people who just happened to be there with a video camera, footage from wars, disasters . . . I guess all of the things they don't . . . can't show you on the six o'clock news. There were films of soldiers being tortured and killed in various conflicts . . . a lot of war stuff."

"And you looked at all these?"

"No . . . God, no. There were descriptions beneath all the links, more or less telling you what to expect if you were brave, or sick enough, to watch."

Don grimaced. "Sounds like tons of family fun."

"Yeah, everything from celebrity autopsy photographs to videos of massacres."

"Isn't that stuff illegal though? I mean, how can something like that be available for public viewing?"

"It had a warning . . . can't remember what it was . . . and a bunch of legalese saying they were protected by FirstAmendment—one word, with a link to whatever they were talking about."

"Jesus. What kind of sick fuck watches something like that?"

Will looked at him.

Don's bushy eyebrows rose. "Ah, I see."

"If you're thinking of asking me why, don't," Will told him, dropping his gaze. "I don't know. I'm not one of those people who get a kick out of watching people being killed. I don't even know why I followed that fucking e-mail link in the first place. But I did, and even as disgusted as I was by all the videotaped atrocities I saw were available, I still, with everything in me resisting, clicked on one. It said: 'Nadejda Petrovna's Execution.'"

"Who's Nadejda Petrovna?"

"A Russian reporter. That's all I know, except of course for the fact that Chechen rebels captured her, and videotaped themselves beheading her."

"Christ."

"Yeah."

"And you watched this?"

"Not all. What I saw was enough though. I threw up right afterward and I haven't slept since."

"I'm not surprised. That would be enough to fuck up anyone's sleep."

Will nodded. "When I do sleep, there are nightmares, except I see the people I love being hurt, not that woman."

"That's to be expected," Don said.

"Why?"

"Well because what you have to realize is that you witnessed a murder. How many average Joes can say that? Just because you watched it on a computer screen doesn't lessen the reality of it. You might as well have been looking through a window. And as any murder witness will tell you, it takes some time for the shock to wear off. Even after it does, they find themselves unable to shake off the horror, the stark reminder of just how tenuous this life of ours actually is, and the guilt."

"Guilt?"

"The guilt of watching that poor woman die, the guilt of giving in to that morbid voyeuristic impulse that exists in all of us, and of course, guilt for not doing something to help her."

Will frowned. "But I couldn't!"

"Exactly. Had you actually been looking at her through a window, you could have tried to help, or called the police . . . something. But you weren't. Remember that this technology—the ability to watch such things from oceans of time and distance away—is relatively new. You wouldn't see it on the news. The movies make it fake enough for you, but when you're essentially there, when the atrocity takes place inches from your face, the mind, sitting in the front row, demands intervention. The impotency that follows as a result of inaction leaves a clear path for guilt, self-disgust and depression."

Will pondered this for a moment. Don had the complacent look of a man impressed by his own wisdom, but despite it, Will felt a swell of gratitude toward him.

There was, however, another problem.

"How does knowing all this help me to deal with it? How does it make me stop seeing death and violence every time I close my eyes?"

"It will pass eventually. That I can assure you. My advice is to find something positive in all of this." Will made to say something; Don raised a hand. "I know, I know. What could possibly be positive about it, right? Well, how about the fact that death, to you, is no longer something that happens to everyone else? Maybe from now on every time you hear about some tragedy you won't—like everyone else does—just shake your head and cluck your tongue before getting back to your crossword puzzle. Maybe it will actually mean something to you."

"That can't be all," Will said, feeling the familiar barbs of panic writhing through him. "I mean, just feeling bad about death can't be the only reason this is happening."

"No, the reason this is happening is because you watched a woman getting her head sawed off."

Will felt his hope dwindle. "So in the meantime I just sit around and . . . what? Isn't there something you can prescribe for me?"

"Other than patience, no. At least nothing that would do you any good."

Will rubbed his hands over his face. "Shit."

"Look, Will. You made a mistake watching that damn video. But it's a mistake you'll get over with a bit of time. The cost of it is suffering through this little nightmare show for a while."

When Will dropped his hands from his face, his eyes were hollow, haunted. "And what if that isn't all?"

That night, Melanie dragged him from his turbulent nightmares with her lips, and her tongue. He moaned in pleasure as she tended to him, rocked his hips as she straddled him, her hair hanging in her face, eyes twinkling in the gloom. The streetlight filled the window behind her with moonlight blue, making a silhouette of her.

"I love you," he whispered.

She didn't reply. He sat up, embracing her and crushing her heavy breasts against his chest; the nipples were hardened points against his own, her legs like a vice around him, locking him into the soft wetness of her. She breathed in short sharp gasps as he ran his fingers through her hair.

Then her breathing caught. Another silhouette rose behind her.

Will froze, his erection wilting immediately.

Slowly, slowly, Melanie threw her head back.

And her neck split with a horrendous zipping sound.

As her body fell away and rolled heavily off the bed, Will found himself staring into the still watching eyes of his wife, his fingers, still tangled in her hair, now the only thing holding her head aloft.

"Help me," she gurgled.

Will screamed.

"Don?" Static crackled over the phone. Will frowned. "Hello, Don?"

"Hey buddy, you there?" Don said. "This line sucks, let me call you back, okay?"

"Okay. Thanks."

A moment later, with Will standing in the hallway, chewing his thumbnail down to the quick and frantically avoiding his reflection in the hallway mirror for fear of the ghoulish visage he might see staring back at him, the phone rang and he snatched it up.

To his relief, this time the line was clear.

"How's my favorite non-paying patient doing?" Don said.

Will cast a glance at Melanie, who sat on the sofa in the living room, nursing a cup of coffee and looking worried. He felt such a swell of love for her he thought it might reduce him to tears, and an equal pang of regret that she should have to bear witness to whatever was happening to him. Although she hadn't said anything about last night, he had caught her more than once massaging her scalp and wincing, which forced him to wonder how hard he had pulled her hair. Guilt forced him to look away, and he turned his attention back to the phone.

"Will?"

"I've been better," he told Don. "Last night was the worst night yet."

"How so? Nightmares?"

Will sighed shakily. "No. They're more than nightmares. Hallucinations, maybe. I find myself watching . . ." He lowered his voice, aware that Melanie was within earshot, ". . . watching them killing Mel."

"Watching who killing Mel?"

"I don't know. Whoever I saw in that video killing Nadejda Petrovna, I guess."

A sigh. "Jesus, bud, this has really burrowed its way into you hasn't it?"

"Yeah. Big time. I'm walking around in a daze from lack of sleep, afraid to close my eyes for fear I'll see the same thing over and over again—some shadowy figure cutting my wife's head off." He heard the faint rustle as Melanie rose and moved away into the kitchen. "I can't do this forever, Don. There has to be something you can do for me."

"I suppose I could prescribe some relaxants for you. Maybe some Valium."

"Will that help?"

"Well, from the sounds of it, anything would be better than lack of sleep. If nothing else, it'll help calm you down, siphon off some of that anxiety. It could be that the apprehension and fear is prolonging these 'hallucinations'—you're expecting to see them, so your mind is obliging. I think maybe one calm, uninterrupted night's sleep will do you the world of good."

"Okay, great," Will said, relieved. "So do I come down there to pick it up, or what?"

"No need. There's a CVS around there somewhere, right?"

"Yeah, over on Sandusky Street."

"Good, I'll call them from here and have them set you up. They'll call when they have the goods for you."

"Thanks a million, Don. Really."

"Don't thank me yet, bud. There's no guarantee this will help, but it should."

"It'll work. I know it will." He ran a hand through his hair. "So what do I do in the meantime?"

"Hang up, light a big fire, grab a bottle of wine from the refrigerator, get Melanie drunk as hell, then take her to bed and teach her the ancient art of bang-fu."

Will laughed. "A note from my doctor might help the request. After last night, I expect she'll be a little gun-shy."

"Gun-shy? Man, Freud would have had a field day with your sorry ass. And what happened last night?"

"Coitus interruptus, in the worst possible way."

"Ah, well . . . say no more, and that's a command, not a request. If I start getting envious of your failed attempts at getting it on, it'll only serve to remind me how empty and pitiful my own sex life is."

The burgeoning strains of cautious relief threatened to turn laughter into a fit of weeping as Will wiped a tear from his eye. Melanie returned to his side, put a hand across his shoulder, her eyes wide with concern.

"Thanks, Don," he said, his voice unsteady.

"For what? I'm well aware that you do this shit just to irritate me, to get me working harder than I care to. Then you stiff me and I'm the one left depressed. Textbook emotional osmosis, pal. Thanks a bunch."

"Would you knock off the wisecracks? I'm serious," Will told him. "I think I'd have gone completely insane without you."

"Bullshit. My ex-wife said the exact same thing and now she's getting porked by pool boys down in Maui, on my tab I may add. Now get off the damn phone and see to business."

"Okay, okay. I owe you one."

"Right. Give Melanie one for me and we'll call it quits."

A rumble in the distance and a sea of static erupted from the phone. "Don?"

There was silence, then the dial tone stuttered in his ear. With a slight shake of his head, Will hung up.

Melanie turned him around to face her, her hands seeking his face. "Are you all right?"

He summoned the best smile he could muster and wrapped his arms around her. "I think so."

She kissed him, a long passionate kiss he didn't want to end. But after a moment he broke away, staring at the small arched window at the end of the hall. Dark clouds had obscured the sun, leeching the light from the day. A moment later, rain began to fall, pattering against the glass and tapping on the roof.

"What is it?" Melanie asked.

Will looked at her, at the slender oval of her face and grinned. "Do we have any wine?"

Sometime later, with a full-blown storm battering the house and premature night pressing against the windows, the phone rang. Sluggishly, already regretting the half bottle of wine he'd consumed before taking Melanie to bed for mercifully uninterrupted and frenzied sex, Will strode naked to the phone. Through the staticky crackle on the line, a voice laden with false cheer informed him that his prescription was ready. He hung up, quickly dressed, and hurried out to his car, the wind wrenching and tearing at him, the rain needling his face.

As he drove the short distance to the store, the wipers working frantically to keep the windshield clear, he realized he already felt better. No hallucinations had spoiled their lovemaking, no shadowy specters had risen from their bedroom floor and afterward, when he'd dozed, there hadn't been any nightmares waiting to thrust him back out of sleep. The dirty feeling still clung to his skin, inside and out, however, a repulsive sensation he knew would take much longer than a day to erase.

He allowed himself a sigh and, one hand on the steering wheel, reached over and popped the glovebox. An almost empty pack of Marlboro Lights tumbled out into his waiting hand. He checked the road ahead and fished out a cigarette, then straightened and thumbed the lighter on the dashboard.

Spindly-legged lightning flashed around the car like negative images of dead branches, briefly turning the rain on the windshield to glimmering jewels. Will coughed, cigarette clenched between his teeth, and drummed his fingers on the steering wheel.

To his right, the CVS sailed out of the dark, and he flipped the indicator, letting the car coast to a stop as he reached the intersection.

The lighter clacked its readiness and he reached for it.

Then froze.

The hair rose on the nape of his neck as a chill scurried down his spine.

I didn't, he thought, fingers still poised before the lighter. *I didn't see anyone in the mirror.*

A gust of wind buffeted the car, rocking it on its axle.

Closing his eyes, but only for a moment for fear unseen hands would grab him from behind, he whispered further reassurances to himself. *The trick is to believe you didn't see it, not just to tell yourself*, he imagined Don telling him. *Force it out of your head, and you'll be okay, bud. Trust me.*

Will nodded slightly, as if Don were with him in the car to see the gesture and swallowed as he straightened.

A car honked behind him, making him jump.

"Just a second, you son of a bitch," he muttered.

The rearview mirror was inches from his face, awaiting him like the sheeted body of a loved one in the morgue. He did not want to look, for ignorance granted him the ability to deny what he thought he'd seen, to deny what might be there.

He cleared the knot of anxiety from his throat and wiped a trembling hand over his face, barely heard the rasp of stubble.

Melanie will complain, he thought. *She'll have beard rash*. He almost smiled, but another angry burst of sound from the car behind him jerked the thought from his mind.

Headlights filled the window like glaring eyes, attempting to blind him, as the impatient driver let his car drift closer to Will's fender.

"All right, asshole," Will said, and straightened in his seat, eyes squarely on the rearview mirror.

For a moment, he saw nothing but the white light making fleeting ghosts that fled across the tan upholstery and the pebbled rain on the rear windshield. But then, there was a woman sitting there, as if she had every right to be, as if she'd dashed in for shelter out of the rain and had just forgotten to thank him, or ask his permission to invade the car.

"No," he moaned and yet could not turn away from the horror that exploded within him at the sight of her raising her bony white hands in front of a face that was slowly slipping to the side, as if she were merely nodding off to sleep. He blinked rapidly, demanding his eyelids scrub away the apparition, ghost, hallucination . . . . whatever it was.

But the woman remained, her eyes deep dark hollows in a moon-shaped face. And *"helllllp,"* she whispered, before the angry red wound that circled her neck began to yawn open.

"Sir, are you okay?"

"Valium . . . um, Will Chambers . . . My psych . . . my doctor called earlier, called in a prescription for me, for . . . for Valium . . . Don Webley . . . Doctor Webley . . . My name is William Chambers."

"Would you like a glass of water, Mr. Chambers?"

"Please, just the fucking pills, please . . . I'm sorry. Please hurry."

"Are you going to be all right? Sir? Sir, are you—?"

I'll get home, he thought in a panic. *I'll get home and they'll be in my house. Those men, those things, those animals, and they'll have my beautiful sweet precious Melanie kneeling on the floor before them. They'll have their hands in her hair and a saw to her throat, and I won't be able to stop them. I won't be able to do anything but regret for the rest of my life that I was fucking stupid dumb piece of shit idiot enough to leave her on her own. They tricked me . . . this is what they wanted . . . this is what they wanted to do all along . . . getting inside my head . . . invading me so I'd leave my wife ripe for them to come and cut her fucking head off . . .*

He got home and barely thought to put the car in park before he was racing up the driveway and yelling his way into the house, not caring that he was dripping rainwater onto the carpet, not caring that at any moment the lights might go out, the power might fail and he'd be left alone, in the dark, with the monsters who had most certainly slaughtered his wife.

The door clattered against the wall and shuddered its way back.

Then the house gloated with silence.

"Melanie!"

No answer. He put his hands to his face, nails primed to tear the skin away if it turned out that his nightmare had taken his wife away from him, if the poison that had marred his soul had reached out and murdered her, if—

"Honey, what's wrong?"

He almost collapsed with relief. Melanie, eyes narrowed at the light, hair tousled, was slowly coming down the stairs, tying the belt on her robe to hide her nakedness from the cold, or from him, who'd become little more than a terrible phantom standing crazed in the hallway.

"Oh Jesus," he breathed, the relief draining him, the adrenaline slowly ebbing away. He leaned back against the front door. "I thought they'd got you," he whispered and with the admission came a huge whooping sob that set Melanie hurrying to cradle him in her arms. "I thought they'd got you," he wept, trembling.

The tears made the dead woman behind his eyes appear to swim.

"Don will call to check on you tomorrow."

Will nodded, already feeling drowsy. The Valium would work. It would have to. The alternatives were looking grimmer by the second and the renewed onslaught of gruesome images were now sharing headspace with thoughts of institutionalization and white padded rooms with screams for cushions and dripping faucets for music.

The bed felt soft and eased the rigidity from his muscles. Beside him sat Melanie, one hand propping up her head, the other stroking his hair like a violinist playing a soundless lullaby.

"I'm sorry," he told her, as the shades began to creep down over his mind's window. "I'm so sorry this is happening."

"Hush," she soothed. "It will be better after you've had a good night's sleep. Tomorrow, we can have a nice breakfast and maybe go for a walk. How does that sound, hmm?"

He composed a smile, but it was not heartfelt. "Good," he said, feeling as if a warm tide were rising in his chest, lapping at his throat. "Good."

"Try to sleep now," she whispered, and her whisper had an echo. He wanted to point this out to her, but the tide had reached his tongue and seized it. He was not alarmed, for it felt sweet as honey and he let it fill his throat until he was lost in its thick, comforting folds.

The phone rang.

Melanie dropped the paperback she'd been valiantly attempting to read in an effort to forget what was happening to Will and hurried into the hallway. With a shaky sigh, she snatched up the receiver. "Hello?"

"Mel. It's Don. Is Will still up?"

"Hi Don. No, he's asleep. Should I wake him?"

"Absolutely not. Let him sleep. He needs it. Besides, it's you I wanted to talk to anyway."

"Wake up, pig."

Frowning, Will's eyes snapped open and he coughed, wheezed and watched in amazement as what appeared to be dust rolled away across a stone floor. He shivered as a deep chill settled into his bones. Suffused white light pulsed across his vision, quickly followed by an acrid tang that was wholly unfamiliar.

"Where—?"

A sharp blow to his stomach propelled him backward and he yelped in pain as his back collided painfully with a solid wall.

Only then was he truly awake.

Jesus . . . he thought, the now familiar terror clawing its way through him with icy nails. *Jesus, they're here. They came while I was sleeping. Melanie . . . oh God, where's Melanie? Where am I?*

"You're familiar with Post Traumatic Stress Disorder?" Don asked her.

"Yes, it's fairly common in soldiers, right?"

"That's right, but it's actually more common than that. Any victim of shock or trauma can suffer from it. Rape, molestation, accident victims . . ."

"Okay."

"The reason I mention it is because I think that's what Will's suffering from."

Before him stood a tall thin man, dressed from head to toe in black.

"Who are you?" The questions pushed against Will's tongue like water through a crack in dam. "How did I get here?"

The man said nothing, but despite the headgear he wore, allowing only his eyes and the wide bridge of his nose to be seen, Will knew he was grinning.

"Get up," the man ordered then, in a clipped accent Will thought might be Russian.

"Why am I here?" Will pleaded with him. "Tell me, please. What . . . what are you going to do to me?" He was trembling so bad he thought he might rattle himself to pieces.

The cold gnawed at him—a merciless freezer cold.

"Stop asking question." It emerged as: *'Stup asging kess-chun'.* The man leveled the large assault rifle strapped across his chest in Will's direction. Distantly Will found the fact that he could discern not even the slightest tremble in the man's hands incredibly disturbing. It suggested a callousness only obtained by familiarity with violence.

Whoever the man behind the mask was, this was a role he had played often.

Will moved, slowly, toward the man, and as

he did so, he realized he was wearing clothes he'd never seen before, and certainly hadn't donned himself—a shapeless, ill-fitting suit of the kind he'd only ever seen on the news. Prisoners in penitentiaries wore them. His heart thumped in his throat hard enough to make his head hurt, eyes brimming with tears.

"How did I get here? Please . . . tell me."

"Stand," said the man. "Stand now!"

Will quickly obeyed, the dusty floor ice-cold against the soles of his bare feet, making his toes curl. *I'm dreaming*, he thought. *Those pills did something to me and I'm dreaming.* But he knew, though he wished he didn't, that whatever was happening now was the proper end for whatever horror he'd been suffering until now, that this was where it had been leading him. And that it was no dream.

I'm going to die, he realized and felt his legs threaten to buckle beneath him.

The armed man nodded his satisfaction and thrust a hand in the center of Will's chest, knocking him back against the wall. Will, winded, looked around at the small room, at the fall of dust motes illuminated by cold white sunlight that slanted through the bars of the room's sole window.

The man spoke something unintelligible and a narrow door opened at the far side of the room.

Three men entered. All of them were dressed the same as the gunman. One of them held a video camera by his side; another held a pistol.

Will felt his skin crawl.

The third man held a saw.

"The symptoms of PTSD are numerous," Don told her, "hallucinations, anxiety attacks, night terrors, memory loss, insomnia, erratic moods, lapses in concentration, depression . . . sound like anyone we know?"

Melanie sagged. "So what do we do about it? Is there a way to treat it that doesn't involve a tight jacket and a cushioned room?"

"Of course. There are Neuro-Emotional Techniques, a relatively new form of 'power therapy' that have proved far more effective than 'talk therapy.' It targets the mind through the body using systems borrowed from the Chi—"

Melanie rolled her eyes. "Don."

"Sorry. But that's your answer. There are numerous treatments available." He sighed heavily. "What I think happened to Will is that after seeing that video, he almost immediately began to visualize the murder, only with him in that woman's place. You can imagine what persistent visualizations like that can do to the nerves. Sooner or later the brain can become convinced that it's really suffering the agonies the eyes have only witnessed. It can even start reproducing the sensations associated with such a death."

Will moaned, his body vibrating with fear as the tall man lunged forward and grabbed him by the collar of his jumpsuit. "Now!" he barked into Will's face and flung him toward the others, who had stopped in the center of the room. The one with the pistol pointed it at Will's head and said something in his own language.

The video man busied himself with setting up the camera, his ministrations oddly calm—he could have been fixing the machine for a kindly old lady, instead of preparing it to film an execution. And Will had no doubt that was exactly what was happening, what was *going* to happen, and that in a few days or weeks, his death would be appearing on a sleazy website he'd once had the misfortune to visit. A horrendous snuff site that justified its existence by claiming it had a responsibility to show the world what they were trying so hard not to see, that they had no business seeing, when in actual fact, it had a far more sinister purpose.

Will knew that now.

What he didn't know was *how* it had been done. How he had gone to sleep beside his loving wife and woken up in a strange place surrounded by masked men who spoke a foreign language?

He supposed it didn't matter now.

He was shoved to his knees, but on the way down, he caught a glimpse of the world beyond the window, and it was not his world at all, but a cold, stark landscape of faltering buildings and slush-laden roads.

Not my world at all, he thought with a flicker of calm. *Not my world. I'm not here. They can't hurt me they won't hurt me they can't.*

A surer voice rose like a bloated corpse to the surface of his mind.

But they will.

He thought of Melanie, stroking his hair last night, and felt a debilitating wave of sorrow at the thought of never seeing her again, of her never knowing how or why her husband had died.

I love you, baby, he thought, willing the words to cross time and space and distance so she would hear them. *So very much.*

They bound his wrists and ankles with thick heavy rope that smelled vaguely of motor oil.

"Please, don't," he pleaded, trying in vain to shuffle away from them. "I didn't do anything to you. I don't even know who you are." Tears spilled down his cheeks. "Please. I have a wife . . ." Terror unlike anything he'd ever known swept through him.

Somewhere beyond the room, a church bell tolled.

Cold steel bit the skin on the back of his neck.

"Don't . . ." he sobbed, as he struggled.

The camera began to whirr.

"Don. Why are you telling me this? Nothing like that is going to happen to Will."

"I know, I know. I'm not saying it will. I use it only to illustrate what the mind can do to someone when it manages to convince itself it's what the body deserves. Atonement for not being able to prevent someone else's suffering. It's a remarkable and tragic condition, but all the seeds are showing themselves in Will, and that's why we have to monitor him closely. You need to stay with him. He needs you now, Mel. You're the only link he has left to the outside world."

"Outside world?"

"Yeah, the real world, because to all intents and purposes it would appear he's losing his grasp on it at a frightening rate. Either that, or whatever dark alternative world he envisions in his head is tightening its hold on him."

Melanie hung up, and hugged herself against the unmerciful cold that Don's phone call had left with her. My God, could it really be so bad? Could she wake up one day to find Will had utterly and completely lost his mind? What would she do? How could she save him?

No, she decided, brushing a single tear from her eye. She would never let that happen. Never. She was stronger than that and she knew Will was too. She'd help him climb his way back from the dark valley into which he'd stumbled.

As she made her way to the bedroom, she brushed the chill from her shoulders. It almost seemed as if the house itself had grown colder. She guessed it was her imagination but told herself to check the thermostat anyway when she returned from checking on Will. A fat lot of good she'd do her husband if she let the heating go berserk.

She cracked open the bedroom door, slicing a wedge of yellow light from the dark inside. "Honey?" she whispered.

Will didn't answer, but she fancied if she strained her ears she could hear him breathing deeply, though it was hard to tell with the rain drumming on the roof.

Nevertheless, she allowed herself a slight sigh of relief. It was fiercely encouraging to see that he wasn't tossing, turning or screaming at ghosts. Perhaps the pills would do the trick after all. She prayed they would.

She opened the door a little wider and entered the room. Will was lying on his back, facing the ceiling, eyes closed. Slowly, she lowered herself down on her side of the bed, wincing at the faint squeak from the mattress springs.

I do love you, she thought, reaching over to stroke his hair. *More than you know.* Her fingers found the soft curls and lightly brushed over them.

He turned his head toward her, eyes still closed, and she quickly withdrew her hand, cursing herself for disturbing him.

"Hush," she whispered.

And watched in stunned, numb horror as

Will's face met the pillow and blood began to flow from his partly open mouth.

"Will?" She quickly stood, and shook him. "Oh Jesus, Will?"

His head rolled free of his body, tumbling down beneath the covers on her side of the bed. Melanie gasped, clutched both hands to her chest as if fearing her heart would burst through it at any moment, and felt the strength leave her.

"Will?" she croaked, staggering back, away from the bed and the ragged bleeding neck still poking up from the covers. She collided with a dresser and fell heavily to the floor, a trembling hand rising to her mouth. Briefly she tried to get up, a scream trapped like angry wasps in her throat, unable to break free. And then the world went black and she fell willingly into its soporific depths.

Melanie stared into her coffee, the steam rising like sinuous ghosts from a black pond, and remembered Don's words, spoken over the phone on the last night she'd awoken from yet another hideous and terrifying nightmare.

This has to be more than a coincidence, Don. What's happening to me?

Her fingers trembled as she traced a line around the rim of the cup.

Cold white sunlight pressed against the windows of the kitchen. From the television in the living room came the sound of a solemn voice relating the details of another atrocity. Melanie put her palms to her face and closed her eyes.

An impassive, bloodless, familiar face shrieked at her in the dark.

She jerked upright in the chair and looked at her hands, at the intensified trembling in them and stifled a sob. Will was dead. Almost five weeks had passed and still she expected him to come waltzing into the kitchen, unshaven and yawning with a dopey smile on his face. She missed him so much, missed the smell of him in the house, the feel of him in the house.

Gone. And she couldn't understand why, no more than she could understand the sudden, soul-freezing fear that had possessed her over the last week or so.

Trauma, Mel. The reason it seems so familiar is because it is. It can manifest itself in different ways, but essentially it's the exact same thing Will went through.

She rubbed her fingers over her temples, chewed her lower lip.

So this is what he had to suffer. You know . . . I wished for his pain. When he was sick, I wished I could take it from him. Now I don't want it. What kind of a person does that make me?

Human, Don had assured her. These days she felt anything but.

Next to her coffee cup sat an unopened pack of cigarettes. She quickly tore the plastic off, discarded the foil that was all that stood between her and the panacea of nicotine, and quickly withdrew one. She lit it and inhaled deeply. She considered calling Don again, but resisted. Sooner or later she would have to conquer the fear on her own, and maybe it was better to start weaning herself off his aid now before she grew to depend on him so much he tired of her constant phone calls, and referred her to someone else. Someone less caring. Someone who didn't understand what had happened to her husband.

I've thought long and hard about it, Mel, Don had told her after the funeral. *And it all keeps pointing to the same thing, though professional skepticism prevents me from buying it outright.* She hadn't wanted to hear it, but let him continue.

Closure, she knew, was needed, or she would forever be haunted by the mystery of Will's death. Would never be able to stop blaming herself unless someone offered proof that it hadn't been her fault. An irrational need, perhaps, but very little about her life these days was rational.

You've heard of stigmata, right? When people, usually religious folks, start showing the wounds of Christ on their bodies? Bleeding feet and palms, and all that jazz?

She'd told him she had and he'd proceeded to inform her of various examples in which ordinary people had suffered extraordinary tortures, with no apparent cause.

There was a colleague of mine in Washington

who documented a case in which an eight year old boy, after witnessing his mother's arm being torn off by a Rottweiler, almost immediately began to develop bruises and small wounds, consistent with bite marks, on his own arm, the same one his mother had lost, though he'd been nowhere near a dog. Three weeks later, the arm was hanging on by strings of flesh and little else, with no physiological explanation for why it had done so. In the end, psychiatrists were brought in to study the boy; they concluded that the boy's trauma at what had happened to his beloved mother was so great, it somehow lent him the ability to experience her pain, by subconsciously willing her wounds onto himself. I imagine if a boy can 'borrow' his mother's wounds to punish himself, then a devout follower of Jesus Christ could conceivably do the same.

The phone rang, jarring the thoughts from Melanie's head. She ignored the persistent shrilling and finished her cigarette. As she'd hoped, it had calmed her, but not nearly enough. She rose and went to the bathroom, locking the door behind her out of habit. As she tugged down her panties and sat on the cold oval of the toilet, she pondered Don's theory, and, as she had when he'd first proposed it, decided it was impossible. But then, wasn't the manner of Will's death also impossible? No matter which way she looked at it, something unnatural had occurred in their bedroom that night, and yet she couldn't force herself to believe that her husband had willed his own death. Trauma could be overcome.

Shock would always fade, and people didn't just decapitate themselves in the dark without a weapon.

Nothing more sinister than empathy.

She covered her face with her hands and moaned. Her body ached, the muscles in her back like taut wires beneath a trembling sheet. There had to be a rational answer to her nightmare but she was no longer sure she wanted to know it. Perhaps there was safety in mystery. At some point, somehow, she would have to start rebuilding her life, even though the mere thought of it felt like a betrayal of Will. Shaking her head, she opened her eyes.

There was a man standing before her, his shadow thick and cold.

Melanie's breath caught in her throat and she looked up, tears threatening to blur her vision, fear like a snare around her throat, tightening, tightening.

Something hit the floor, and rolled and when at last she gathered the courage to look upon it, she found herself staring into her husband's glassy eyes.

She screamed and grabbed her hair, her nails digging, then dragging down her face, drawing blood, as all the horror, the loss, and the grief erupted, spewing from her open mouth as she slid from the toilet to her knees, even as instinct tried to tug her away from the head on the floor and the still, silent form of the dead man it belonged to.

And still she screamed.

And screamed.

Until the scream became a tortured gurgle as a slim but deep wound began to draw its way across her throat.

Born and raised in Dungarvan, Ireland, **Kealan Patrick Burke** is the Bram Stoker Award-winning author of five novels (*Master of the Moors*, *Currency of Souls*, *Kin*, *The Living*, and *Nemesis: The Death of Timmy Quinn*), over a hundred short stories, three collections, and editor of four acclaimed anthologies (*Taverns of the Dead*, *Quietly Now: A Tribute to Charles L. Grant*, *Brimstone Turnpike*, and *Tales from the Gorezone*.)

When not writing, Kealan designs covers for print and digital books through his company Elderlemon Design. To date he has designed covers for books by Richard Laymon, Brian Keene, Scott Nicholson, Bentley Little, William Schoell, and Hugh Howey, to name a few.

In what little free time remains, Kealan is a voracious reader, movie buff, videogamer (Xbox), and road-trip enthusiast.

You can find him on the web at www.kealanpatrickburke.com.

LONG SHADOWS (2011)
Book cover art for *Long Shadows, Nightmare Light* by Mark Morris for PS Publishing

SHADOWS (2012)
Book cover art for *Locke & Key: Crown of Shadows* by Joe Hill & Gabriel Rodriguez for Subterranean Press

MORE THAN MIDNIGHT (2011)
Book cover art for *More Than Midnight* by Brian James Freeman for Cemetery Dance Publications

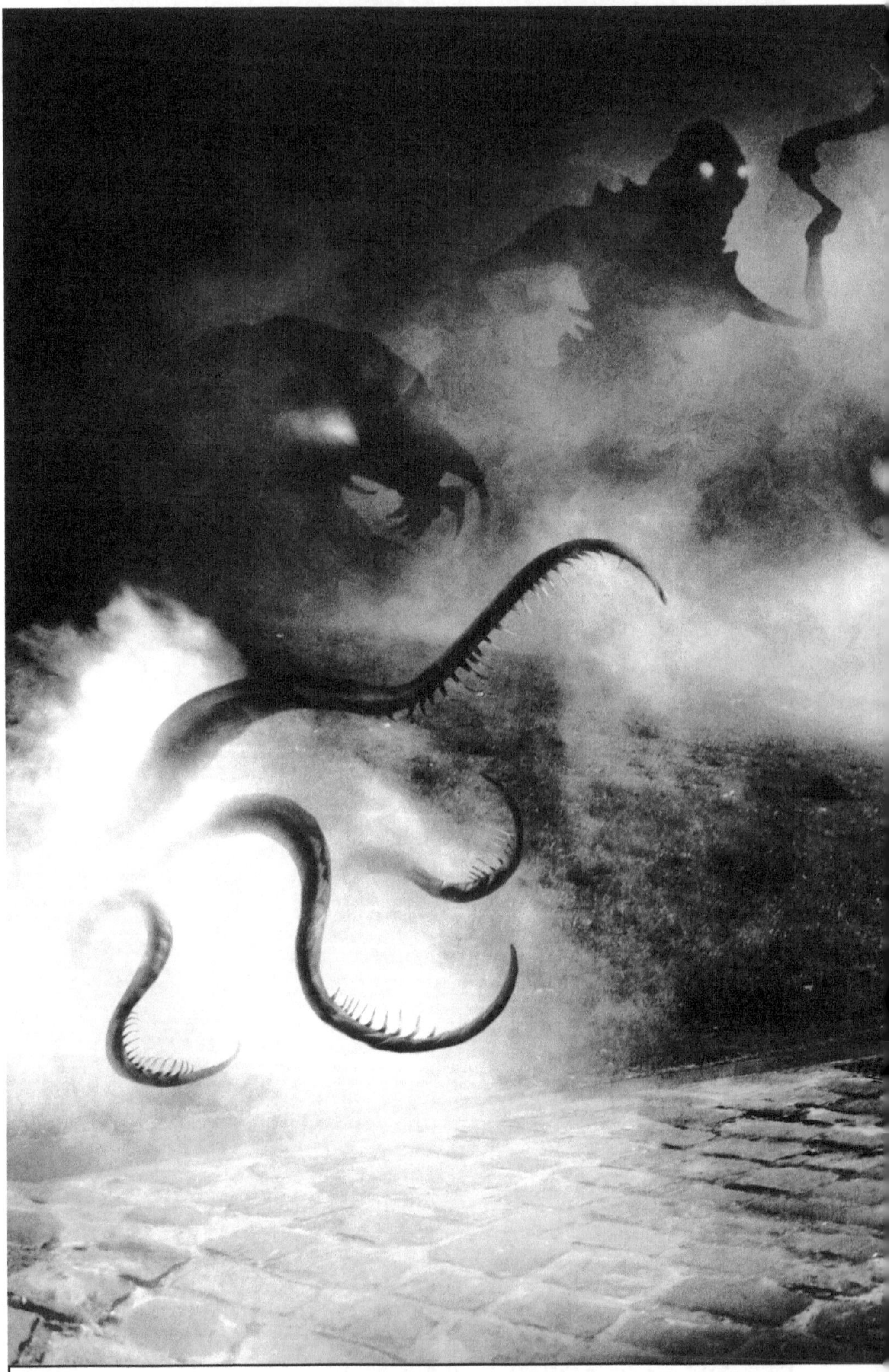

A KILLER AMONG DEMONS (2012)

Book cover art for *A Killer Among Demons* by Various for Dark Prints Press

FADE AWAY (2012)

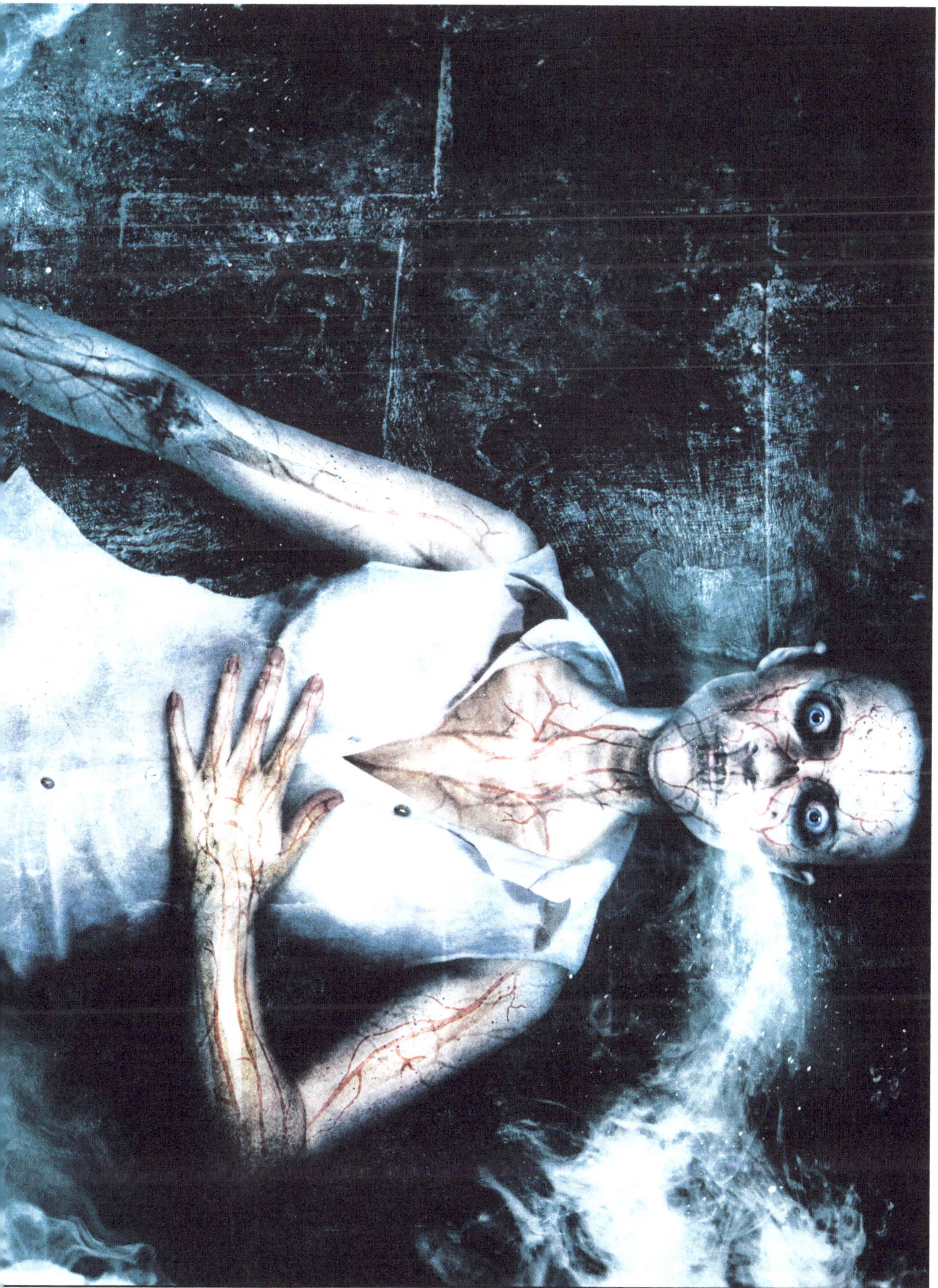

Book cover art for the lettered edition of *Doctor Sleep* by Stephen King for Cemetery Dance Publications

THE END OF THE WORLD (2012)

Magazine cover art for *Cemetery Dance* magazine #69 for Cemetery Dance Publications

BAD FAIRY (2012)
Book cover art detail for *Drawn & Quartered* by Shane McKenzie for Thunderstorm Books

LIVING WITH THE DEAD (2011)

Book cover art for *Living with the Dead* by Martin Livings for Dark Prints Press

A Brief Conversation with Vincent Chong

Paul Fry

Paul Fry: Hi Vincent, thanks very much for taking the time to talk with me. I'll keep this brief as I know how incredibly busy you are.

You've been a professional illustrator for a while now haven't you, what's been the highlight of your career to date?

Vincent Chong: There's been many highlights, but one that sticks out was when I was invited to be Artist Guest of Honour at the 2011 World Horror Convention in Austin, Texas. The organizers were all wonderful and put on an amazing Con and I was very well looked after. So I had an absolute blast and met some fantastic people over there. Austin's a cool city and I still have very fond memories of a BBQ place we found downtown there one night (I don't think I've ever seen so much meat piled onto a plate!).

PF: What's it like getting paid for doing something you love?

VC: It's fantastic! Sometimes I still can't believe that this is my actual job. From a young age at school, I knew that I wanted to do something art related for a job, and always loved book cover art and such, so it's amazing that it's now what I get to do on a daily basis and get paid for it. There are some commissions that I enjoy more than others, and there's some things I prefer illustrating, but I'm still finding it all fun and challenging. I do wish that I had some more time to spend on personal projects though; as much as I enjoy illustrating other people's work, I would love to do more work based on my own ideas.

PF: Congratulations on all the many awards you have won so far in your career. Are there any in particular that you're really proud of?

VC: The first time I won a British Fantasy Award meant a lot to me; I was happy just to be nominated and never expected to win. Around that time, I'd been starting to get more commissions but I was only working as an illustrator part time, and was still very much a newcomer to the scene. So getting the award felt like people were really starting to notice my work and appreciated what I was doing, and that my hard work was starting to pay off! I was also thrilled when I was shortlisted for a World Fantasy Award in 2011, even though I didn't win it.

PF: If you weren't an illustrator what would you like to be doing?

VC: I've often wondered about that myself . . . I never had a back-up plan in case the illustration career didn't take off so have never seriously considered any alternative careers. Having worked for myself for a while now, I think I would find it extremely difficult doing any sort of typical, 9 to 5 office-type job working for someone else. My immediate reaction would be that I would still like to do something related to the creative fields in some way, though I'm not sure what that would be exactly. Having said that, if I decided I had had enough of being an illustrator one day, I might want to do something that was completely different and totally unexpected . . . Of course, in a dream world, if I wasn't an illustrator and had plenty of money, I'd just be taking holiday after holiday!

PF: Are you currently working on any exciting projects? Or have any lined-up for the future, ones that you can talk about that is?

VC: I'm working on the Subterranean Press limited edition of *The Shining* right now, which is my biggest project to date. Besides the cover design, I'm doing a number of full page colour and duotone illustrations as well as various spot illustrations, so I'll be producing over forty images for the book. I've done interior illustrations for books previously, but have never done this amount of artwork for a single project before, so it's definitely a challenge. I wasn't sure it was something I could handle when I was first approached with this, but it was too good an opportunity to pass over, and it's going well so far, so I'm glad I decided to take it on. I've done covers for a number of Stephen King's books but *The Shining* is one of my favourites so it's cool that it's this book of his that I'm getting to do all this artwork for.

For a while now I've been wanting to do more personal work, as I mentioned earlier, and a big thing I'd like to do is create my own illustrated story. I've had a few ideas which I need to spend more time developing, so I'm hoping that it's something I will be able to find more time to work on in the near future. And who knows, maybe it'll actually materialize in a few years' time . . . Watch this space!

PF: I've just ordered your art book *Altered Visions: The Art of Vincent Chong* from Telos Publishing (telos.co.uk), which I'm really looking forward to receiving! Have you any more art books lined-up or currently in the works?

VC: I don't have any other art books in the pipe-line at the moment, but I would definitely like to do more in the future and already have some ideas of what I'd like to do for them. *Altered Visions* came about in an unexpected way; I was doing the cover for Simon Clark's *Humpty's Bones* for Telos, when the publisher, David Howe, had the idea of producing a small art book of my work that would accompany a special limited edition of the book. Ultimately, he decided not to put out the special edition of *Humpty's Bones* but still wanted to go ahead with my art book as a publication on its own to launch at the 2010 World Horror Con in Brighton. As such, it's only a small collection of my work, so I'd love to produce a bigger coffee-table book that's a much more comprehensive collection of my work to date, and also featuring some behind-the-scenes material like roughs sketches and such.

PF: It's been a pleasure talking with you, Vincent and I look forward to seeing *lots* more amazing work from you!

PHOTO: BRIAN HODGES

RAY GARTON

AN INTRODUCTION

Ray Garton is the author of over 60 novels, novellas, short story collections, movie novelizations and TV tie-ins. His work spans the genres of horror, crime, and suspense. His 1987 erotic vampire novel *Live Girls* was called "artful" by the *New York Times* and was nominated for the Bram Stoker Award. In 2006, he received the Grand Master of Horror Award at the World Horror Convention in San Francisco. His 2001 comedy thriller *Sex and Violence in Hollywood* is being developed for the screen. His most recent novels, *Trailer Park Noir* and *Meds* (a thriller with deadly side effects), are available in paperback and as ebooks from E-Reads, and his seventh collection, *Wailing and Gnashing of Teeth*, was recently published by Cemetery Dance Publications. "The Man in the Palace Theater," a short, emotional horror story, and his erotic noir novella *Serpent Girl* are available for Kindle and Nook. You can see his bibliography and keep up with new releases at his website, RayGartonOnline.com. He lives in northern California with his wife Dawn.

Something happened to me back in my drinking days, when I cleverly avoided hangovers by never sobering up, that I have enjoyed repeating ever since because the story never fails to horrify. It delights the little boy who still lurks in me, a boy who will shove a frog into a little girl's face just for the fun of watching her run away screaming.

I shuffled around the bathroom in my robe one night, getting ready for bed, my movements and thought processes slowed by vodka. As I brushed my teeth with the usual toothbrush and toothpaste, an unusual flavor filled my mouth, something other than minty freshness, followed by a familiar smell in my nostrils. It was the smell of grass. Freshly cut grass. But it was late at night and no one had been doing any mowing.

When I spit toothpaste into the sink, it contained something extra. I looked closely and finally identified them as the amputated legs of a spider. I spit again and more of the dismembered spider came out of my mouth. In an instant, I realized what I had done.

We had more spiders than usual that year. They were everywhere. They made their way into our house and we found them on pillows, on the ceiling, in the bathtub, skittering across floors. They were mostly wolf spiders—robust, hairy arachnids that range from half an inch to two inches in length and are capable of delivering a nasty bite. One of those wolf spiders had been perched on the bristles of my toothbrush when I applied toothpaste to it. It seems odd that the spider did not hurry away when I picked up my toothbrush, rather than sitting there and letting me cover it in toothpaste, but that's what had happened. Maybe it was already dead when I picked up the toothbrush, I don't know. In my inebriated state, I didn't notice it and I put it in my mouth and crushed it against my teeth and smeared it over my gums.

When I became aware of what I had done, I

gasped in horror as I dropped to my knees and began spitting and gagging into the sink. My whole body shuddered and became cold and clammy as I retched and groaned, trying to get that front-lawn taste out of my mouth and imagining the spider guts probably oozing between my teeth. I looked up to see my wife Dawn standing in the doorway, frowning at me.

"Are you sick?" she said.

I tried to respond, but all I could do was continue spitting into the sink. When I tried to speak, nothing but incoherent sounds of disgust came out of me.

"Are you choking?" she said. She grabbed a glass, filled it with water and handed it to me.

I rinsed my mouth several times, swishing the water around in there, trying to make sure I got all of the spider out of me. When I was finally able to explain to Dawn what had happened, she made a horrified sound and shuddered as she turned and walked away.

That story gets 'em every time, and every word of it is true, it really happened. It's a good example of what horror can do. Anyone listening to that story is at first made comfortable by a familiar setting and familiar activity. Everybody has a bathroom routine before bed, it's common to all of us. They know exactly what I'm talking about when I begin the story because they've all done that and the familiarity is almost soothing. Then something strange is injected into the story—the taste and smell I experience while brushing my teeth. Then . . . the horrifying reveal. Without the set-up, the reveal isn't really a reveal, it's just a disgusting idea. The set-up not only prepares the listener for the reveal, it traps him in a familiar situation where he thinks he's safe.

For me, that's how horror works best. I enjoy the change of expression that takes place on faces as I reveal what I inadvertently had done with that spider. It's more than just a response. The story alters the way they feel as they put themselves in my position and the experience becomes their own.

When it's done right, when it works, the horror genre alters the way we feel. It rips us out of our mundane existence and puts us in the worst circumstances imaginable, making us think and feel things we would not otherwise have thought and felt.

Douglas E. Winter's oft-repeated quote, "Horror is not a genre, it's an emotion," is oft-repeated because it is true. Comedy makes us laugh, tragedy makes us feel pain, and horror makes us experience the emotions of fear, terror, dread, and . . . horror. The thing I love most about horror is that it can embrace all of those things—comedy, tragedy, and horror—within a story.

But why would anyone want to make themselves feel that way? many ask.

Like our muscles, our emotions need exercise to keep them from withering away. Without our muscles, we would be useless husks, and without our emotions . . . the same thing.

The horror genre makes for great escapism and entertainment, but underneath all that, among other things, it also helps to keep us human. It reminds us that, as bad as things might seem, at least we aren't possessed by a demon or the target of some sinister conspiracy or the captive of a serial killer.

The first horror movie I ever saw was William Castle's *13 Ghosts*. I was five and had never seen anything like it before. First, it scared the hell out of me and made me hide my eyes as a headless ghost cracked a whip at a ghostly lion. But when it was over, I wanted to do it again.

After that, I sought it out, and lucky for me, there was plenty of it around on TV back then. Shows like *The Twilight Zone*, *The Outer Limits*, *Dark Shadows*, *Night Gallery*, *One Step Beyond*, *Kolchak: The Night Stalker*, and *Creature Features* on KTVU 2 from San Francisco, hosted by Bob Wilkins, who offered up two horror movies every Saturday night, from classic Universal and Hammer films to the schlockiest of the schlocky.

For me, horror was more than just a casual escape, it was a refuge. I was a pretty sensitive kid with a vivid and active imagination being raised in a strict Seventh-day Adventist family, and as far back as I can remember, I lived in fear of the horrifying "last days," a time of unparalleled horror and suffering that would precede the second coming of Christ. At home, in school (I attended an Adventist school), and in church, I was constantly reminded that the "time of trouble" could begin at any moment—tomorrow, next month, a year from now, or in ten minutes—and vivid descriptions of that coming time were burned into my mind before I even started school.

I was in a constant state of fear. When I watched a horror movie or TV show, it scared me, but it was a *fun* kind of scared. I was safe because there was no such thing as vampires or werewolves. The movies and TV shows manipulated me into a tense state of fear for a while and then resolved everything and left me grinning and feeling relieved. It was like a roller coaster ride. My fear of the last days, however, remained; it was, as far as I knew, a rock-solid fact and it was only a matter of time before it started and turned all our lives into a living nightmare. But those movies and

TV shows were fun and they gave me an outlet, a way of expressing the fear that was always inside me, and releasing it. Screaming in church would not be well received, no matter how much I might have wanted to, but crying out as I slapped my hands over my eyes while watching a horror movie on TV was perfectly acceptable.

I discovered the man who made me want to be a writer at a flea market. There was a booth there with stacks and stacks of paperback books, and among them, I found a worn old collection of short stories called *Shock* by Richard Matheson. I think it cost a nickel, but its value could not be measured in money. The stories spanned the genres of horror, science fiction, and fantasy and I gobbled them up. When my family went back to the flea market the following Sunday, I returned to that table and looked for more books by Richard Matheson. I found *Shock II* and *Shock III* and *The Incredible Shrinking Man* and *Hell House* and *I Am Legend*.

Matheson brought real humanity to horror. His characters were no different than you or I, real people going about their lives and dealing with problems with which we are all familiar. And then Matheson would throw something horrific at them—ghosts, vampires, aliens, helplessly shrinking to the size of a thimble. There were no castles or counts or rampaging villagers. Richard Matheson dropped the horror genre smack in the middle of my life. He brought it home.

A few years later, Stephen King came along and brought tremendous commercial success to horror fiction. He cemented in me the desire to write. I was already doing it. I cranked out one story after another for the amusement of my friends, and in the sixth grade, I started writing novel-length stories. They were terrible, of course, but only because I was in the process of learning how to do it.

A little aside here. That's what writers do, by the way. They write. All the time. Whenever someone says to me, "I'd like to be a writer. How do I go about it?" my answer is always the same: Write, keep writing, and when you're not writing, read everything. Don't talk about it or read how-to books about it or take classes to learn how to do it. If you're not already writing because you just can't help yourself, because you can't *not* write, then you're probably not a writer.

A couple of years after finishing high school, I dropped out of college, accidentally found an agent, and sold my first novel, *Seductions*, which was published in 1984. Luck was on my side because horror was hotter than the sun at that time, and everywhere you looked—book stores, grocery stores, drug stores—there were paperbacks with garish, elaborate covers that featured dripping blood and fanged creatures and evil children and plenty of women in distress. It was the golden age of horror fiction, kick-started by the huge success of Stephen King, and publishers were buying.

And that's how I ended up here, writing this column.

The horror genre is a large umbrella that covers a number of subgenres. One of them is "splatterpunk," which came about in the mid-1980s. Because much of my fiction contained explicit sex and violence, I was given that label. I resisted it, though, because I didn't think it quite fit my work. It seemed to me that explicit sex and violence were the raison d'être of splatterpunk, and I was trying hard to make those elements grow out of whatever story I was writing rather than the other way around. But I was being hypocritical.

My 1988 novel *Crucifax* included a long, disgusting scene in which Mace, a mysterious man with a tongue that could extend to a length of three feet, performs a cunnilingual abortion on a young woman and then eats the fetus. Both my agent and my editor insisted that the scene went way too far, went on far too long, and wasn't necessary to the story. I strongly disagreed, but I was young, drunk, and stupid at the time and didn't know what I was talking about. The scene was watered down for the Simon & Schuster paperback but published intact in *Crucifax Autumn*, the limited hardcover edition published by Dark Harvest. I have come to see that my agent and editor were correct in their assessment of that scene. I had gone for the gross-out in a big way and it brought the story to a halt. I now prefer the edited version.

My tastes have changed over the last thirty years. Back in the early 1980s, when VCRs were new and revolutionary, I could rent a stack of really gory, low-budget movies in which people were killed in imaginative and bloody ways and watch them back to back, and I would be happier than a great big fat guy in a hot tub full of fried chicken and waffles. I find movies like that impossible to watch now. They don't challenge me in any way and they offer none of the things I'm looking for.

Although my tastes have shifted, I find that I still cling to the elements I grew up loving in horror movies and fiction: a strong story, characters with whom I have some kind of emotional connection, and the injection of something terrifying into the mundane routine of life. If explicit violence grows out of that, I'm all for it, but I'm not entertained when it is the driving force behind a movie, novel, or story.

I discovered just how much I've changed when I wrote a novella called *Threesome*, which was published in 2011 by Sideshow Press. One of my guilty pleasures are "true crime" TV shows. A favorite is *Wicked Attraction* on Investigation Discovery, about couples who kill. How does each couple discover that both of them want to kill? That question is never answered on *Wicked Attraction* and I wanted to write about it. That was my intention with *Threesome*. But as stories so often do, it got away from me and became something else. I did not enjoy writing it. I had to stop at times for a break. It was an unpleasant writing experience.

I discovered that I no longer had the stomach for the amount of torture and bloodshed in *Threesome*. Maybe it's a result of getting older, valuing life more, becoming more compassionate with experience and buddying up with my own mortality as I age. I don't know. But that was the last piece of fiction of its kind that I'll be writing, I suspect. There will still be bloody violence in my work when it's called for, and it will still be painful and unpleasant because I think violence *should* be painful and unpleasant when depicted in fiction. But it won't be emphasized in my work the way it has been in the past. These days, I'm more interested in how people live than in how they die.

That doesn't mean people won't be dying in my fiction anymore. I don't think anyone should be safe in horror fiction, and I'll probably be killing off the characters you least expect until I've written my last word. But I think, at times, I've lost sight of the fact that horror—for me, anyway—has always been a very human and humane genre, and I don't want that to happen again. I don't want to be read because of the violence and bloodshed in my books, I'd rather be read in spite of it. I don't want readers to take delight in that violence, I want it to make them wince and squirm and feel uncomfortable. And then I want them to be relieved when it's over. I know I don't always succeed at that, but that's the goal.

If we're going to be meeting here regularly to discuss this genre we love so much, I wanted you to know my general thoughts on the subject, which is why I've written this rambling introduction. I'll have more specific topics in the future, now that you know me a little better.

Until next time . . .

PHOTO: CARO SOLES

Award-winning author **Nancy Kilpatrick** has published 18 novels, about 200 short stories, and has edited 13 anthologies, most in the horror/dark fantasy field. She also published the non-fiction book *The goth Bible: A Compendium for the Darkly Inclined* (St. Martin's Press) and has written many articles and reviews. Her two most recent—award-winning—titles are (as editor) the anthology *Danse Macabre: Close Encounters with the Reaper*, and her sixth collection of short stories, *Vampyric Variations* (both from EDGE Science Fiction and Fantasy Publishing). She lives in Montréal with her calico cat Fedex, but travels frequently searching out crypts, ossuaries, mummies and original Danse Macabre artwork. Check her website for updates: nancykilpatrick.com. But join her on Facebook if you want the latest news. She doesn't bite. Much.

NANCY KILPATRICK

Hello Fans-of-the-Dark-Side. I'm thrilled to be here, writing a column for *Beware the Dark*. This first one is a reprint which I know most readers haven't read because it was published in a newsletter of the British Fantasy Society, available only to members. But, I thought you'd enjoy knowing about these two spots, unique in the UK. I'm very much looking forward to jumping into the fray with articles and opinions about the field I love the best—horror and dark fantasy. Do let me know how you like this first one via BTD's website, or message me on Facebook.

Bones in England

Photos by Hugues Leblanc

I always find it curious the number of people who seem to be blithely unaware of treasures in their own—proverbial—backyard.

When it comes to bone crypts, plenty can be found in Europe, like the popular catacombs beneath Paris, and the bones-forming-objects at the Sedlec bone chapel in Kutná Hora, Czech Republic.

Until recently, few knew there were bone crypts in England. As it turns out, two exist, and they are open for viewing beginning in the spring of each year.

Holy Trinity Church, Rothwell

Rothwell is a small town near Leicester. To reach it, either drive, or take the train to Kettering, then a taxi from there to Rothwell, about four miles away.

Much of Holy Trinity Church dates from the 13th century, although the oldest parts are from Norman times, nearly 1,000 years ago. Here you'll find the longest nave of any church in the country. Built of local sandstone, Holy Trinity is located in the centre of Rothwell, with a lovely cemetery adjacent.

As the story goes, that lovely cemetery was

HOLY TRINITY CHURCH, ROTHWELL

PHOTOS: HUGUES LEBLANC

St. Leonard's Church, Hythe — Photos: Hugues Leblanc

instrumental in discovering the bone crypt. A gravedigger dug too deep and fell twelve feet through a hole into pitch blackness. In that hole were so many bones that the poor man was shocked enough to lose his mind. A good story, true or false.

The bones at Holy Trinity are from the cemetery. On two occasions, remains were dug up and some of the bones stored in the crypt beneath the church. The second occasion occurred when digging began in 1580 for the Jesus Hospital on church property.

At last tally, approximately 1600 individuals are accounted for with skull and thigh bones (the skull and crossed bones we associate with pirates going back in time to the idea that only these bones were needed for resurrection). DNA tests have determined that there are two distinct ethnic groups represented, Danes and Anglo Saxons. The skull belonging to the youngest crypt-dweller is that of a twelve year old, the average age of skulls of the formerly living is forty years. There are no skulls of young children, which is odd, given the centuries where mortality rate was high among infants and children.

Femurs are stored in two wooden bins in the center of the charnel house. There are skulls atop but most of the skulls sit on parallel wooden shelving by the door. Holy Trinity is in consultation regarding display.

St. Leonard's Church, Hythe

Hythe—which means 'haven'—is close to Dover and closer to Folkestone, a lovely town in its own right. Drive, or take the train to Folkestone or the slower train to Sandling. From either station a taxi will get you to Hythe in about 10 minutes.

St. Leonard's began as a Norman church in 1080, undergoing the usual additions and building catastrophes over the centuries. It stands atop a hill which overlooks the town and, on a clear day, you can see France. Being located in a port town has affected its history at various times and over the centuries brought an influx of visitors, including pilgrims en route to Canterbury.

Beneath the church is a lovely Gothic crypt which houses bones. When these bones were brought here and by whom, no one knows, but theories abound, among them: These are the bones of Saxons killed in a nearby battle in AD 456. Or a different battle fought against the Danes in AD 843. Time-wise, the best guess as to when the bones found their way into the crypt is the early 13th century when the chancel was extended into the former churchyard, but another idea is that they arrived in the 15th century.

St. Leonard's crypt houses about 2,000 skulls and 8,000 thigh bones, not quite the right configuration. One skull shows a hole indicative of a medieval trepanning operation and it has been determined that the patient survived. There are also jaw bones with teeth in fairly good condition, and some hair that remains intact. Other interesting material is on display in wood and glass cases, as well as a few old stone crosses. This lovely vaulted crypt displays the skulls in wooden Gothic frames, one on each side of the door, placed there in 1851 and 1908. Femurs are stored in neat piles in the center of the room.

DNA tests are underway at St. Leonard's to determine just who these bones belonged to, at least culturally, which might help determine the time-frame of their interment.

Both ossuaries are worth a visit for all sorts of reasons, not the least of which is that these crypts are a British heritage that citizens should be proud to own.

http://www.rothwellholytrinity.org.uk/
http://www.stleonardschurchhythekent.org/

PHOTO: KAYA LAUWERYS

Nightlight

Robert Morrish

Welcome to the inaugural installment of "Nightlight," which I'm thrilled to be launching in the likewise inaugural issue of *Beware the Dark*. For those who don't know me, I've been involved in the horror genre for more than 20 years now. I've edited two magazines (*The Scream Factory* and *Cemetery Dance*), published articles and reviews in a variety of both genre and non-genre magazines, contributed to major horror reference works, and even published a couple dozen stories in anthologies (including one in *BTD* editor Paul Fry's *Cold Flesh*). I also run a website, TwilightRidge.net, that's devoted to horror small press book publishing, with news, reviews, and interviews.

More to the point, I've written—or am still writing—several other ongoing columns, and the one thing they've all had in common is a theme:

• "The Small Press Box," as its name implies, covered the small press, albeit almost exclusively magazines.

• "The Re*fear*ence Shelf" reviewed non-fiction books that focused on the horror genre.

• "Spotlight on Publishing" continues to feature interviews with small press publishers, along with small press book news and reviews.

• "What the Hell Ever Happened To...?" continues to track down folks who in the past achieved some degree of notoriety in the horror genre, only to later disappear from the scene.

Faced with a clean slate and the opportunity to take this column in any direction I wanted (as long as it remains horror-centric), I thus proceeded to give a fair amount of thought to what potential themes this column could have. I'm going to share the results of that brainstorming, as it provides a fair amount of insight into the sorts of topics that tend to interest (or obsess) me.

Themes I considered include:

• Cross-genre horror hybrids—for example horror/science fiction, horror/war, horror/fantasy, horror/western (the latter is a US-centric phenomenon), and so forth.

• A UK-themed version of "Spotlight on Publishing"—In my existing version of this column, I've already covered a few UK-based presses, such as PS Publishing and Gray Friar, so this would simply have been an extension of that . . . but wasn't entirely comfortable with recycling a topic that I'm already covering.

• A UK-themed version of "What the Hell Ever Happened To...?"—I gave this potential topic a *lot* of thought, because it remains near and dear to my heart, but again, felt like maybe trying something different was more advisable.

• Collecting horror fiction—My concerns with this notion were that John Pelan already did a good job of covering this topic via his column "Collecting Horror Fiction," which had a long run in *Cemetery Dance*, and that I'm not (quite) the obsessive collector that I used to be.

• Obscure horror films—I definitely have some interest in this topic, and there are plenty of films that could be written about, but then again films are not my greatest area of knowledge, and there are other folks out there who are already digging up hidden gems and writing about them.

• Horror on television—Considerations stacking against this topic: A) Mike O'Driscoll is doing a good job covering this topic in *Black Static*, and B) I'm so far behind in my television-watching that it would be difficult for me to be timely. The DVR is definitely my friend.

• Horror non-fiction and reference works—Another

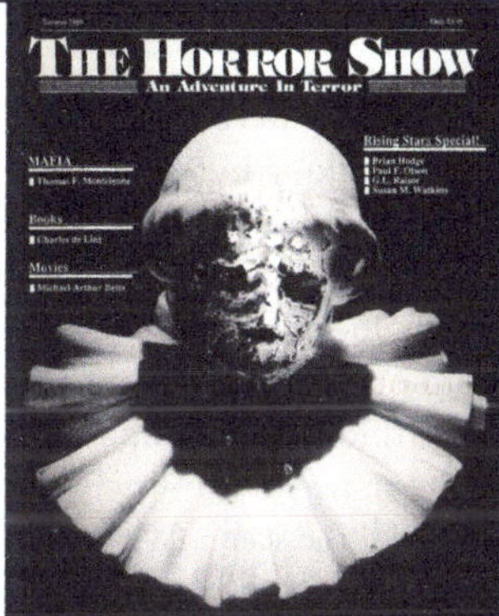

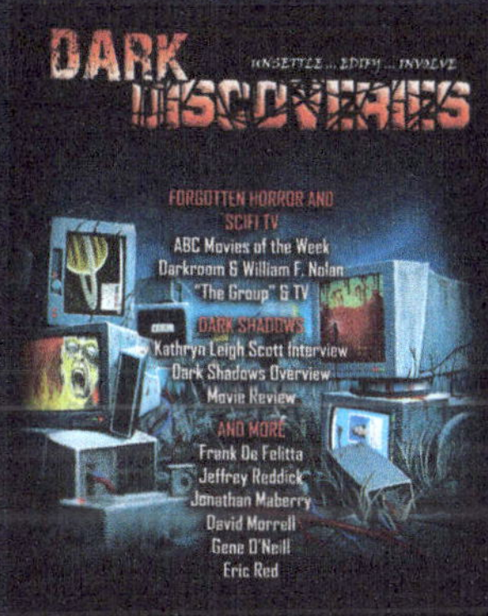

topic where I've already "been there, done that," and I also wasn't sure how many *BTD* readers would be interested.

• Horror-oriented websites—This theme sort of ties in to my "day job," which has involved working for software and internet companies in Silicon Valley, but has only limited appeal to me, for some reason (maybe at the end of the day, I just want to get away from all vestiges of work!).

So, after entertaining all of the notions listed above, which one did I decide on? Well, none of them. And all of them.

Meaning that I've decided to go theme-less (which for an inveterate theme-lover like me is the equivalent of flying without a parachute). But while there won't be a single, consistent theme to the column, odds are that most of what I write about will tie in to one of the topics above, which is why I bothered to go into such detail. As an example, the first thing I want to talk about is . . .

The state of horror short fiction markets

"The Small Press Box" column that I mention above ran in 10 issues of *The Scream Factory*, from 1991 to 1996. For part of that time, I was also co-editing a "best of small press horror" anthology called *Quick Chills*, although I gave that up after just one volume (although reviewing selected publications for the column was manageable, trying to read everything in the field in order to make selections for an annual "Best Of" anthology was just far too time-consuming). Regardless, the point I want to make is that, between reading for the column and (briefly) the anthology, I was slogging through a tremendous amount of small press magazines and anthologies. And that's because there *was* a tremendous amount of them—the market was thriving back then, before postal and printing costs started skyrocketing, and long before the web offered a way to publish more quickly and inexpensively.

Magazines such as *Deathrealm* (31 issues), *Eldritch Tales* (30 issues), *Ghosts & Scholars* (33 issues), *Grue* (18 issues), *The Horror Show* (24 issues), *Peeping Tom* (33 issues), *Terminal Fright* (14 issues), *Whispers* (24 issues) and *Weirdbook* (30 issues) were long-running markets for horror fiction, and a significant portion of a generation of horror writers cut their teeth in those and other small press markets, before graduating to works of greater length and publishers of greater stature.

Needless to say, it's much more manageable to track the state of the field nowadays. In the realm of print periodicals, there are relatively few remaining. We have stalwarts like *Cemetery Dance* (published irregularly, with 69 issues to date), *Black Static* (bimonthly, 34 issues), *Dark Discoveries* (quarterly, 23 issues), and *Supernatural Tales* (triannual, 23 issues), and relative newcomers such as *Midnight Echo* (irregular, 9 issues; the official magazine of the Australian Horror Writers Association), *Shock Totem* (irregular, 7 issues), *Shadows & Tall Trees* (biannual, 5 issues; recently announced it will become an annual anthology), *Unspoken Water* (biannual, 4 issues; recently announced it will become a non-paying market), and *Nameless Digest* (irregular, 2 issues).

And I would certainly be remiss not to mention *Weird Tales,* the magazine that has refused to die, even as it has undergone countless changes—361 issues published since 1923, from numerous publishers, in various formats and with differing focus, with its most recent changes being a gradual return to its roots since its acquisition in late 2011 by Marvin Kaye.

There are also a handful of long-running "B-listers," as I deem them for one or more of the following reasons: lower production values; highly irregular publishing schedules; lower or non-existent pay rates. These include titles such as *Not One of Us* (irregular, 46 issues), *Albedo One* (irregular, 41 issues, cross-genre), and *Dark Moon Digest* (quarterly, 12 issues).

Additionally, there are some online/digital magazines worth mentioning, although not as many as one might expect:

• *Apex Magazine*—Monthly, 50 issues; content includes fantasy and science fiction as well as horror.

• *ChiZine*—Extant since 1997, but as of this writing the site is currently down for redesign, so I'm unable to note the number of issues published or the planned frequency going forward.

• *Clarkesworld* —Monthly, 82 issues; but focused more on fantasy & science fiction than horror.

• *Innsmouth Magazine*—Triannual, 13 issues; a Lovecraftian publication that also features a frequently updated website.

• *Nightmare Magazine*—Monthly, 10 issues; a highly-regarded newcomer, published by book publisher Creeping Hemlock Press and edited by John Joseph Adams.

• *Spinetinglers*—Monthly, 91 issues; not generally of the quality of the other online publications on this list.

• *Subterranean Magazine*—Quarterly, 27 issues; more focused on fantasy and science fiction than horror.

Add it all up and it still makes for a pretty paltry list, especially in comparison to the robust roster of periodicals that thrived during the 1980s and '90s. The Ralan.com website has been compiling lists of speculative fiction markets since 1994 and thus provides a fairly accurate barometer of the field. Having followed Ralan.com for that entire time period, I have to say it's sad to see how the number of listings has declined over the years.

Meanwhile, the market for small press horror anthologies has not, at least in terms of sheer numbers, declined as severely as the market for magazines. A survey of the output of the small press horror publishers that I track on TwilightRidge.net (see http://twilightridge.net/blog/the-list/ for a listing of the 184 horror book publishers) reveals that there are many, many anthologies included amongst their output. But what *has* declined, I would argue, is the number of small press anthologies paying pro or semi-pro pay rates. A depressing number of current anthologies pay only in contributor copies, royalties, or "recognition," making them of interest primarily to writers who are desperate for any publishing credit—and who are often lacking in talent.

Between the decline in quantity of small press magazines and the decline in quality of small press anthologies, the market for short fiction has changed profoundly over the last twenty years, and I can't help but think that change has had, and will continue to have, a negative impact on the number of new writers joining the scene. Without a chance to hone their craft at short-story length, and gain some confidence and genre notoriety in so doing, a potential new generation of horror writers may wilt on the vine.

Lists, why I love them . . . and a new kind of list

I've always loved lists, particularly horror-themed lists, and particularly "best of" lists—everything from the annual "short lists" of nominees for awards (such as the HWA Bram Stoker Awards and the Shirley Jackson Awards) to annual "year's best" anthologies (like the *Quick Chills* antho I formerly edited) to magazines' "best of" lists to entire books dedicated to the subject (like *The Book of Lists: Horror* by Amy Wallace, Del Howison, and Scott Bradley, and *Horror: 100 Best Books* edited by Stephen Jones and Kim Newman). Across all these various types of lists, I've been endlessly fascinated by others' opinions—and, in some cases, have used those lists as a basis for growing my collection.

And it's worth pointing out that lists are not always focused on the "best of." While I was co-editing *The Scream Factory*, we rather infamously published an issue that focused on "The Worst of the Horror Genre," and included a variety of "worst of" lists. And that issue was in turn inspired primarily by a couple of lists that the *TSF* editors had seen previously—a compilation of the 50 worst horror films ever made by *The Monster Times*, and a list of "The Thirteen Worst Stinkers of the Weird," in *Rod Serling's Twilight Zone Magazine.*

But even though there have been a few "worst of" lists to offset all those "best of" lists, it occurred to me that one thing I've never seen listed is the "most disappointing" efforts in a particular genre or medium. Although any such list would obviously be highly subjective, that's no different than any "best of" or "worst of" list. So, in an attempt to possibly break some new ground, I'm going to offer a list of my top 10 biggest disappointments in the realm of horror fiction.

*

A word or two of explanation first—in order for a writer's work to be deemed extremely disappointing, the author obviously must have previously written something that was so excellent that it greatly heightened my expectations for their next work.

10. Ramsey Campbell, *The Influence*—This one just edged onto the list, because it's certainly not a bad book. But after the example set by such excellent work as the novels *Incarnate* and *The Hungry Moon*, and the collections *Demons by Daylight* and *Dark Companions*, *The Influence* was a plodding snoozer.

9. Simon Clark, *Vengeance Child*—Clark has produced some great books in his career, and I read this shortly after the wonderful *She Loves Monsters*, which only served to highlight just how trite *Vengeance Child* is.

8. Ira Levin, *Sliver*—This pedestrian, formulaic effort, produced by the author of *A Kiss Before Dying*, *Rosemary's Baby*, and *The Boys from Brazil*, to name a few? Say it ain't so, Ira.

7. Laird Barron, *The Light is the Darkness*—Coming on the heels of his two outstanding collections, *The Imago Sequence* and *Occultation*, Barron's first novel was something I had high hopes for. Unfortunately, it was inconsistent and very pulp-ish at times. But I nonetheless have high hopes for his second novel, *The Croning*.

6. Dan Simmons' gradual move away from horror, culminating (?) in *Flashback*—Coming from an author who's produced stellar horror novels such as *Carrion Comfort* and *Summer of Night* (and tremendous science fiction such as *Hyperion* and *Endymion*), the move to doorstop-sized historical novels *Drood* and *Black Hills*, and then to the political morass of *Flashback*, has been mystifying. Hopefully his forthcoming supernatural historical novel *The Abominable* will set him firmly back on track.

5. Anne Rice, *The Mummy*, and what came after—Although they were at times more historical drama than horror, I really enjoyed *Interview with the Vampire* and its first two sequels. But then came *The Mummy or Ramses the Damned*, a turgid melodrama that was unfortunately a sign of things to come for Rice.

4. Whitley Strieber, *Catmagic* and what came after—Following his brilliant early novels *The Wolfen* and *The Hunger*, Strieber produced the less-successful but still worthwhile *Black Magic* and *The Night Church*, but then came the mixed-up jumble otherwise known as *Catmagic*, which seemed to presage the post-*Communion* quagmire that would overwhelm Strieber's fiction career.

3. Karl Wagner's *Why Not You and I?*, and what came after—In the wake of the unbridled brilliance of Wagner's debut collection, *In a Lonely Place* (1983), the collection *Why Not You and I?* four years later was much more of a mixed bag, with magnificent moments offset by puzzling passages. Seven years later, Wagner was dead, essentially from alcoholism, and a tremendously promising career was cut far too short.

2. Stephen King, *The Tommyknockers*—Up until this book came out, I'd faithfully read, and mostly loved, what King had produced. But after reading the confused mess that is *The Tommyknockers*, I became an infrequent reader of King. It wasn't until years later that I learned that he'd written this book at the nadir of his drug addiction . . . which explained a lot.

1. Clive Barker's career since 1987—When the six-volume *Books of Blood* appeared in 1984-5, they were collectively the most exciting thing to hit the genre in years, as evidenced by the famous "future of horror" quote from Stephen King. But after the subsequent novel *The Damnation Game* and novella *The Hellbound Heart*, Barker's horror output has largely been limited to the movie screen (notable exceptions being the novels *Coldheart Canyon* and *Mister B. Gone*). Sure, some of his fantasy novels such as *Weaveworld* and *The Great and Secret Show*, are excellent, and contain definite horror influences, but in terms of the sheer, balls-to-the-wall horror that Barker displayed in the *Books of Blood* . . . there's been precious little in nearly 30 years. And horror fans are left mumbling about what could have been . . .

Let me say again, for emphasis: the only reason the works listed above were so disappointing is because they paled in comparison to the truly brilliant work previously produced by the authors.

To offset this list of disappointments, perhaps I'll put together a list of my most unexpected pleasant surprises in my next column. :)

Until next time . . . don't turn out the nightlight.

PHOTO: KYRA SZEPIETOWSKI

Ty Schwamberger is an award-winning author & editor in the horror genre. He is the author of a novel, multiple novellas, collections and editor on several anthologies. In addition, he's had many short stories published online and in print. Three stories, "Cake Batter" (released in 2010), "House Call" (released in June 2013) and *Dinin'* (optioned in July 2013), have been optioned for film adaptation. He is an Active Member of the Horror Writers Association. You can learn more at: http://tyschwamberger.com.

Ty Schwamberger
The Dark Spot

In each issue of Beware the Dark *magazine, author & editor, Ty Schwamberger will be taking you on a two-pronged, terror-filled ride deep into "The Dark Spot." The two stabs to your gut will consist of: an article and an interview. In this issue; Ty talks about the trials and tribulations of being a writer with a day job. This is surely something the majority of writers in today's economic environment have to deal with on a daily basis. Some don't mind working during the day and writing a night. But, to some, working for someone else during the day can be a struggle—emotionally and creatively. Ty discusses all this, and more, in the first installment of his new column, "The Dark Spot."*

"Being a Writer (with a day job) Ain't Easy"

Back in June I posted this as my status on Facebook:

"Being a writer and having a day job ain't easy. Story ideas and/or your current WIP are constantly running through your mind. Add in having to deal with unruly customer, bosses, deadlines, etc., can really put a damper on your ultimate goal—writing full-time. It's a tough gig for sure. Just remember to keep your eyes on the prize. With a lot of hard work, and a little bit of luck, you'll one day be able to do what you were put on this planet to do—write till your fingers cramp up and bleed. And, oh yes, you'll love every minute of it. Onward and Upward, my friends."

I wrote this after having a rather difficult morning at my 'day job.'

Actually, I feel like this most mornings.

Who am I kidding . . . I think about this all day, every day.

It can be difficult working for someone else until the time comes you can quit the 'day job' and make enough from your writing to live on. It might surprise some after looking at my bibliography that I still have a day job. Besides, having 10 books, a bunch of short stories, audio books, some films, etc., it would appear I make enough to sustain myself on writing alone.

Unfortunately, that's not the case.

At least not yet.

Of course, that's my ultimate goal—to write full-time. But, while I do make a nice supplemental income with my writing, it's still not enough to sustain me and my wife's current lifestyle. The fact of the matter is; we like nice things. We enjoy vacations, nice cars, eating out, buying new toys, doing fun things with my daughter, etc. We also just got married this past June. Our honeymoon to the Caribbean is later this year. We plan on selling our condo and buying a large house in the next 6 to 12 months. We also plan on starting a family of our own, soon. All this takes money. A LOT of money. Now, we could scale back and not do as much, not go on the fancy honeymoon or buy the dream house, but that's what we want in our lives together. I'm not bitching about needing to keep the day job in order to do all those things. Not one bit. That's part of life. You take the good with the bad. The fact of the matter is; my wife earns substantially more in her job than I do. We could probably live on her income alone. Of course, if we did, we probably wouldn't be able to do all the things we want. So, until the day comes when I make enough with my writing as I do in my current 'day job' I'll continue to wake up each morning, put up with idiots on the road during the commute, struggle with unattainable goals and deadlines from my bosses, deal with unruly customers, etc. I work with numbers during the day. This isn't my strong suit, of course. I've done this since graduating in 2000 from college. That's one helluva long time to be doing something you can't stand. Then again, I doubt the majority of people like their jobs (my wife is one of the rare breeds that enjoys what she does for a living). For most, I think it's just something you do to earn money to pay your bills and enjoy yourself a little bit. But, to a writer, needing/having a 'day job' can be even more difficult than for most. A writer will constantly have a new story idea or their current WIP running through their mind. They never stop surveying the world around them for new characters, storylines, etc. Their brain is constantly churning, wanting to spew-forth a meaty new story upon the world. Writing is what we were born to do, not sit in a cubical like a caged animal all day while taking a beating from a tiny man with a whip (hummm . . . now that might just be a good story idea . . . I better jot that down).

For me, having a 'day job' is horrid. I don't particularly care for someone (other than my wife, of course) telling me what to do or yelling at me for not doing something the way THEY would like it done. Many times I have to restrain myself from screaming: *If YOU want it done that way, then how about YOU do it your damn self?! Oh, I'm being paid to be your bitch? Damn, you're right. I'll just sit here like a wet dog and let you beat me into submission. After all, I'm a nobody in your eyes. You're so much smarter* (which according to my IQ is probably furthest from the truth) *than me. You LOVE earning money for a company that already has millions, don't you? Of course YOU do. Besides, YOU'RE the one earning so much more than me, but have half the responsibility! You bastard.*

Or something along those lines.

Whew.

Okay.

I'm better now.

Back to what I was saying . . .

Writing is a lonely affair. When you're pounding away at the keyboard there's no one there to help if you back the story into a corner. You have to figure it out yourself. You have to put in long hours, weeks, months, perhaps even a year, to pen the best story possible. Then once you're done and send it to your publisher, he or she might not like it, or might want you to make this or that change to the manuscript. It can be a tedious process. BUT, even with all the hours crafting the story, then editing it for your publisher, it's still a shitton better life than having to work for someone else. A writer is their own boss. You don't have to take any shit from anyone. You can write when/if you want. Then again, if you don't produce, you don't get paid. So that's one drawback. Even so, I would rather pound at the keyboard till my fingers bleed, eventually wearing my fingertips down to the bone, than work for someone else.

At least that's how I feel. Perhaps you have a day job that you enjoy. If so, I'm not sure if I should be envious or tell you in a very matter-of-fact way that you're one sorry sonofabitch. Or perhaps I'll just give you a big 'thumbs up' while a shit-eating grin is stretched across my face. Eh . . . I'll just decide on a case by case basis.

But, if you're like me, and want to write full-time, but for whatever reason still can't, let me reiterate what I said on Facebook:

Just remember to keep your eyes on the prize. With a lot of hard work, and a little bit of luck, you'll one day be able to do what you were put on this planet to do . . .

TO WRITE!

Yeah, that's right.

Now, finish up reading the rest of this twisted mag, then get your ass back to writing!

Besides, that's what WE writers do.

Onward & Upward, my writer friends.

Interview with Kasey Lansdale

Kasey Lansdale was born into the world of writing. Daughter of renowned author Joe R. Lansdale, she was first published by Random House at the tender age of 8 for the short story, "The Companion."

Her non-fiction article "Growing up Lansdale Style," was published in 2012 in *The Horror Zine* online magazine created by editor Jeani Rector and later published in *The Horror Zine* print anthology, *A Feast of Frights*. She is the editor of the horror anthology, *Impossible Monsters* recently published by Subterranean Press. Her short story "Blind Love," will appear in Harper Collin's 2014 *Dark Duets*. Lansdale is also known for her work as a singer/songwriter and has just completed her first novel.

The Dark Spot Interview Series
Ty Schwamberger

In each issue of Beware the Dark *magazine, author & editor, Ty Schwamberger will be taking you on a two-pronged, terror-filled ride deep into "The Dark Spot." The two stabs to your gut will consist of: an article and an interview. In this issue; Ty sat down with Kasey Lansdale, daughter of legendary Joe Lansdale. If you've never heard of Kasey before, you're in for a treat. We at* Beware the Dark *magazine love her stuff (she's pretty easy on the eyes too), and we think you will too. If you already follow Kasey, well, you know what's in store for you: A multi-talented musician and actress that continues to climb the ladder to stardom. We feel very fortunate that Kasey took time out of her busy schedule to venture deep inside "The Dark Spot." So, without further ado, here's the interview.*

INTERVIEW WITH KASEY LANSDALE

Ty Schwamberger: Hi, Kasey. Thanks for being here.

Kasey Lansdale: Hi Ty, thanks for asking me!

TS: Before we delve into the *real* questions; what do you prefer to go by: Kasey, Miss Lansdale or The Multi-Talented Blonde Texan Goddess?

KL: Wow. That last one sounds really good . . . but for the sake of time and space, Kasey is just fine.

TS: Now that's settled, we hear you have a new CD out called, *Restless*. Tell us a little about it? Do you have a favorite track?

KL: Well, the CD actually won't be released until August 20th, but you can hear some of the sample tracks now as well as get your pre-orders in. It's produced by John Carter Cash at the Cash Cabin in Nashville and has some really great people that were involved in the making. I wrote on 7 of the 11 tracks and I'm really proud of where it ended up. It's got that country blues thing going for it, and I think it really represents where I am as an artist. As far as a favorite track, you can't choose which baby you like the most. It changes based on my mood, what I'm wanting out of a song, etc.

TS: You've had the opportunity to perform all over the world. What place can't you wait to visit again?

KL: I always find myself returning to Italy and have a special feeling for that country, but really I am always happy just to be invited somewhere and get to perform.

TS: Earlier this year you wrote an article for *The Horror Zine* about "Growing up Lansdale-Style." I found the entire piece quite interesting. However, there was one part that really caught my attention. You said: *"Being a singer is so much more than just getting up on a stage and belting out some tunes. When you're little, you don't think much about it. You think you will just perform your songs, people will love them or not, and your hard work will pay off. Unfortunately, it doesn't always work like that, especially these days when the music business (and so many other creative businesses) are in such financial hardship."* As you mentioned, I think this hits home for all sorts of artists, especially right now. Do you think changes in the music & publishing world have finally hit a plateau and we'll start to see some stabilization or will things continue to be in flux for some time?

KL: This is such a difficult and broad question, but I think that we are the generation (all ages) that has to figure out the new model. I think that the days of being a millionaire based solely off of your merchandise sales are over. People are going to have to be inventive and more widespread in what they are doing because no one wants to pay $40 for a book or $25 for a CD anymore; it's just not in the cards. I think the other problem, besides the economic factor is that so many people don't consider "art" a necessity. But when you step back and look around, the whole world runs on it. It's easy to have little respect for it when you have unlimited and often times free access to it, but if it all disappeared over night, people would be up in arms. It has become disposable in today's society, (I am of course speaking broadly) but finding a way to show the importance will be a step in the right direction. Understanding that math and music for example, though different, have their equal positive effects will be groundbreaking.

Regarding the quote above though, I think I meant more just that I thought growing up it was about the art, but I know now it's about money and numbers and the right marketing a lot more than maybe talent sometimes. Not to say it's one without the other, but it seems like this is a country (world?) where people have to be told what to enjoy, and if only a handful of people at the top are telling you what to like, it's not going to be a broad selection to choose from and without variety, I think this hurts sales. People just have to do what they love and hope that the cream will rise to the top.

TS: What can artists (be it a singer or writer) do to help themselves through this minefield of change?

KL: It's different for everyone of course, but I think being open to other avenues that you may not have previously considered is a good idea. I am a singer songwriter, but I like to do other things that are creative as well. The days of being one thing are over. You have to be the Reba of business. Clothes line, Broadway, TV, music. . . . You get the point.

TS: You recently made your editorial debut with the anthology, *Impossible Monsters,* through Subterranean Press. (It has a great TOC, btw.) We all know you're a talented musician and actress, so how did editing a horror anthology come about? Is this something your dad put you up to or have you always had a love for creatures and monsters that run amok?

KL: I grew up in this world, so it seemed second nature. In fact, everyone in the book is a friend in one way or another and that's pretty cool if you ask me. When I was 8, myself, my dad and brother all wrote a horror story that was published by Random House so I feel like it's something that was inevitable, and actually have some more pieces coming out soon. Dad & I just finished a short for an anthology for Christopher Golden, as well as some other projects that are being wrapped up. I also have some work I do independently of my father, but we work well together, so why not try a little bit of everything. Maybe it works, maybe it doesn't, but only one way to find out.

TS: Okay, I know you're traveling in Europe right now, so let me ask the last *real* question. Artists of every kind have an ultimate goal. Singers might want to be at the top of the Billboard Music Charts, while an author might want their name on the *New York Times* Best Seller list. So what's your ultimate goal?

KL: I guess the ultimate life goal is just to be happy. Maybe that's not what you wanted to hear, but it's the truth. The goal is to not have to work a 9-5 job and wish I had done something different. For a strictly tangible answer, CMA Best New Artist of the Year Award would be okay with me too.

TS: Okay, I lied. One more question. Where can folks order *Restless*, as well as find out more about your other work?

KL: Right now, the website, www.kaseylansdale.com is the only place to order. However, presales everywhere, (iTunes, etc.) should start July 24th. (If I filled out the paperwork they sent correctly.) I update daily on www.facebook.com/kaseylansdalefans and am on twitter as kaseylansdale too. Look me up, say hey.

TS: Thanks, Multi-Talented Blonde Texan Goddess, err, Kasey, for dropping by "The Dark Spot." This was a lot of fun. Good luck with everything!

KL: Was a pleasure. Thanks for the interview and the time. I look forward to seeing what "The Dark Spot" brings to the world of Horror.

~K

PHOTO: RUM PUNCH PRODUCTIONS LLP

Writer/Director Luke Brady Talks

YOUNG, HIGH AND DEAD

Vi Reaper

Since a very young age **Luke Brady** possessed an unhealthy passion for blood and gore, especially special effects makeup. He geared his entire education towards a career in film and studied Special Effects in Film and Television at South Bank University. For his graduation piece he made a short film and became obsessed with making films and music videos. He also began writing at this point but it was many years later when he wrote *Young, High and Dead*. His background is made up of both technical and creativity, he's tech obsessed so he's a huge champion of the digital revolution. He also has strange hobbies including collecting bottle tops, hoping one day that the price of metal goes up and they become a rare commodity, his current collection stands at over 8,000. Other collections include analogue camera equipment and axes. His zest for chopping wood is quite extraordinary. If he's not chopping wood, collecting bottle tops or making films he's probably asleep dreaming about his next film and shiny axes.

Vi Reaper: I understand this is your first film. Were there any influences (other films, directors, writers) that helped you set the tone and content for YHAD?

Luke Brady: Absolutely, I am a huge fan of many filmmakers including Hitchcock, Tarantino and Robert Rodriguez. But it was Robert Rodriguez's book *Rebel Without a Crew* that pretty much inspired me to physically take action and go and make my own film. At the same time that I was reading this book I was managing a Casting studio in London and was working on the film *Shifty*, the two filmmakers Ben Pugh (Producer) & Eran Creevy (Writer/Director) were making a low budget British film for £100,000 and these guys were the same age as me but making a feature film. I pretty much thought, hey if these guys can do it, then why can't I? So I started writing *Young, High and Dead.*

VR: From initial idea all the way through to the finished product, how long has the film taken to complete?

LB: From the first initial idea, the film has taken more or less five years. I wrote the first draft of YHAD in 30 days, then spent 18 months re-drafting the script, we then prepped the film in about 9 months, shot the film in 10 days and have spent the past 3 years in Post Production.

VR: How much did the film cost to make and where and how did you get the funding for the film?

LB: I won't disclose exact figures but it's a lot less than people think. Many people have guessed the budget to be around the £150,000 to £200,000 mark but they are way off. The film was self-financed and made with hard work and effort instead of money. The fact that I am pretty poor is a good indication of the films budget, I don't have any rich relatives, no savings and I don't earn a lot so YHAD was made with 99% passion and obsession.

VR: The film has a number of co-directors. How did these collaborations come to be and what do you think these people brought to the film?

LB: The crew that I got together were all like-minded filmmakers who I had worked on many different projects with, including many low budget music videos. I knew Daniel Fenton from my days back in University we both studied at South Bank Uni in Elephant and Castle. Thabo and I had made several music videos together and in a weird but not stalker way we met through Myspace online! But he has come to be a great filmmaking partner and a dear friend. Jon my brother is also in the industry he is a VFX artist so it's kind of natural that we collab together. Portia I knew through Dan, me and her had worked together in casting and I loved the strong female voice that she bought to an otherwise quite male dominating group. One of the greatest things about YHAD is the collaboration between us as filmmakers, the film itself has a unique voice that the UK film industry CANNOT create. No one in the industry would ever gamble on a film like *Young, High* especially the way we all worked on it, they simply wouldn't let us make the film this way. But I knew that each of us would bring such a strong look and style to each scene, something that I think we really did pull off.

VR: With so many collaborators involved how much did other people's opinion change the film while you were making it and were there some things you stuck with even against other people's advice?

LB: In huge ways! Once the script was given to each of the crew they all went way and made notes. We then spent months re-working the script and injecting different ideas into the characters and the story. I cannot claim all the credit for everything in YHAD, it was a true collaborating and artistic project. This sound pretentious but it was exactly that. We were young and confident enough to run with these ideas.

On several occasions we were offered money to make YHAD but it would have meant the script and story changing in various ways. Essentially the money people wanted me to make *Young, High and Eden Lake*! Don't get me wrong *Eden Lake* was good, but it's a completely different film. I felt no connection to that type of story and didn't want to sell out at the first hurdle.

PHOTO: RUM PUNCH PRODUCTIONS LLP

VR: Charlie is not your typical raving lunatic type baddie and I found the scene with him in the DIY store especially chilling because of the character's lack of movement. Did you give the actor who plays Charlie any specific direction about how he should move or interact with others?

LB: Poor Charlie! He is so misunderstood. David Partridge who played Charlie did the most amazing job. On paper Charlie was weird for sure but David ramped up the cringe, he made Charlie so awkward in his skin it's very creepy to watch. I was so lucky to have such fantastic actors on my debut film. I hardly had to do much directing. I would give notes that allowed them to experiment with the scene but David had this character so on point I felt there was no point in

PHOTO: RUM PUNCH PRODUCTIONS LLP

intervening too much. If it's not broken. . . .

VR: I also liked how the 'locals' in the film view the group of main characters with suspicion bordering on hatred. What was your thinking behind this decision?

LB: This is the one of the basic elements to YHAD. I wanted the main characters to feel real enough so that you as the audience are with them each step of the way, feeling every awkward stare and look. As a born and bred Londoner you always get suspicious looks from people the minute you speak with a South London accent, eyebrows get raised and people guard their bags. I have experienced this a lot so I simply threw it into the script. The truth is that the locals in the film are weirder than the main cast. I wanted each extra to have the possibility that they might feature in the film further down the line.

VR: The music in the film is excellent, almost Hitchcockian in the sense that it becomes like another character. What influenced you in your music choice?

LB: The music is amazing and full credit goes to Kwesi "Blue Daisy" Darko for that. The guy clearly has dark mental issues, because what he scored on *Young, High and Dead* makes me sick to the core! We chatted early on before the shoot about the kind of style, the script definitely has an 80's horror vibe and Kwesi pretty much nailed exactly what style of music I had in mind. Big long droning bass lines, with grinding synths.

VR: Some of the camera angles you used, while not gratuitous in the least, really makes the viewer feel involved in the violence. Was this your intention and if so why?

LB: Indeed, even from writing the script I knew I wanted to show less on screen, obviously this also works great for having virtually no money, but that aside I didn't want YHAD to be too gory. I think the audience do the best job of scaring themselves so it's better to let them imagine the worst in their head. In real life you would look away, so it makes sense to treat the camera in the same way. I think too often violence in films loses its impact but more importantly it can lose its message. Audiences have pretty much seen it all and lots of horror films just try to outdo each other with 'glamour gore,' that's all well and good but I genuinely think it serves very little to the story.

VR: You have released a number of podcasts where you go in depth on the making of the film. Why did you decide to make those and how do you think it helped you personally?

LB: The podcasts started out as one of my hair brain ideas to create content for YHAD. But they proved popular so I kind of kept going, I didn't really know what purpose they would serve other than for me to document the process but for me they have also worked as a filmmaking therapy session. You kind of go a bit nuts making a film at this level and your sanity rides on the edge. The podcast has been a great comfort for me to gather my random thoughts and put my opinion across. This is something not many filmmakers are able to do. I also didn't realise how much fun I would have doing them, so hopefully the show will continue. Either way I hope to make more podcast content.

VR: Having mentioned that the 'money people' wanted you to make a different type of film that apes what has come before what is your opinion on the state of British horror today and how do you think it can be improved?

LB: This is definitely a touchy subject with me and I am extremely conscious about what I say and who I talk about. The UK Horror industry will NEVER compete on the global stage. Yes we have the odd hit film but these are predictable and boring ventures that the same people work on and if you aren't with the 'In crowd' you are pretty much screwed. So someone like me from a state educated background and who doesn't speak BBC English is not going to get on very well, or worse ever, even get a chance of making a film like *Young, High and Dead*. The UK film industry is full of middle class snobs. The content they create does not reflect our diverse society, that's why there are hardly any black film producers, Indian actors, Muslim Directors. I could go on and on. So with such an exclusive elitist white middle class club you get nothing but *Notting Hill* & *The King's Speech*! Will this ever change? I fear not. For UK horror fans expect things like *The Woman in Black 2*.

VR: Do you plan on taking the film to any film festivals and/or horror conventions?

LB: I will take YHAD wherever there is demand for it. I hope to grow an open community with the film whereby people can link with me online and hopefully we can help each other's projects. *Young, High and Dead* is a film for the people. It wasn't made by suits and therefore its marketing and screening strategies are pretty diverse. I know what the film is so I don't need awards, but it will be good if it does hit a few good festivals. I am just glad there is no pressure for the film to perform like a dancing bear.

VR: What are your plans for the future? Are there any more films you are currently working on?

LB: Retire from film and become a plumber. Sadly I have come to that crossroad in life whereby I have to have a secure career, I love filmmaking with all my heart but financially and for my own sanity I wouldn't be able to make another film in the same way as YHAD. What I mean by this is that I couldn't do another film part time. I would have to be getting paid and working on it full time. That's every filmmaker's dream, to get paid to do your own stuff, but I am a realist. I am always writing so that will stay with me, if someone pays me to make films then absolutely, I have 3 projects burning a hole in my filmmaking pocket.

VR: Finally, if you could remake any Hollywood horror and make it uniquely British, what film would it be and how would you make it cater for us Brits?

LB: A dangerous question! But if I had to choose it would have to be *House* (1986) I genuinely don't think the UK could do a film like that justice though, I wouldn't dare mess with it I love and respect it far too much!

VR: I would like to thank Mr Brady for doing this interview and urge everyone out there to watch *Young, High and Dead* and then tell your friends to go and see it too.

PHOTO: RUM PUNCH PRODUCTIONS LLP

The film is released in the UK on Friday 13th of September, 2013 and will be released in the US this Halloween, 31st of October, 2013. It's available exclusively to Vimeo.

younghighanddead.com

Vi Reaper lives in England. She shares her house with a loveable but tough German Shepherd and a very loud green canary. Her favourite author is Edward Lee and she'd like to have lunch with Hannibal Lecter as long as she wasn't on the menu.

Veins AND SKULLS
daniele serra
artbook | hardcover
december 2013
SST

GLENN CHADBOURNE
WWW.GLENNCHADBOURNE.COM | CHADBORN@ROADRUNNER.COM
Available for commercial and private commissions

Young, High and Dead
Written & Directed by Luke Brady
Rum Punch Productions/Salani Films (2013), Horror, 89 min
UK Release 13th Sept 2013, US Release 31st Oct 2013

Review by Vi Reaper

Dan and Katy decide to celebrate their engagement by joining with three friends and going to spend the night in the woods. Getting high, drunk and having a good time is top on their list of priorities but what the five don't expect is to find themselves in a nerve jangling struggle not just for their lives but for their sanity too.

Right from the start this is a film that creeps under your skin. The opening scene of a searching torchlight picking through the darkness catching just a glimpse of movement here and the rattle of chains there, all the way through to the sickeningly twisted but ultimately satisfying ending leaves your nerves shredded. There are very few moments when you are not tense watching this film. Even the most every day of scenes is somehow given an edge by the tone, camera angle or acting. Even within the group of the five friends there is a tension, a jealousy or a controlling aspect to the characters and every second that they are gathered around a campfire you just know they are not alone, you know they are in danger and that sooner rather than later something or someone will come for them, emerging through the thick woods that surround them as they are blissfully unaware that they have unwittingly stumbled into a hunting ground. You, as the audience are clued up somewhat by short scenes of the hunter that stalks them, sometimes it's just a flash, a jump cut of something awful that constantly reminds you to be on guard and even though you know that the characters are essentially on borrowed time the film is never predictable. In fact, the way in which these people's good time is severely ended is quite a shock as what you expect to happen does not and the fate of the group is once more thrown in to turmoil and the viewer once again gets no respite. It is also intriguing to see the way group react to each other when placed into a highly dangerous, stressful and violent situation. Will they rely on each other with trust and compassion or simply seek safety for just themselves and forego any bond of loyalty?

This is one of those horror movies that shows you don't need a large budget or a famous cast and crew to make an intelligent, thrilling and frightening film and although there is plenty here for any gore hounds out there, the blood splatter is used as violence should be used; to shock and disturb. Along with the top-notch acting, writing and direction, also of note is the music of the film that, almost like an invisible cast member, sets the tone from the very beginning with haunting melodies that shriek and tear at your rapidly dwindling reserves of bravado.

Anybody with an interest in horror should watch this film. It deserves to be seen and I expect big things in the future for all the talent involved. Britain can make top-notch horror too. This film will remind you of that.

Splatterpunk 2
Edited by Jack Bantry
Splatterpunk Zine, Dec 2012, 44 pages
Print Zine £2.99

Review by Vi Reaper

This zine is amazing. Within its minimalistic pages are four superb short horror stories. Whether it's an obese man who gets a not too friendly visit by a fat-eating demon or guy who is forced to go to extraordinarily violent lengths when his wife discovers his infidelity, all the stories are sharp, nasty, brutal and brilliant. Also included are two articles. One by Mark Sieber, the editor of the *Horror Drive-In* where he discusses the 1968 book *Image of the Beast* and how the introduction of mature sex has affected and infected the idea of horror literature for the bitter and the better. Wayne Simmons, author of many books including *Flu* and *Fever* discusses his interests in slasher flicks and how gore is definitely good. Another good reason to read this zine is a revealing interview with horror god Ray Garton. He frankly discusses the state of horror in literature, the difficulty in getting published and some of the hard times he himself has been through. All this along with an informative list of book reviews, a great editorial piece by Jack Bantry and some first-rate illustrations make up a superb zine that should be read not only by horror fans but by established authors and publishing houses alike.

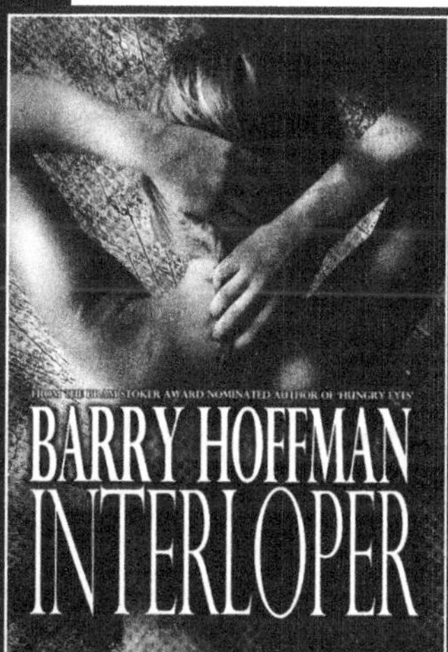

Interloper
by Barry Hoffman
Splatterpunk Zine, 2012, 40 pages
Limited Edition Chapbook £5.00

Review by Vi Reaper

The themes covered in this chapbook would be enough to fill maybe hundreds of pages. Things like religion, guilt, the meaning of love and loss, lust and the ultimate power of life and death. So to condense all those deep psychological and philosophical quandaries into something barely over thirty pages is quite a feat. There's also the chance that such probing thoughts could overtake the story leaving no proper tale to tell. Thankfully, the story does not get bogged down, instead the multitude of notions behind the book really lift it towards something bordering on epic.

After an accident that claims the life of her lover, Diana starts having dreams of people's demise. The dreams formulate over time as she relives them time and time again. Confused and scared by these dreams Diana seeks counselling from her priest. Instead of easing her mind, Diana is left stricken with guilt over her sexuality and the burden of this 'gift' she did not want. She sets about to stop these victims in her dreams from dying in real life, often helping others along the way. But Diana is not alone in this game of life and death. Shanicha also receives dreams of the deaths. A seemingly emotionally bankrupt character, she repeatedly tries to sabotage Diana's rescue attempts. The two women are thrown together in a struggle for power that quickly erupts with lust and while Diana debates Shanicha's motives and conscience, she begins to realize that her adversary might also turn out to be her saviour.

What this book lacks in length is more than made up for by the power of the story. It will have you debating with yourself and questioning many assumptions you may have.

This book is a prequel to *Born Bad.*

Legends of Urban Horror: A Friend of a Friend Told Me

by Gloria Bobrowicz (Editor)
Sirens Call Publications, 2012, 256 pages
Paperback $14.99

Review by Vi Reaper

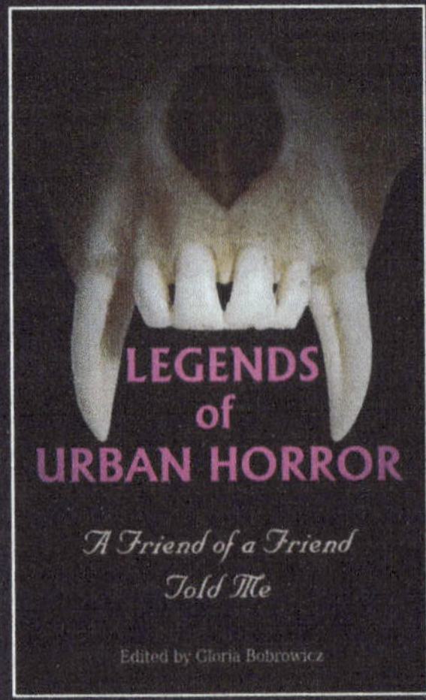

Urban Legends live and die by the way they are told. By their very nature they must be well known, passed along from person to person, each embellishing the tale a little here and there almost transforming it into something new with each retelling. This is how each legend survives but it is also how each legend can become boring, overly complicated and stagnant. So, for a group of writers to come along, take on a legend and try to make it fresh, unexpected and exciting must be a very hard task. Thankfully, the group of writers gathered in this collection definitely exceed expectation and succeed where others may have fallen.

There are ten short stories in all. Some take on very famous myths like the one about the lone woman stranded on a road in middle of the night who may have an unwanted passenger lurking in the backseat of her car, while other stories re-imagine 'local legend' small town tales such as a mysterious wild man with long toenails who lurks in the tree tops ready to attack anyone unlucky enough to travel through his neck of the woods, a myth about an escaped psychopath that likes to gut people and hang them from trees just like hunted rabbits or an overheard rumour that propels a group of kids into seeking a pit that is so deep that it is said that it leads straight down to hell. Other stories are not so much myths but rather tales of curses and underlying evil that exacerbates negative human emotions like jealousy, false bravado, stupidity and ignorance that leads the characters involved down a path of madness, regret and an untimely grisly death.

This is an excellent collection. It doesn't rely heavily on over the top gore but rather it unsettles you, niggling at your brain. The stories are all well told and edited and well worth reading. You may think you've heard all these stories before. You may think you know what will happen. Believe me, you have no idea.

Days with the Undead: Book One

by Julianne Snow
Sirens Call Publications, 2012, 272 pages
Paperback $14.99 / eBook $3.99

Review by Vi Reaper

Zombie Apocalypse stories are everywhere. Whether it is books, television, film, video games or comic books, the undead section in media is virtually overflowing. While there are many people out there for whom zombie tales never become boring (of which I count myself one) I can easily see why other people maybe have become quite jaded with the whole living dead theme.

So, what can this book do to engage both diehard zombie fans and those who may think there's nothing new left to do when detailing the undead? Well, for one, the characters involved in this story aren't your usual stereotypical survivor types. There's no macho guy. There's no annoyingly dumb woman. There's no awkward love story. Instead, you have a small group of people who are smart as they desperately try to outrun and survive the undead whilst dealing with all the little, but ultimately human emotions that come with the stress of imminent nasty death. The book is written like a series of blog entries. A day to day journal of a group of five people always on the move. There is no dialogue in the entire book and while you get to know the other four members of the group, you only get vital information on the author of the blog at the very end. This new angle allows the reader to engage with the characters, you like them, you want them to survive so badly that when inevitable disaster or threat strikes you want to skip through the pages just to see if all will live another day. The writing is quick and clever, with contrasting bleak humour and terrible tragedy that will keep you constantly enthralled. This book excels because of the characters. They are believable in an imaginatively designed damaged world. You should read this book not only because it's an excellent work of fiction but because, in a practical way, this book could save your life when the real zombie apocalypse begins. You have been warned.

Where the Dead Fear to Tread
by M.R. Gott
Untreed Reads Publishing, 2011, 196 pages
eBook $4.99

Review by Vi Reaper

Although this is ostensibly a horror novel complete with horror staples such as werewolves, ghosts, poltergeists and vampires there is so much more to this book. Part detective story, part literary noir, the eclectic mix of characters and settings raise this book above easy generalisation.

We start with the character of William Chandler, a man intent on raining down violence on perverts and child abusers. A past of deep sorrow and loss fuels his hate but as he infiltrates a child sex ring he is suddenly thrown into a world he could never have imagined. A world where past tragedies take ghostly form, dark shadows watch with glowing eyes and behind many a human face lurks a monster. While William could be seen as the hero of this piece, his actions blur the line between right and wrong as he seeks justice with bullets and fists instead of police and judges. He is a very well-drawn, unique character who, despite his actions, you really root for throughout the piece. As we meet other characters any preconceptions of where they might stand on the scale of evil is always being challenged by the writer, pulling heroes from the stereotype of villains and the opposite which, in turn, leaves the reader double-guessing each action or decision in the hopes of seeing where the heart of each character lies. When the face of true evil does show itself, it is ugly and the violence that erupts is brutal, nasty and awash with gore.

As a whole this book is quite fresh in the horror field, beautifully describing a world of the supernatural and paranormal that easily inhabits our own. With a bullets pace and many twists and turns along the way, it is very entertaining and thrilling with the only let-down being a slightly unsatisfactory ending. But, as we are promised a return of William Chandler maybe this is just a precursor to bigger, better things.

Authors and publishers wishing to have their work considered for review, please don't send any books/eBooks/magazines/movies before you query first. Please email magreviews@sstpublications.co.uk with all the details of the title that you'd like considered for review. We will then add it to the review list to see if any of our reviewers are interested in reviewing your work. If someone is you will be asked to send the title directly to the reviewer please.

The Function Room: The Kollection
by Matt Leyshon
Morpheus Tales Publishing / lulu.com, 2012, 156 pages
Paperback £6.99

Review by Vi Reaper

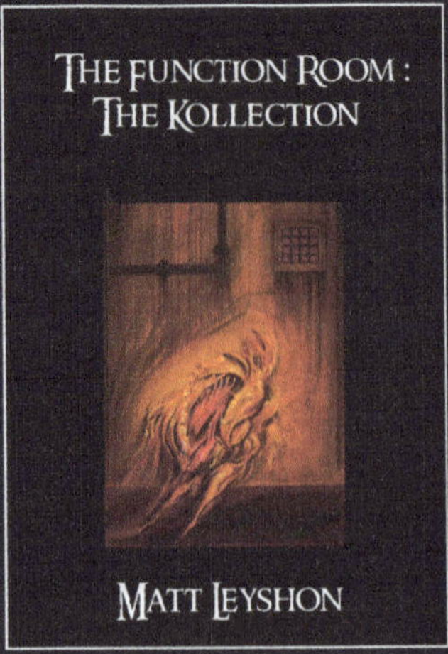

Although this is technically a short story collection, this book can be read just as easily, like a novel. Various characters appear in many of the tales as storylines overlap, timelines twist and scenarios fold into themselves then expand again in a different direction. Most of the stories circle around a town called Leddenton which, as described in the introduction, is a place between worlds and through mirrors. It is definitely not the type of place you would like to visit as it populated with crow men, psychotic cannibal butchers, sex-crazed police detectives, zombies and slime dripping junkies. As the stories tumble over each other in a maze of violence and gore, The Function Room lies at the heart. From the outside it is just a dilapidated building but within it is alive, literally alive, a seething mass of bloody human tissue that the writer does an exceptional, albeit disgusting, job of describing.

So, if you love your horror steeped in guts but with a strong line of intelligence, give this collection a go. You'll never see small towns in the same way again.

Morpheus Tales Apocalypse Special Issue
Edited by Sheri White
Morpheus Tales Publishing, Feb 2013, 74 pages
Print magazine £5.00 / eBook £1.99

Review by Vi Reaper

There is an over-abundance of Apocalypse stories out there now, which makes it very difficult to come up with new, interesting and surprising ways to end the world in a fictional sense. But personally I love a dying world tale and never get sick of reading them so I went into this short story collection with high-hopes and enthusiasm. I wasn't disappointed.

The twelve stories included cover a wide range of End-of-Day's themes. Whether it's a monster emerging from the earth at a fairground, a mysterious vomiting illness or a bizarre worldwide catastrophe caused by a love of ponies, the stories are all very well written and highly entertaining. Each story is also deeply personal, attaching you to a single character or a couple and making you witness Armageddon through their eyes like a pregnant woman's fight against a suicide virus, a father and daughter's touching last moments together as earthquakes drain the oceans or a bored housewife's stark realization of what really is important in life, all the stories make you feel for the characters involved. Plus, you've got all the well-used apocalypse themes such as comets, zombies, starvation and social disintegration as backdrops to each story. All this, along with an excellent editorial, makes this a fine, high quality collection of Ragnarok fiction.

How to Kill a Vampire: Fangs in Folklore, Film and Fiction
by Liisa Ladouceur
ECW Press, Canada, 2013, 190 pages Print & eBook

Review by Nancy Kilpatrick

The last volume devoted exclusively to destroying vampires is a decade old so we were due for an updated refresher, and here it is. *How to Kill a Vampire: Fangs in Folklore, Film and Fiction* is a fun investigation into the demise of everyone's favorite non-zombie undead.

Liisa Ladouceur has been known as an alternative-music and counter-culture critic for quite a while, penning pieces for *Rue Morgue* magazine and hosting a weekly all-horror podcast on Rue Morgue Radio. In 2011 she wrote her first book, *Encyclopedia Gothica*, an alphabetical listing and description of goth culture's terms and well-known entities. Her new book focuses on another of the subjects she holds dear.

Ladouceur begins with what is fairly common knowledge about vampires from the early 1800s to now. By chapter two we're into lesser-known revenants, like the Chinese Chiang-Shih and the Greek Vrykolakas. Once she's established the cultural array of predatory supernaturals of the fanged variety roaming the planet in mythology, folklore, fiction and film—and proved the need for gathering knowledge to eradicate them—the author drives her stake towards the main reason for this tome—how to dispatch these resuscitated corpses. She also profiles the more famous slayers, from Abraham Van Helsing to Buffy Summers, and even suggests the necessary contents of a Vampire Dispatching Kit, should the reader want to build one.

Much has been written about vampires, but little specifically focused on their execution. This is that everything-you've-been-dying-to-ask book about how to bring about the final gasp of humanity's cleverest predator. It contains a wealth of mortal options presented with a wordsmith's skill, underpinned by a scholarly approach to research, and offered with blatant humor and the infectious awe of a long-time aficionado whose tongue is, appropriately, firmly planted in her cheek.

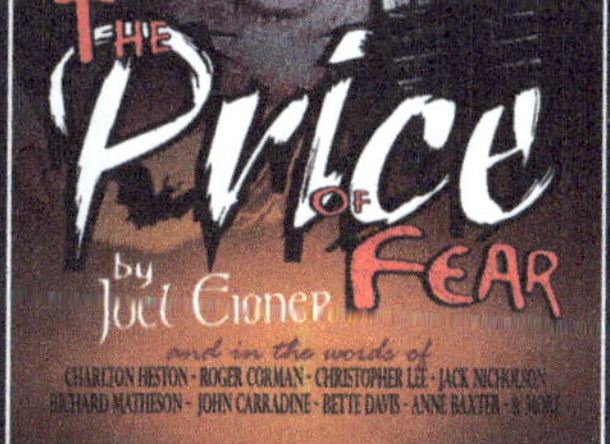

The Price of Fear
The Film Career of Vincent Price: In His Own Words
by Joel Eisner
A Black Bed Sheet/Diverse Media Book, 2013, 216 pages

Review by Nancy Kilpatrick

The Price of Fear is presented as 'The only authorized biography directly from the master himself.' Foreword by Peter Cushing—in the form of a brief 'letter' to Price the year after his death. Many actors and directors Price worked for or with also comment on the actor or the production, including Roger Corman, Christopher Lee, Richard Matheson and John Carradine.

This book provides quite a bit of plot synopsis for each film and play. Readers unfamiliar with Price's earlier works can see the types of roles he was selected for and the range of his acting abilities. Combined with reminiscences, there's a glimpse into old-time movie-making, when actors did their own stunts, and frightened studio commissary workers by wearing monster makeup to lunch!

Amusing stories abound. For instance, Price's first stage role as Prince Albert in *Victoria Regina*. He recounts sussing out Albert's actual wardrobe and discovering a corset made of metal rods for posture beneath the antique clothing. He recreated that corset for himself—only to pass out from wearing it at rehearsal.

Price recounts the drinking scene with Basil Rathbone in the *Tower of London* which they had to rehearse so much, "I nearly threw up after drinking goblet after goblet of fake wine, which was in reality diluted Coca-Cola."

In *Scream and Scream Again*, Christopher Lee describes the famous fight scene when his character forces Price's character "back and back, until he finally, quite willingly and without my saying a word, immerses himself in a vat of acid. I'll never forget that stately figure, desperately trying to keep a straight face, and me too . . ."

Roger Corman and Vincent Price were a mutual admiration society. *House of Usher* was made in fifteen days, ". . . but I loved every minute of it!" Price enthused. "Where else would I have been given the opportunity to bury a beautiful young girl alive and then die a sickening death by having a burning building collapse on me? I still think it was the best of all the Poe films." Corman even let Price "pick the artist to do the portraits of the members of the Usher family that were used in the film."

Price loved some of his work, but did not think highly of much of it. He claims he often took roles partly out of a sense of adventure, partly because of alimony and child support payments.

This book touches on his other interests, collecting fine art, which he'd done from an early age, and cooking. He and his second wife Mary Grant (from 1949 to 1973) wrote bestselling cookbooks together. They also donated art and endowed the *Vincent Price Art Museum* in LA in the 1960s. Mary was the mother of Vincent's only daughter, Victoria, who wrote an intimate biography of her father: *Vincent Price: A Daughter's Biography*.

Price's third wife, the colorful Australian actress Coral Browne, is barely mentioned, though he converted to Catholicism and she took out US citizenship in order to wed, and they were married from 1974 until her death in 1991.

Price was that most sophisticated of gentlemen, a Renaissance man who possessed wit, charm and style layered with intelligence, and that comes through in his comments, and in the comments of those in the industry who adhere to the Hollywood code of utilizing flattering terms like 'funny, generous, wonderful, gentleman.' This is Vincent Price the beloved screen idol to many, perusing his career with a touch of humor and insightful clarity.

If you hope for personal information about Vincent Price, you will be disappointed. This is a book focused almost exclusively on his work, with a few personal snippets tossed in. The chronology of his theatre and film life feels more real than his private life. And although the book opens with his childhood memories, after that the private feels like an outline. For example: (about Edith Barrett, his wife from 1938 to 1948, and the mother of his son Vincent Barrett Price), the author writes: "They were delighted when they got a day off during rehearsals. It was spring: love was in bloom, and so was the countryside in and near New York. They got into a car and Vincent drove into Connecticut. On the way home, he told Edith how he felt about her. She felt the same way about him. Vincent and Edith were later married on April 22, 1938 at the St. Thomas Episcopal Church on New York's 5th Avenue. He was 26 and she was 31 . . ."

To create this book, Joel Eisner interviewed Price at length in 1985 and then by phone over the years until Vincent's death in 1993. He admits to going through three literary agents, two publishers and several format changes before hitting this current incarnation. A former publisher that went out of business managed to procure an ISBN before collapsing and the book is listed in Books In Print for 1993 but did not see print. Only an author deeply in love with his subject would endure this much grief, and Eisner has clearly been a huge Price fan all of his life.

Eisner authored *The Official Batman Batbook* (and a recent revised edition), co-wrote *Lost in Space Forever*, and *Television Comedy Series: An episode Guide to 153 TV Sitcoms in Syndication*. Which is why I was annoyed by the multitude of errors in the print book. Many missing articles, misspellings, incorrect punctuation, format issues . . . I contacted the author who admitted that the publisher encountered data-transfer problems but is correcting them. The ebook does not have these issues, I'm told.

The book includes approximately 20 pages of mainly movie stills and lobby card images, a couple of small, fun quizzes at the back, and offers an unproduced *Dr. Phibes Rises Again* script from 1972. *The Price of Fear* is well worth the money, but if possible, opt for the ebook, or wait for the second—hopefully error-free—printing.

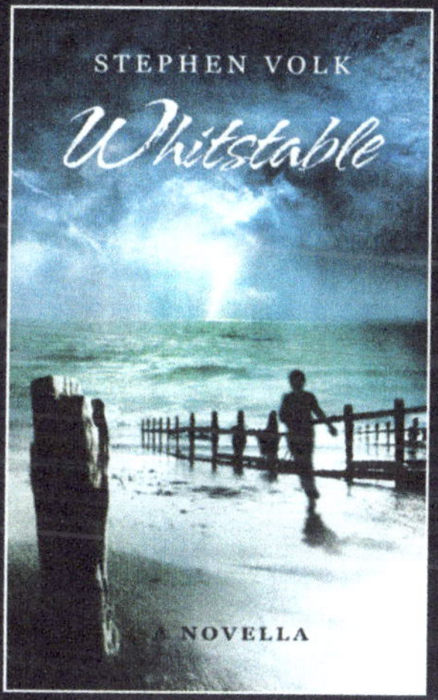

Whitstable
by Stephen Volk
Spectral Press, UK, 140 pages, £21.00 hardcover, £12.50 paperback, £1.99 eBook

Review by Nancy Kilpatrick

Rare it is when an author can credibly write a person recently deceased into a story. But that's just what Stephen Volk has done with the late British actor Peter Cushing, his main character in *Whitstable*, a novella-length tale of grief, sadness, crudeness, cruelty and redemption.

Volk is best known as a screenwriter, his most notable films *Gothic*, directed by Ken Russell, and the recent hit *The Awakening*, a smart, chilling ghost story. He has also scripted for television, for example, the *Afterlife* series. His fiction includes short stories, film adaptations and novellas, and it's no surprise that this intelligent writer of emotional works has penned a gripping tale that delivers on all counts.

Whitstable is set in the seaside town where Cushing lived with his beloved spouse Helen. The story begins with Peter Cushing nearly crushed by grief from the recent loss of his wife, who he relied heavily upon to help him—an exceptionally meek, mild, insecure yet courteous man—through his life. Alone, he is floundering when he meets a young boy with a serious problem. What's lovely about this 1970s story is that Volk never lets Cushing act out of character of the real man. Cushing is a gentle fellow possessed of extraordinary morals and holding to a solid belief in both religion and the afterlife. Compelled to help the tortured boy who has ultimate faith in him because of his heroic movie roles, he must find a route that is entirely his own and that suits his character. Whether you know Peter Cushing only from his Hammer horror films, or have some knowledge of his life, this story will resonate. The author cleverly utilizes his own background in scriptwriting to synopsize scenes from Cushing's movies that relate to the events taking place in the story, cinematically reflecting the situation.

Whitstable is touching and troubling at the same time, a tale that evokes morality and presses the existential questions most of us struggle with, especially prominent at the time of a great loss. Volk has always been a sensitive writer and this novella certainly fits perfectly into his oeuvre. That 2013 is the 100th anniversary of Peter Cushing's birth makes this commemorative a sweet and poignant tribute to a beloved actor lingering in the hearts and minds of many. At the same time, the story acts as a memento mori for all of us.

It is easy to come away from this exquisite novella wishing that Peter Cushing had been a friend.

Vi Reaper lives in England. She shares her house with a loveable but tough German Shepherd and a very loud green canary. Her favourite author is Edward Lee and she'd like to have lunch with Hannibal Lecter as long as she wasn't on the menu.

Award-winning author **Nancy Kilpatrick** has published 18 novels, about 200 short stories, and has edited 13 anthologies, most in the horror/dark fantasy field. She also published the non-fiction book *The goth Bible: A Compendium for the Darkly Inclined* (St. Martin's Press) and has written many articles and reviews. Her two most recent—award-winning—titles are (as editor) the anthology *Danse Macabre: Close Encounters with the Reaper*, and her sixth collection of short stories, *Vampyric Variations* (both from EDGE Science Fiction and Fantasy Publishing). She lives in Montréal with her calico cat Fedex, but travels frequently searching out crypts, ossuaries, mummies and original Danse Macabre artwork. Check her website for updates: nancykilpatrick.com. But join her on Facebook if you want the latest news. She doesn't bite. Much.

Vincent Chong is an award-winning freelance illustrator and designer. Since 2004 he has brought his creative vision and distinctive visual style to a wide range of projects from book and magazine covers to CD packaging and websites. Currently living in the UK, he has worked for clients all around the world and has illustrated the works of renowned authors such as Stephen King and Ray Bradbury. In 2010 he released his first art book, *Altered Visions: The Art of Vincent Chong*. Vincent has received the British Fantasy Award for 'Best Artist' on multiple occasions and has been shortlisted for World Fantasy and BSFA awards as well as being nominated for a Hugo Award this year. You can learn more about Vincent at his website, www.vincentchong-art.co.uk and blog, vincentchongart.wordpress.com.

Vince Natale has been creating illustrations and fine art professionally since 1985. He attended the School of Visual Arts in New York City and graduated from the duCret School of Art in Plainfield, New Jersey.

His works range from magazine editorials to book covers as well as fine art, and spans the genres of romance, horror, fantasy/science fiction, portraiture, and military subjects. Vince has also created many illustrations for advertising clients in fashion, pharmaceuticals, and high tech.

He has received numerous awards for both his commercial and fine art work, and has been represented in several annual exhibitions of the Society of Illustrators in New York and Los Angeles. Vince's works also appears regularly in the Spectrum annual book of *The Best in Contemporary Fantastic Art* and various other art publications.

As well as having produced work for private commissions, his personal/gallery work has found homes in many private collections in the US and abroad.

Alongside his professional artist/illustrator duties, Vince is also an instructor at the Woodstock School of Art.

vincenatale.com

Alfred Klosterman lives in Philadelphia and has long worked as a graphic artist for printing firms. He's read and collected fantasy and science fiction most of his life, which fills much of his spare time. He's contributed artwork to many genre small press publications for a number of years. These include titles such as *Cemetery Dance*, *The Horror Show*, *Eldritch Tales*, *Space & Time* and *Dark Horizons*. He is totally devoted to black & white work, inspired by the many fine illustrators he's enjoyed while looking through vintage magazines.

Alfred's other interests include gardening, caring for pets, political activism and listening to extremely loud music while enjoying a cold beer.

Luke Spooner a.k.a. Carrion House currently lives and works in the South of England. Having recently graduated from the University of Portsmouth with a first class degree he is now a full time illustrator for just about any project that peaks his interest. Despite regular forays into children's books and fairy tales his true love lies in anything macabre, melancholy or dark in nature and essence. He believes that the job of putting someone else's words into a visual form, to accompany and support their text, is a massive responsibility as well as being something he truly treasures.

www.carrionhouse.com / www.facebook.com/CarrionHouse

Glenn Chadbourne is a freelance artist specializing in the horror/dark fantasy genre. His work has appeared in over fifty books as well as numerous magazines, comics and computer games. His trademark pen and ink drawings have accompanied the works of today's hottest authors including Stephen King.

Glenn has worked on several Stephen King books, including: *The Dark Man*, *Full Dark, No Stars*, *The Secretary of Dreams: Volume 1* and *The Colorado Kid*.

Eleanor Bennett is an award-winning photographer and visual artist. Eleanor's photography has been published in *The Telegraph*, *The Guardian*, *The British Journal of Psychiatry*, *Life Force Magazine*, British *Vogue* and as the cover of books and magazines extensively throughout the world. Her art is globally exhibited, having shown work in New York, Paris, London, Rome, Los Angeles, Hong Kong, Copenhagen, Washington, Canada, Spain, Japan and Australia amongst many other locations.

Stephen Cooney has always been a fan of art for as long as he can remember. He's always been into horror and fantasy art since an early age after watching fantasy films, which he then would try to copy. In his teenage years heavy metal music and album covers influenced his art in a major way. He has always wanted to work on designing album covers for heavy metal bands. After school he went on to study Art at Exeter College but soon found out he did not fit in at art school because his teacher did not understand the dark side of his art. After years of painting he then meet up with a tattooist who loved his work so much he asked him to design some tattoo flash for him. Unfortunately, the designing side of tattooing just wasn't enough for him so he went on to start tattooing himself with the help of a professional tattooist. After years of successfully tattooing many clients he then decided to give painting another go. Stephen is still enjoying painting to this day. Although most of his work has been to do with horror and fantasy he's always willing to do new projects on different subjects. Influence wise he would have to say Derek Riggs, Ken Kelly, Edward J. Repka, and all artists who design album covers. If he's not playing the guitar, then painting is his first love.

He is married to Amanda and has two children Hayley and Steven Jr.

Allen Koszowski has been getting art published within the SF/horror/fantasy genres since 1973. Since then he has had over four thousand pieces published in such magazines as *Fantasy Tales*, *Weird Tales*, *Whispers*, *Eldritch Tales*, *Asimov's SF Magazine*, *F&SF*, *Weirdbook*, *Cemetery Dance*, *The Horror Show* and many others. He has done work for many publishers such as Subterranean Press, Midnight Marquee Press, Gryphon Press, PS Publishing, Centipede Press and many more. Along the way he has won a World Fantasy Best Artist Award among others. He has been the artist Guest of Honor at The World Fantasy Convention, The World Horror Convention, The EerieCon, The Albacon and more. He currently edits and publishes his own magazine *Inhuman*.

www.allenk.com

Daniele Serra is a professional illustrator. His work has been published in Europe, Australia, United States and Japan, and displayed at various exhibits across the U.S. and Europe. He has worked for DC Comics, Image Comics, Cemetery Dance, *Weird Tales* magazine, PS Publishing and other publications. Winner of the British Fantasy Award.

www.multigrade.it